The Lavender Ladies

Detective Agency:

THE END OF
SUNSET GROVE

Also by Minna Lindgren

Death in Sunset Grove
Escape from Sunset Grove

*The Lavender Ladies
Detective Agency:*

THE END OF
SUNSET GROVE

Translated by Kristian London

Minna Lindgren

PAN BOOKS

First published 2015 by Teos Publishing, Finland

First published in the UK 2018 by Pan Books
an imprint of Pan Macmillan
20 New Wharf Road, London N1 9RR
Associated companies throughout the world
www.panmacmillan.com

ISBN 978-1-4472-8935-7

English edition published by agreement with Minna Lindgren
and Elina Ahlback Literary Agency, Helsinki, Finland

1 3 5 7 9 8 6 4 2

A CIP catalogue record for this book is available from the British Library.

Typeset by Palimpsest Book Production Ltd, Falkirk, Stirlingshire
Printed and bound by CPI Group (UK) Ltd, Croydon, CR0 4YY

Visit **www.panmacmillan.com** to read more about all our books
and to buy them. You will also find features, author interviews and
news of any author events, and you can sign up for e-newsletters
so that you're always first to hear about our new releases.

The Lavender Ladies
Detective Agency:

THE END OF
SUNSET GROVE

Chapter 1

Siiri Kettunen woke up and thought she was having a night-mare. She was standing next to her bed, swollen feet jammed stoutly into her slippers and grey hair a fright, staring at the glowing red wall before her. She could tell she was alive, because the familiar fifth-octave A was ringing in her ears.

'Good morning, Siiri! Your caregivers today are: No staff on duty! For details on the past night, press 1!'

Siiri tried to swipe at the animated digit, which danced and smiled next to a little goblin face. Siiri was communicating with her smartwall. It wasn't a television or a computer, or even a tablet like Irma's green flaptop, but a wall loaded with infinite amounts of intelligence. It brought security and meaning to an old person's life. Her hand was trembling so furiously that initially the 1 didn't react to her touch. In the end, she supported her swiping hand with her other hand, concentrated hard, and somehow managed to hit the dancing number with her forefinger. Upon being selected, it bowed in gratitude.

'Time in bed 8 h 25 min. Sleep 7 h 5 min. Total amount of

uninterrupted sleep 3 h 47 min. Sleep efficiency 88%. Intermittent snoring 27 min. Number of movements 229, duration 1060 sec. PLMD events 0. Pulse 52. Stress reactions 25%.'

Siiri could make neither head nor tail of the significance of this cheerfully presented information. Was it cause for concern if one moved 229 times over a period of 8 hours and 25 minutes? Was that too little? Or too much? The snoring amused her. She had always grumbled about her husband's snoring, and now she suffered from the same affliction herself. His had been constant, of course, not intermittent. He had always dropped off quickly, and the rumble started immediately and continued till morning. Siiri sighed deeply as she thought about her dearly departed husband, with whom she had shared a bed for fifty-seven happy years, despite the snoring.

The smartwall roused her from her wistful reverie: 'For personal updates, press 1!'

The wall flashed so eagerly that apparently it had something important to tell her. Some sort of cartoon character was bouncing around the screen, perhaps a bear cub, or maybe a fish. It hopped there comically, trying to stimulate a drowsy old woman to take an interest in herself.

Siiri concentrated so she would be able to catch the capering number 1. She wanted to know what the smartwall knew about her.

'Today is your 97th birthday! Congratulations from Awaken Now!'

As if she wouldn't have known without being reminded. Ninety-seven was nearly one hundred. She and Irma had determined not to turn one hundred; doing so would only cause trouble. A lady from the A wing had received a reminder from the paediatric clinic on her 105th birthday. Evidently all five-year-olds were called in for tests to measure their motor skills and psychological development, and now that she had turned 105, the computer system thought she was a pre-schooler. Apparently it didn't recognize numbers over one hundred. Siiri thought the lady should have gone in; she certainly would have. The tests were rather fun; you had to draw a triangle and walk in a straight line, which was no simple feat for a 105-year-old. But instead of going in, the lady made a huge fuss, sent off a barrage of complaints, and then died before the complaints arrived at the appropriate authority.

'Thank you very much,' Siiri said to the smartwall, which was pushing a virtual bouquet of flame-red roses at her in honour of her birthday.

Siiri jabbed randomly at the smartwall, because she still hadn't figured out where the controls were located and how to make it do what you wanted. But this was par for the course at Sunset Grove these days: one spent one's days swiping and prodding surfaces. Intelligence was everywhere, gobs of it, a flick of the wrist and something terrifically smart happened. Siiri's little one-bedroom flat was jam-packed with electrodes, sensors, chips, transmitters and cameras that tracked her existence. Somewhere in the depths of her mattress lurked that vigilant gadget that monitored her incessantly while she slept and counted every movement for lack of anything better to do. If she took a tumble and didn't pick herself up in an allotted amount of time, smart-nodes in the floor would alert emergency services, and an ambulance carrying a brigade of medics would rush over to hoist her up. This ensured that old folks didn't die on the floor. Finns were in unanimous agreement that dying on the floor of one's home was more tragic than dying in a bed at the public health centre. An emotionally charged debate on the issue had even taken place during one of the plenary sessions in Parliament, which Siiri often watched with Anna-Liisa and Irma.

Living in a smartflat was a gas if one maintained a receptive attitude towards the surprises the machines threw one's way. A trip to the refrigerator, for instance, was always a grand adventure. One never knew what the appliance would get it in its head to say.

'Remove. Half. Litre. Carton. Of. Spoiled. Milk. Immediately. Expires. Today.'

Siiri's fridge was a young woman, rather energetic but a little full of herself. Irma had insisted on an older man's voice for her own icebox, which had proven funny indeed, as her refrigerator turned out to be the former announcer for public radio, whom they all knew from the foreign exchange rates and maritime weather conditions over the years. Irma had immediately started calling her refrigerator 'her cavalier', and she had hopelessly tried to teach it to say 'cakesies' instead of 'cake'.

'I'd have more luck with a parrot,' she had huffed angrily when her painstaking instruction didn't generate results.

Initially a talking fridge had seemed like nothing more

than a day-brightener, the sort that put one in a good mood when one had neither a cat nor a spouse, but the fact of the matter was that it saved old people from food poisoning and diarrhoea: so many of them ate spoiled food as a result of not checking expiry dates. Or they forgot that bit of salmon from last week at the back of the fridge that eventually turned to green slime. Such lapses smelled so foul that one woman's odour alarm had started blaring, and Siiri and Irma thought they were in the middle of an air raid.

To put her refrigerator's mind at ease, Siiri started her breakfast with the expiring half-litre of milk. If she tried to put something in the fridge that should have been eaten the day before last, it launched into an unpleasant tirade, and Siiri didn't know how to soothe it. She was having constant problems with her liver casseroles.

'You did not follow instructions. You did not follow instructions. You did not follow instructions,' the fridge might repeat for hours on end in an unvarying tone, over-stressing the beginning of each word. It was torture, enough to put an end to an old person's life, drain her of her will to live as she numbly suffered the refrigerator's sermon in her dining room chair, while the barely spoiled liver casserole she had bought on special offer warmed up in the frying pan.

'But I'd rather listen to a sermon from my cavalier than these volunteers,' Irma would have said if she had been participating in the present conversation 'online' and 'in real-time'. Sunset Grove's sprouting army of volunteer caregivers used such terms when helping residents adjust to their new environment. There were no longer any staff per se. No exercise teachers or activity leaders, no kitchen staff, social workers, directors, caregivers, or even interns in theoretical caregiving or immigrants temporarily employed to further the integration process, only machines and an ambiguous band of volunteer helpers who indoctrinated residents into the pleasures of a machine-centred life.

Although still at its former location in Helsinki's Munk-kiniemi district, Sunset Grove was no longer your average terminal centre for the elderly. The renovation, which had lasted well over a year, had proved much more extensive than anyone could have imagined. The place had been gutted and rebuilt, and the end result sold off to an inter-national conglomerate. Now the retirement home was a pilot project in monitored elder-care, its establishment and oper-ation funded by three ministries. Politicians and businessmen believed that turning the elderly into laboratory animals would save society in the future and serve as the global solu-tion to one of the world's most pressing problems: old people. Finland would rise out of economic distress when various health and caregiving technologies conquered the world and demonstrated yet again the sort of miracles Finn-ish engineers were capable of working.

'This is our last service to society,' Siiri said to herself, wiping the remnants of her breakfast from the table top with the leg of her old pyjamas. She had forced down one hard-boiled egg and some crispbread, as she no longer felt hungry and ate primarily out of a sense of duty.

While Siiri was so occupied, Irma's head appeared in gar-gantuan size on her smartwall, as if Irma had heard her mumbling to herself amid the sensors and devices. Irma's curly white hair flopped untidily this way and that; she had cakesie crumbs in the corners of her mouth and enormous diamonds in her ears.

'Dratted contraption!' Irma shouted, not looking at Siiri but glaring angrily off to the side somewhere. 'I'm at my wits' end! Say your name and press enter . . . fiddlesticks! . . .'

There was a peculiar clatter and Irma vanished from Siiri's wall. *The Marriage of Figaro* blared in the background. Siiri listened for a moment and decided it was the first act. Count Almaviva had found the pageboy Cherubino under a dress in the chambermaid Susanna's room. Then Irma reappeared and fixed her penetrating gaze on the centre of the screen, as if she were furious with Siiri.

'Ir-ma Län-nen-lei-mu. Enter! How does this ridiculous wall work? Open Sesame! Let me out! I can't get out of my apartment! For God's sake, will someone help me? Is there a single one of the institutional caretakers formerly known as maintenance men still left in this world? Can anyone hear me?'

Irma had wandered out of view of the camera, but Siiri had no trouble hearing her muttering and the consternation the discovery of Cherubino in the wrong room inspired in Almaviva's court. The bray of the gossiping music teacher's tenor rose above the other sounds. Irma grew increasingly panicked, she squealed and swore, sighed and moaned, and intermittently flashed past the camera, hair straggling. Suddenly the music ended. All was still, rather dreadfully silent, until Irma began trilling Alessandro Stradella's 'Pietà, Signore' high and loud.

Siiri threw on her robe and rushed to the rescue.

Chapter 2

Irma was stunned when Siiri materialized in her flat with her own key. Or actually it was no key; it was a small oval fob that magically opened doors and signed off on purchases in the canteen and the MeDoc kiosk downstairs. The fob knew everything about them, more than they did themselves. One no longer needed to even remember one's social security number, which was undeniably a relief for many residents. One simply had to flash the fob at the blob on the wall at the door to one's apartment. But of course you had to find the dratted thing first. Many residents hung their fob around their neck, some didn't know the difference between the fob and their medical alert bracelet, Irma's was generally misplaced, and Siiri had attached hers to the strap of her wristwatch. Flashing the fob was always a time-consuming process, as the door-blob couldn't be bothered to obey the first time, and one had to coax it to life by waving the fob around in various trajectories. When successful, a green light lit on the blob and the door opened slowly and impolitely right into the face of the person trying to enter. Doors that opened with a simple push or pull of a handle no longer existed.

'Yes, just imagine those poor people who earned a livelihood making signs for doors, the ones that tell you whether you're supposed to push or pull. Do you suppose they've all lost their jobs? I must say I find it peculiar. Inventing one contraption after the other that take people's jobs from them. And what about those poor souls who glued the stickers to the doors?' Irma said, bustling about the kitchen looking as if she meant to offer Siiri something but couldn't think what.

Siiri offered a helping hand: 'Cakesies would be nice. Or did you already finish it with your breakfast?'

Irma whirled towards Siiri in alarm and snapped almost angrily: 'How did you know I had cakesies for breakfast? Was it announced on some smart-alec wall for the whole world to see? This place is driving me mad. According to the wall, my sleep efficiency was 78 per cent, even though I clearly remember I didn't sleep a wink.'

Irma couldn't stand the thought of being under constant surveillance. That was why the antennas and cameras had been set up: someone was sitting somewhere monitoring their every move, even when they were asleep. At this very moment, some bored surveillance officer out there – perhaps some former Push sticker-gluer or stick-exercise class leader who had been let go – was observing their morning rituals. Irma was sure the electronic jungle cost the residents of Sunset Grove a pretty penny; after all, who would be paying for it if not the residents? The government's funds only covered start-up and construction. The ultimate intent was to launch new elder-care monitoring centres in India and

South America with export subsidies from the Ministry of Economic Affairs.

Irma took a breath, and Siiri said with a smile: 'You have cakesie crumbs in the corner of your mouth.'

'Hmm, well. Does that offend your sensibilities? I'll get my serviette; it should be here on the table. Why isn't my serviette on the table . . . the pink one with my initials appliquéd on it so beautifully? An engagement present, lovely durable linen. I don't like putting it in the laundry, which is why I keep it here on the table where I eat. Why did you have to start talking about cakesie crumbs now? Oh, I'll just use my hand, there. Better now? Where were we?'

Siiri couldn't be bothered to explain to Irma that she and her cakesie crumbs had accidentally appeared on Siiri's wall. Some sort of ethereal connection had been established between their apartments so they could contact, as the idiom was, each other without getting up from the couch. Presumably one could establish such a connection with any of the residents' walls if one had the skill and the interest. Irma's and Siiri's fobs allowed them to enter each other's apartments, and Anna-Liisa's, too, in case an electrode dozed off and one of them happened to die at that very moment. Every resident had been asked to choose two 'safety buddies' whose locks were programmed into the fobs. The residents looked after each other in this fashion; it was called 'communal caretaking'.

But now they were at Irma's breakfast table, stimulatingly simultaneously and in real time, discussing how awful it looked when so many residents went around with a three-week menu on their shirt-fronts. Couldn't they see the mess themselves? Now that there were no nurses, there was no one around to tell these residents that they might want to wear a bib while they ate or at the very least change their shirt once a week. Irma remembered a cousin who was paralysed on one side of his face, so a steady trickle of food dribbled out of the corner of his mouth onto his shirt. No matter how gargantuan a bib was tied around his neck, a mess was inevitable. It had been very embarrassing, especially at family gatherings, which people had still had the energy to organize back then. Irma spent a moment reminiscing about her amusing cousins, all those spirited girls and boys who loved card games and proposing toasts and inviting the entire family over on Sundays to dine on delicacies.

'Oh dear, oh dear, I've had a lovely life,' she said, trilling and clapping her hands. Then she looked at Siiri and grew serious. 'But they're all dead, my high-spirited cousins.' She sighed dramatically twice, breath quivering. 'I have no one left but you, Siiri.'

'You poor thing.' Siiri said, gathering that she was cold comfort in comparison to Irma's countless cousins.

They ate their cakesies and drank their instant coffee in silence. Both of them wished they had a newspaper, but complaining about that no longer felt invigorating. They had been outraged for months when all the newspapers moved to the Internet. They had written to the editor-in-chief of *Helsingin Sanomat*, the director of the Sanoma Group, all the CEOs, even those in the Netherlands, the head of customer service, the chair of the board of directors, and the corporate social responsibility officer, but had only received one response to their painstaking missives. It read: 'We've streamlined our customer service feedback to Twitter. Remember to use the hashtags @sanoma #feedback #bouquetsandbrickbats #satisfiedclient.'

Irma's green flaptop contained the daily paper as well as all the archive clouds and special issues one could ever want, but no matter how hard they tried reading the newspaper from the tiny screen, it simply wasn't fun. The flaptop got sticky when you tried to swipe the pages with cakesie-moistened fingers – not that they were real pages, they were graphics that looked like newspaper pages.

'"Graphics", that's a beautiful word,' Irma said, savouring it. 'It has a certain gravitas and solidness to it, like "gravestone". Graphics. Do you suppose Anna-Liisa has got a gravestone for Onni yet? Wasn't she having all sorts of trouble with it?'

'You'd never believe how much!'

Due to his bevy of ex-wives, Onni's name hadn't fitted on the original gravestone, and so Anna-Liisa had been forced to purchase her husband a new, larger one, in beautiful black granite. She had had her own name engraved on it in golden letters as well, which Siiri and Irma found slightly comical and above all pointlessly costly.

'Jesus, Mary and Jehoshaphat!' Irma suddenly squawked, nearly frightening Siiri to death.

A rat had emerged from behind the curtains. A real, live, sleek-coated rat that scanned its surroundings for a moment and then scampered off purposefully, its paws clacking against the plastic flooring. They gasped, unsure of how to react. Siiri felt a horrific stabbing at her temple, and Irma splashed coffee on her blue dress. When the rat jogged between their legs, they both screamed so loudly that the creature disappeared without a trace and the smartwall woke up.

'Unidentified alarm! Check your smoke alarm!'

Try as she might, Siiri couldn't catch her breath. She felt as if she'd run eight hundred metres backwards, followed by three somersaults. Her heart was pounding ferociously, paused for a frighteningly long time, and then started pounding again. She couldn't get a word out; she just gaped in turn at Irma and the smartwall, which once again was of absolutely no use.

'It went over there!' Irma screeched, pointing towards the kitchen. Her diamond ring flashed as if it were also on alert.

The smartwall was as vigilant as Irma: 'Danger over! No smoke!'

Irma bravely rose and rushed into the kitchen. She clanked and clattered, shooed and shouted to frighten the rat, but the animal had vanished without a trace. Siiri laboriously pulled herself up and out of her chair and slowly made her way to join Irma in the kitchen. The blood was rushing through her ears as if she were standing under a waterfall. Her eyes went dark.

'You're fainting! Siiri, don't – oh for Pete's sake!'

Irma caught Siiri before she collapsed to the floor and dragged her friend over to the small floral couch, where she raised Siiri's legs onto the armrest. Siiri didn't believe she lost consciousness, but she was too immobilized to do anything sensible. Irma was remarkably calm and collected and went to fetch Siiri something to drink from the kitchen. As she passed the smartwall, she gave it a peevish punch.

'What are you staring at, with those stupid exclamation marks?'

'Press 1 for ambulance 2 for customer service 3 for building maintenance,' the wall replied amiably, dropping the exclamation marks. The yellow ball marking each option had eyes and a smiling mouth.

Over on the sofa, Siiri caught a whiff of Irma's cloying perfume mingled with a hint of light menthol cigarettes and Mynthon mints. She understood she couldn't be smelling all of this, but one smell reminded her of another, and eventually an image emerged of Irma sitting on her 1930s Stockmann sofa upholstered in Sanderson fabric, a mint in her mouth and a cigarette in her hand, which she smoked solely to open up her blocked nostrils. The vein at Siiri's temples was throbbing, but the rushing in her head had faded so that the fifth-octave A rang clearly again in her left ear. She felt vaguely nauseous. Was it the rat that had caused all of this? How was that possible? She didn't remember ever having been afraid of rats, and in her youth they had been a common occurrence in Helsinki's streets, courtyards and cellars. Rumour had it that some people had trapped and eaten them during the worst years of famine.

'Drink this, you skittish city girl,' Irma said cheerfully and handed Siiri a coffee cup decorated with pink songbirds and filled with red wine. 'You'll feel stronger. Skål!' She had filled her own glass to the brim but slurped it masterfully from the side so that not a single drop splashed onto the flowered sofa or her blue dress.

Irma was right. A couple of swigs of the slightly sour red wine worked wonders. Siiri felt her blood circulating again, from her humming head to her stiff legs, and she wanted to sit up at Irma's side. Irma had her work cut out, hoisting Siiri's old limbs from the armrest to the floor, but the moment passed cheerfully with Irma singing her favourite Schlager, 'Siribiribim'.

'So we have rats,' Irma said in satisfaction, since the day hadn't turned out to be a typically dull one, of which they had far too many. 'Is this the beginning of the end now? Like in Camus' *The Plague*?'

This rat was healthy and alive, unlike in Camus' book, where rats spat up blood, died in the streets and spread the plague. They spent a moment pondering if the rat had come looking for food, but decided that was improbable. Surely more tempting victuals were to be found in the skips of Munkkiniemi, enough for a rat to feed on to its heart's content. What if the creature had smelled a body? Had someone died again?

'Trained rats could be a good solution to the problem of old people dying in their retirement-home flats without anyone noticing,' Siiri said.

Such things happened on occasion, an old person might languish dead for weeks before some cleaner or light-bulb changer noticed them. There had recently been talk on the radio about the dangers of dying alone. One of the city's bureaucrats had suggested that retirement homes and assisted living centres be required to check on each resident's state once a week.

'To see whether they're alive or dead!' Irma said, and started cackling. She wiped the tears from her eyes with a lace handkerchief and couldn't stop laughing. They pictured some caregiving trainee, some seventeen-year-old Jemina, knocking timidly at the residents' doors asking whether they were alive or dead and reporting the result with her smartphone. A trained rat would be much better suited to the task.

'Or we could volunteer to do it ourselves. I might be rather good at it; I'd rap on the door and ask if there are any good dead boys or girls at home.'

Irma emptied her handbag onto the porcelain table she had painted herself in a floral pattern, found her pack of cigarettes and had just managed to light her first nasal-opener of the day when there was strident throat-clearing at the door. Someone had entered Irma's flat.

'We're alive!' Irma crowed in her piercing falsetto, developed during the private singing lessons of her youth.

A tall, slim woman appeared before them. Her age was hard to determine, because she was by no means young, but compared to Siiri and Irma she couldn't be considered old. She had shiny hair, dyed black, large plastic spectacles, and beady eyes that scanned the apartment inquisitively.

'Ili, I'm Sirkka.'

Their visitor didn't have a last name; no one did, these days. She was just Sirkka. Bewildered, they studied the intruder, who offered no explanation for popping by. She was wearing a blousy turquoise knit top, tight trousers cut from upholstery fabric, and bright green heels.

'At least ten centimetres. How can she keep from toppling over?' Irma said to Siiri, as if they were watching a television programme and not a living person.

'Did you come to check if we're dead?' Siiri asked, hoisting herself up from Irma's low sofa to greet their guest. Sirkka's grip felt alarmingly cold and bony.

'My name is Siiri Kettunen; I live next door,' Siiri said, looking Sirkka warmly in the eyes. They had a peculiarly penetrating gaze. 'How can we help you?'

'If you're collecting money, I don't have any. I can't find my magic button anywhere. All I have is a debit card, and I don't know if it has any money, either,' Irma added, still puffing away on the sofa.

She was right of course. There was no point collecting money, even for a worthy cause, the Red Cross or the Disabled War Veterans Association, because no one carried cash, and one couldn't even get it from the bank any more.

'I understood an alarm went off here,' Sirkka said in a high, reedy voice. She was wearing an abundance of make-up, and her carefully drawn eyebrows rose above her spectacles.

'No, that was me,' Irma said, waving the cigarette smoke out of her face with a jangle of her gold bracelets. Siiri loved the sound. She looked at her friend happily, who began explaining at length to their uninvited guest how shrilly she could squeal, or sing if necessary. She offered a couple of masterful samples of her vocal skills, and when she arrived at the Queen of the Night's staccatos, the smartwall popped on, once again imagining that there was a fire in the kitchen.

'Look! That wall has lost its mind!' Irma pointed accusingly at the screen, which once again suggested three solutions to the problem: 1 Fire blanket 2 Emergency services 3 Maintenance company. Sirkka furrowed her foundation-caked brow, looking like nothing more than Snow White in ugly clothes.

'Have you heard about the Holy Spirit?' she then asked. That was the only option the smartwall hadn't yet proposed that morning.

Irma burst out laughing, but Siiri tried to be polite and look engaged, because she didn't like judging people on the basis of their religion. Who knew, perhaps this Sirkka had something interesting to tell them? But Sirkka didn't wait for their reaction. She had already reached into her green shoulder bag and pulled out brochures and pamphlets, which she now laid out on Irma's porcelain table like lures to tempt them into conversation. Upon seeing the Prayer Clinic brochures, Irma got upset. She popped up angrily and announced that she was offended that someone would trespass on her home in this fashion simply because her singing was mistaken for a fire alarm and that someone was monitoring her life with espionage equipment of every description.

'Are you the one who saw me raise my voice a little, cooped up in the bowels of the cellar monitoring us? I know you have a surveillance centre down there, where you spy on us more eagerly than the Stasi and the KGB put together ever dreamed of? Did my squealing bring you rushing up here with a handbag full of the Holy Spirit? Are you completely out of your mind?'

Sirkka rose to a threatening height and ran a hand across her sleek hair. Siiri sincerely hoped she wouldn't start asking them about the meaning of life. They were far too old to be interested in such poppycock.

'I heal in Jesus's name; I drive out evil spirits. When you receive the Holy Ghost as the wellspring of your life, you are reborn and no longer try to rule your own life. It's that simple. In order to take yourself over to divinity, all you have to do is allow the Holy Spirit into your heart. It will be granted to you as long as you stay close to Jesus. I free you from the powers of Satan. I'm here to listen to you and pray for you. It's that simple.'

Irma took a step backwards so she wouldn't be standing too close to the strange woman, who emanated strength and animosity. Siiri could see that Irma was on the verge of bursting with rage but couldn't figure out how to address this creature. She looked at Siiri, eyes boiling with anger.

'Maybe you could pray for us that the rats would leave us alone,' Siiri said.

This caught Sirkka off guard, even though she must have been a seasoned itinerant preacher. In all likelihood she had grown accustomed to hearing about violence, rape, alcoholism, insomnia, drugs, unemployment, loneliness and paedophilia, but no one had ever turned to her for assistance with rats. As she hesitated as to how to react, Irma had an inspiration.

'We're also fine with you praying for the rats and leaving

us in peace. Feel free to pick a side depending on which of us is more possessed by the Devil, the rats or us. It's that simple!'

Irma walked into the hallway so Sirkka would take a hint and skedaddle. When she didn't budge, Siiri took her by the elbow and escorted her to the door. Sirkka fidgeted with the strap of her shoulder bag but couldn't find the right words for the moment. Irma winked at Siiri and gave the door a push. As the door opened painfully slowly, they spied a fat rat in the corridor, bathing in the autumn sun.

'Cock-a-doodle-doo!' Irma crowed. It came instinctively from her repertoire, and in this instance was rather appropriate. The rat dashed off, the smartwall in the living room came on, and Sirkka the Saver of Souls collapsed to the floor.

Chapter 3

The swooning volunteer preacher attracted well-deserved attention in the lobby of Sunset Grove as she was escorted over to the sofa, still in a state of discombobulation. Looking dignified in her black dress, as straight-backed and august as ever, Anna-Liisa wasted no time placing pillows under Sirkka's neck. Then she posed the patient a few questions the others found puzzling and to which Sirkka the Saver of Souls did not respond.

'I am going to survey your neurological status,' Anna-Liisa announced. 'Can you stick your tongue out? Make a face? What is your favourite colour?'

The sudden appearance of a meaningful task vitalized Tauno. Back hunched and cap teetering on his head, he rocked about, hands fanning at his sides, and commanded the troops as effectively as only a front-line officer accustomed to wartime exigencies could.

'Water! Bring water! Lift her legs – make way; I'll take her pulse.'

Tauno couldn't find a pulse, which didn't surprise anyone. Sirkka gave off such a frigid air when she was in full fettle that her pulse must have been nearly imperceptible after major athletic exertion, let alone on the brink of consciousness.

Margit attempted to abort her session in the automated massage chair, but to no avail. She spent time every day in the ugly black artificial leather contraption; its iron fists pounded one's bones and muscles so brutally that Siiri felt like she'd been dragged off and beaten from head to toe after her one and only treatment. Each mauling cost five euros, paid for with a wave of one's fob, but Margit wasn't one to count her pennies when the chair's vibrators were kneading her vast carcass. She let out such moans that the others couldn't help but be reminded of her dear departed husband Eino's virile years and the echo of the couple's afternoon lovemaking down the corridors of Sunset Grove, now but a distant memory.

Sirkka the Saver of Souls started coming round. 'Holy Spirit . . . Gift of the Spirit . . . God's strength in me . . .' Tauno slapped her pale cheeks a couple of times, prompting her to open her eyes.

'I've been touched by the Holy Spirit! The moment of clarity has come!' Sirkka rose to sitting, an entranced look on her face, and no longer seemed the least bit frail. 'I was reborn Tuesday, 29 April 1997. My prayers have finally been answered. Thanks be to God!'

Then she returned to earth, scanned the crowd of concerned nonagenarian faces surrounding her, and was overcome with a girlish shyness. 'Tell me . . . How did I . . . Did I speak in tongues?'

Sirkka the Saver of Souls didn't seem to grasp that she had fainted. She believed a gift of the spirit had been visited upon her due to the steadfastness of her faith, that her loss of consciousness had been a sign of some sort of anointment – the sort that, among neo-charismatic revivalist movements, was anticipated more feverishly than death was in retirement homes.

'You didn't speak any Swedish, I can tell you that much,' Irma said. 'You just fainted. This time your Holy Spirit was a rat, a very plump and healthy specimen. I've seen much skinnier. The ones that overran cellars and rubbish bins in the 1940s were often terribly malnourished, seeing as how there wasn't enough food for humans at the time, not to mention rats. They had mangy fur and funny tails longer than the poor rats themselves. But this rat of ours was very handsome; its fur had a beautiful sheen.'

Sirkka didn't hear any of what was said to her. She lifted both of her hands and raised her voice to a dreadful volume.

'And these signs shall follow them that believe: in my name shall they cast out devils; they shall speak with new tongues; they shall take up serpents; and if they drink any deadly thing, it shall not hurt them; they shall lay hands on the sick, and they shall recover. The Gospel according to St Mark, chapter sixteen, verses seventeen and eighteen.'

'For heaven's sake, drink!' Anna-Liisa ordered Sirkka the Saver of Souls so brusquely that the other woman stopped blathering, lowered her hands, and accepted a glass of water. She downed it in one swig without looking at the contents.

But she believed she was immortal, and took superhuman courage from the fact.

Anna-Liisa fixed her flinty gaze on Sirkka. With her mourning wear, dark, flashing eyes, and hand clawed around her cane, Anna-Liisa was a spooky sight, and not only to the volunteer. Since her husband's death, Anna-Liisa had dressed exclusively in black, refusing to compromise on this principle in even the most scorching weather. It was insanity, but Anna-Liisa was resolute. Black drained the colour from her face, making her look pale and frail.

Sirkka handed the glass back to Anna-Liisa and wiped her mouth on her sleeve, leaving behind an unpleasant smear of lipstick. Siiri knew the stain would be hard to get out in the wash.

'Bless the Lord, O my soul, and forget not all his benefits. Psalms, chapter one hundred and three, verse two.'

'No need to involve anyone else; I'm the one who brought you the water. Now perhaps you can walk out of here on your own two feet, as, to my understanding, we no longer require your assistance,' Anna-Liisa said, pointing her cane at the main door. Sirkka ran a hand across her black coiffure, tugged at her loosely knit top until it offered some semblance of coverage for her shoulders, rose briskly, and exited with a clack of her high heels.

'God bless you all,' she intoned upon arriving at the door. Her smile was beautiful, as blissful and happy as only that of a bride of Christ who has witnessed a miracle could be.

'Did we get rid of her yet?' bellowed the tattooed drunk of a doctor who always wanted to go to the Ukko-Munkki for a pint and sit on her balcony in the sun without any knickers. During the renovation, every apartment at Sunset Grove had been outfitted with an external glass cubicle that served as a balcony, and from hers Siiri could see everything the doctor and the other residents did in their display windows. It was far from pleasant. Ritva Lehtinen, that was the doctor's name. Now Ritva walked over in sandals, ripped dungarees, and a summer top. She always went around in a sun visor these days, rain or shine, and lately it had been shining. She smelled powerfully of tobacco after having fled the swooning saver of souls for a smoke in the courtyard.

'That's right, you're a doctor, aren't you?' Anna-Liisa said sternly, fixing an accusing eye on Ritva.

'Medical examiner, how many times do I have to tell you? Nothing but corpses for me, thanks,' Ritva replied, hacking up a cigarette-roughened laugh.

Whenever she ran into Ritva, Siiri reflected that the other woman was young enough to be her daughter. Both of Siiri's sons had died so long ago of affluenza-related diseases that she had stopped counting the years. And with her daughter unreachable at a French nunnery somewhere, Siiri had, for all intents and purposes, become childless in her old age. But she had no interest in adopting Ritva, peculiar as she was, as a foster child.

'She certainly recovered fast,' Tauno marvelled, twisting himself around awkwardly onto the sofa. It was the same old couch that had served as the centrepiece for the communal area since the beginning of time, a massive and rather uncomfortable National Romantic behemoth that some dead resident had left behind. At least the furniture hadn't been replaced with virtual substitutes during the renovation. The baize-covered table had been allowed to remain in its spot in the corner, with its motley collection of chairs that deceased residents' heirs had turned up their noses at.

'The Holy Spirit healed her,' Irma remarked cheerfully and crossed her hands, pretending to pray for fresh miracles from above. 'Perhaps the spirit will heal my digestive tract, too. Sometimes my stomach stews so badly I think I'll die from the pain. Do any of you ever experience that?'

'My digestion works regularly and effectively,' Margit brayed, cheeks glowing after her treatment in the massage chair. 'You should try this chair sometime, too.'

'What you've got stewing in there is the Devil. An evil spirit, that's why it smells so horrible!' Siiri said. Everyone burst out laughing.

'You're saying it's that abusive chair that keeps your intestines in line?' Irma asked Margit while rummaging around in her bag for a pack of cards.

'Diverticula,' Ritva said laconically, coughing up a rather large glob of phlegm. She clearly was at a loss what to do with it; apparently it was too large to swallow and she had too much presence of mind to spit it out, despite her general lack of decorum. After a moment's consideration, Irma sacrificed her lace handkerchief to Ritva's sputum.

'I can always throw it in the wash,' she whispered to Siiri so loudly that Tauno smiled from the sofa.

'We actually did see a rat,' Siiri said, to steer the conversation elsewhere. Everyone was very interested in the animal, and Siiri had to recount over and over how it had appeared like the saviour's son or a volunteer staff member out of nowhere and inspired Sirkka the Saver of Souls to fall into a neo-charismatic trance.

'They're everywhere around here. I'm lucky if I can go to the toilet in peace,' Tauno said. He declined to participate in the card game, as did Ritva.

'I've never seen a single one!' Irma cried.

'They're here to convert us. To take the few last pennies we have. There's always an account number at the end of every prayer,' Tauno continued.

'Wait a minute!' Anna-Liisa's resonant voice cracked like a whip, for the first time in ages. Siiri was overjoyed, because most days Anna-Liisa no longer bothered to upset herself over illogical leaps in topic the way she used to. 'Are we talking about rats or the volunteers from Awaken Now! Association?'

None of them knew what they ought to be talking about or if they were to blame for confusing the flow of conversation. Ritva started explaining that diverticula were harmless yet painful sacs that formed in the intestines, particularly common among women, and could be treated with an operation. Irma pulled out her living will with surprising agility and pronounced that she was prepared to fight to the last fart to avoid surgical procedures. Tauno slouched against a stack of pillows on the sofa and didn't understand a word of what was going on. He had a difficult time sitting normally, since his spine had been so badly mangled in the war. Anna-Liisa frowned in frustration and ordered Irma to deal.

'Canasta,' she said, rapping the baize table top with her knuckles.

'I had a very interesting conversation with one of the volunteers yesterday,' Margit said, as she sorted her hand. 'It was a man, nearly our age, although he must have been a little younger, but he had impressive whiskers, like a walrus, and the same kind of glasses as President Paasikivi in the 1950s. Have you met him?'

'President Paasikivi?'

'He's not a volunteer!' Tauno shouted with surprising fury. Irma was so startled that her cards fell to her lap and her box of pastilles to the floor.

'President Paasikivi?'

'But . . . he doesn't even live here,' Margit said.

'Ha! He must be the one who spies on us from the basement!' Irma exclaimed. She tried to bend down, but her rotund frame refused to cooperate. 'Dratted pastilles!'

Siiri picked up the box from the floor and laid out her first canasta. The others were dumbfounded; they'd barely had time to organize their cards.

'You're cheating!' Irma crowed.

'You can avoid diverticula by eating a handful of seeds every day,' Ritva said.

'Why would you want to feed rats seeds?' Margit asked, a little anxiously. Her hearing wasn't the best.

'He's my friend,' Tauno said.

'A rat?'

'For heaven's sake, this conversation,' Anna-Liisa roared, slapping her cards back onto the pack, hands trembling.

'Could you please try to concentrate for a moment! Who exactly is your friend, Tauno?'

'We all are, aren't we?'

'Silence, Irma. During the course of this conversation we have spoken about intestinal sacs, digestive tracts, volunteers, President Paasikivi and rats, and then Tauno said some specific individual, if not a rodent, was his friend. I'm eager to hear clarification on the matter from Tauno.'

'I've heard rats are kept as pets these days. Snakes are also popular,' Irma interjected, before Tauno could get a word in edgeways.

'Are you saying the rat escaped from a resident?'

'Oiva is my friend,' Tauno said, with an unexpected reverence.

'You named the rat Oiva?' Margit asked. Apparently, to her mind, some other name would have been more fitting.

'If I had a rat, I'd name it Musk. Then it would be Musk Rat, like in the Moomins,' Irma said with a laugh.

'Oiva is no rat,' Tauno said very softly.

'I'm happy to hear that. My cousin was married to an Oiva for a while, but he was quite the scoundrel, bounced cheques and jumped into bed with any girl to cross his path, so although divorce doesn't generally sit with me, in my cousin's case it was the only sensible solution. She was left alone with an enormous brood of children. We did what we could to help her, baked *pulla* for the poor dears and gave them our hand-me-downs. Is it my turn now?'

Siiri wondered what was upsetting Irma so. She always babbled uncontrollably when she found a situation unpleasant or embarrassing. But they were just playing cards. There was absolutely nothing out of the ordinary about their confounding conversation.

'No, Irma. It's my turn. And I meld,' Anna-Liisa sighed, face pale as death. She had decided to continue playing, by force if necessary. 'And when it comes to these volunteers, I find their activity entirely unacceptable – if, indeed, it is even legal.'

Chapter 4

'First you must become an empty vessel, as you can accomplish nothing with your own flesh.'

The pleasant-voiced man mildly looked every member of his audience in the eye before leafing through the Bible in his hand. It made an amusing sound, a soft rustle-crackle, as his nimble fingers sought the right page. Three old women were sleeping in wheelchairs, confounding the Holy Spirit's efforts to enter their flesh. But the new resident of the C wing, a Somali-Finnish woman barely seventy years old, hearkened attentively, as did Siiri's widowed neighbour Eila, a few residents Siiri didn't recognize, and Margit. Siiri and Irma sat at a safe distance to avoid being counted as part of the silken-voiced man's congregation, despite being curious to hear what he had to say. It was a normal Thursday, but the volunteer was dressed in a dark suit; he had left his Sunday shoes at the door and was now standing in his stockinged feet in one corner of the communal area. His voice echoed in the lobby, which was mostly deserted. One old woman who'd forgotten a curler in the back of her head was parked in her wheelchair in the middle of the walkway, holding a robot seal – or rather, a seal pup. It was white and had long black lashes, and if held in human hands, would purr like a cat. If you looked it in the eye or spoke to it in a tender voice, it wagged its tail adorably. But other than this, there were no signs of life in the communal area. No hurried slap of nurses' sandals, no ponytailed stick-exercise leaders bouncing around fishing for residents to rehabilitate, no chipper-voiced activity directors calling out bingo numbers.

'Romans, chapter eight, verse eleven, is important here. The idea is that if the Spirit of God resides within you, he will quicken your mortal body. If the Spirit of God lives inside you, he will bring you life.'

One of the women sleeping in front of the preacher coughed, started, and slipped into an even deeper sleep, accompanied by a snore. The speaker's compassionate gaze lingered on the row of wheelchairs for a moment and then moved on to more fertile pastures.

'He who does not believe in the gospel is damned. Those who believe speak in tongues and lay their hands on the sick so as to heal them. They do not work these miracles themselves; they are worked by the Holy Spirit within them. The Holy Spirit. The same Holy Spirit that raised Jesus from the dead. The same Holy Spirit that has been poured into us. All we have to do is allow the Holy Spirit to fill our lives and guide us and deny our own will. It's that simple.'

'Deny our own will? This one is a real blockhead,' Irma said tactlessly, as there was no call to disturb the others' contemplatory convocation. The man looked Irma dead in the eye. 'Oh dear!' Irma said in a panic, and started touching up her lipstick without a mirror. Thanks to decades of solid experience, she managed it flawlessly. She pinched her lips together to put the finishing touch on her maquillage and flirtatiously returned the preacher's gaze, but he refused to be unsettled by her feminine wiles.

'Your will is in the Devil's hands if it prevents you from allowing the Holy Spirit to enter you and fill you. When you are guided by the will of God, you are reborn. The will of God. It is the fulfilment of the Holy Spirit. It is the beginning of a new life and abundance, of salvation and repentance. It all begins with allowing the Holy Spirit in. The Holy Spirit. It's that simple. Believe, and you shall be blessed with health and strength.'

The speaker's audience looked neither healthy nor strong. He had his work cut out for him: he would have to do much more missionary work, preach about the pouring out of the Holy Spirit and the horrors of damnation before this herd of wandering souls experienced the sort of miracle that would even allow them to stand on their own two feet. Siiri and Irma whispered inappropriately, and when they started to laugh, decided it was time to leave. They tried to coax Margit to join them, but she refused; she was focused on fishing around her purse as the preacher had reached the climax of his sermon.

'Feel free to donate any sum; even a mite is pleasing to the Lord. If you don't have cash, you can make a donation through the Awaken Now! Association website with just a few clicks from the link that reads 'The Gift of Sacrifice'. It's that simple.'

Siiri and Irma made a break for what was left of the dining room, now that the kitchen had been removed, along with the cook and the other human employees. They had been replaced by an automated line where the residents served themselves, that is if they were coherent enough to know what they wanted and where they were. A stack of sticky, machine-rinsed trays stood at the head of the line, after which one equipped oneself with the requisite weapons, in other words forks, knives or spoons, followed by glasses. Up to this point, everything was as simple as coming to Christ.

'Oh, how I despise this contraption,' Irma huffed, jabbing at the 'Milk/Non-fat' button on the drinks machine. Nothing emerged from the rubber teat. Just to be sure, Irma pressed 'Water/Spring' a few times and then 'Milk/Non-fat' again.

'You forgot to flash your fob. That's how you pay for your drinks,' Siiri said.

With surprising speed, Irma retrieved her fob from her décolleté, like an opera singer revealing a secret letter from between her breasts, and flashed it at the automated machine. A deluge of non-fat milk showered into her glass and over the rim. Siiri thrust her own glass under the spigot, and it filled up too. There seemed to be no end to the stream of bluish liquid. Irma shrieked out every possible command she could think of in her falsetto and turned the milk to water.

'Do you suppose the Holy Spirit did that?' she said in surprise, filling a second glass with water.

'Press here,' Ritva said, jabbing the word 'Exit' and staunching the flood.

'Thank you so much!'

Irma took a fresh tray and moved down the line as if nothing had happened. When she arrived at the MealMat, she sighed deeply and glared defiantly at the towering cabinet of gleaming steel. This was their restaurant, cook and waiter in one, as a doctor of technology or what have you had illustrated during his overblown introduction to the miraculous MealMat.

The machine represented the future of technology; it would solve the problems of globalization and bring production closer to the consumer. The secret to this was an invention called a 3D printer. The residents had gradually come to gather that '3D' was English, like all fashionable abbreviations, and meant three-dimensional. Anna-Liisa had audibly wondered if the abbreviation was written with a capital or lowercase d, and the presenter had eventually huffed that both were used, but the issue was of no relevance. OMG! (Tauno and Margit were sure that OMG was the manufacturer of the MealMat, like BMW or AGA, but Ritva had informed them that it was also abbreviated English and came from the words 'oh my god'.) The printers could be used to make anything from cars to old people's meals. Thanks to them, the Chinese no longer needed to work their fingers to the bone for a pittance, since factories were being replaced by handy home appliances. The printer was able to load any manner of implausible materials, which it then transformed into a perfect object, say a stool, a spark plug, or a darling pair of earrings.

Eventually the machine man had got around to the Meal-Mat. He had explained that it was filled once a week with various powdered nutritional ingredients. Apparently the machine kept the powders edible for thirty years, which had been tested on manned expeditions to Mars.

It was the latest technology. Everything was 'the latest' these days; they heard the term everywhere they turned. The MealMat consultant had reminded them that the machine needed its rest, too, which was why the Swedish 8–4 diet had been adopted at Sunset Grove. The underlying principle of this regimen had been unfamiliar to the residents, and so the by-now-bored machine man had been forced to explain that as well: it meant that from then on, food would only be served at Sunset Grove between the hours of 8 a.m. and 4 p.m.

To make eating fun, powders of various colours were dumped into the MealMat's compartments. The customer also got to select the geometry of the food they would be enjoying: broccoli-shaped, something resembling a sphere, tubes, flat triangles or stately pyramids. They all tasted like bland root-vegetable mush, but the residents were used to that. The shapes and colours undeniably brought variety to their mealtimes.

'Green tubes, red triangles and . . . What else? Should I take some white balls?' Irma pondered as she stared at the

MealMat's screen. Every option came with an illustrative image: all one had to do was press it and the lump formed on the plate, if one happened to get it under the right nozzle at the right time. 'White balls are no fun; I think I'll take green balls and . . . Was it red triangles? Which leaves . . . This is worse than algebra and trigonometry!'

'Just close your eyes. That's what I do,' Siiri said.

In the end, it made absolutely no difference what shape and colour their tasteless baby food was. Anna-Liisa claimed the root-vegetable powder wasn't even made from fresh vegetables; she had heard that leftover food from nearby grocery stores and schools was brought to Sunset Grove and ground to a pulp, after which a few handfuls of nutritional supplements designed to combat malnutrition and lack of appetite were tossed in the mix.

'Do you believe this is made from food that was going to be thrown away?' Siiri asked Irma. After a prolonged battle with the MealMat, they were finally sitting at a window table with Ritva, their geometric servings in front of them.

'It has nothing to do with what I believe,' Irma said. 'But to be perfectly blunt, I don't even know what "food waste" means.'

Siiri had heard about it on television and the radio. Food waste had become a major problem, since people weren't buying enough groceries from the stores and children skipped their school lunches. This generated skips-full of waste that wasn't really waste, but food.

'Food that no one else would touch, is that it? Is that what they grind up for us and feed into that printer for thirty years at a time?'

'Imagine, if we didn't eat these green triangles, they would have ended up at the dump,' Siiri said, feeling useful. There was all sorts of trouble with waste depots now, too, since there was too much rubbish and it needed to be sorted and treated and recycled. Which was wise, of course: reusing everything. That's what they had always done back in the day, too. A bedspread turned into a dress, which then became a hat; Siiri had sewn herself stylish clothes this way, over and over again from the same piece of fabric.

Suddenly they heard a racket from the food printer. Green mush was oozing to the floor and the machine was spraying what looked like blood all over. It wasn't blood, though; it was Tauno making a mess. His back was so hunched he had a hard time reaching the screen and pressing the pictures there, not to mention the fact that his hands shook so violently that it was impossible to know what button he was trying to press. Ritva rushed over to help him, which was surprising, because generally Ritva was the first to remove herself the moment anyone needed assistance. But of course this was no health-related emergency, and Ritva knew how to handle machines as skilfully as she did corpses. Like a magician, she put a stop to Tauno's rampage with a few strokes of her hand, and peace was restored to the dining room.

Solitary residents sat at their trays; the room was void of cheerful banter. Every now and again, the elevator's mono-tone narration echoed from the lobby: 'Going. Up.'

Ritva and Tauno joined Siiri and Irma at their table, but before they had taken their seats, a little round cleaning robot had started bustling about at the floor in front of the food line.

'Now that one I like!' Irma said. 'So cute and efficient. Just look at it!'

The cleaner was black and white, and thanks to its curves had an oddly human appearance. It thrummed busily and importantly back and forth in the catastrophe zone of Tauno's creation. Water squirted out one side, brushes thrust forth from the other, and sponges dried up the traces. The end result was astonishingly tidy. Upon finishing its work, the little robot seemed to thank its audience, flashing a red light and then a green one before returning to await the next emergency.

'Bravo, bravo!' Irma cried, giving the little worker a rousing round of applause. 'Or is it a girl? Should I be shouting brava?'

'It's so quiet, too,' Siiri said thoughtfully as she eyed the robot. 'Maybe some of this automated tomfoolery really is intelligent.'

'This morning I thought the window was rainy, but because my husband didn't make it into the polytechnic school, we're going to have to give the dog away, too,' Ritva observed.

Siiri stopped eating and studied the doctor, whose eyes projected their usual common sense and vaguely inebriated fatigue. Tauno didn't appear to pay any attention to what Ritva was saying. He was shovelling long red tubes into his mouth as if they were particularly delicious field rations.

'Did you have many dogs?' Irma asked blithely.

'Who can be bothered to count dogs, they'll die come winter anyway. But my enormous aphids grew in my mother's garden.'

'Beg pardon?'

'We brought those flags all the way from Ahvenanmaa, we always had to have flags everywhere and sometimes flowers too, red flowers, those pretty ones . . .'

Ritva stopped talking, and her fork dropped to the table, leaving a green stain that escaped the attention of the cleaning robot in the corner. Irma and Siiri exchanged nervous glances and waited to hear what Ritva would come up with next.

'What are those flowers called?' Ritva asked, looking each of them in the eye in turn. Then she started laughing her rough cigarette laugh. 'Geraniums, that's what I meant! Goddammit, this happens to me sometimes, not being able to remember totally normal words. They just vanish, even though there's nothing else wrong with my memory. I know it's completely normal, but it's still annoying.'

Ritva continued eating serenely, and after emptying her plate offered to carry everyone's trays and plates over to the DishGullet.

'I may as well take them while I'm at it,' she said, gathering up the dirty dishware, sorting it quickly at the automatic dishwasher and calling from the door: 'Anyone care to join

me for a pint at Ukko-Munkki? Of course not. Just thought
I'd ask.'

'Poor woman,' Tauno remarked, appropriately so. 'She's
getting demented without realizing it. Oiva's like that too,
sometimes. You never get used to it.'

And so it was. Any one of them might suddenly start spouting
off all sorts of gibberish, but that was nothing to be afraid of.

'Who is this Oiva?' Siiri asked. She could tell Irma wanted
to learn more about Oiva, too, and for once her friend
seemed satisfied that Siiri beat her to it. Tauno gazed out of
the window and didn't reply. Despite it being late September,
it was still unseasonably warm. An uncomfortably long
moment passed without anyone saying anything. The elevator had time to announce it was going up twice before Siiri
spoke.

'Where does he live?' she asked, to ease Tauno's burden.

'Oiva is . . .' he said and paused to take a deep breath.
'Oiva lives in a municipal retirement home in Haaga. We
weren't assigned to the same place because . . . well, there
wasn't room. I had to come here.' His voice faded until it
was practically inaudible.

'But Haaga's not far from here!' Irma said encouragingly,
and started blabbering about taxis that carried you wherever
you wanted to go without any trouble, and her cousins who
lived in various retirement homes around town unless they
were already dead, as the greater part of them were, of
course, even though their family was very long-lived. 'Oh
dear, oh dear, now I have to settle for you two. *Döden,
döden, döden.*'

Siiri paid Irma no heed; she just let the chatter babble in her ears as she watched the enigmatic Tauno. She was very fond of him, one of the new friends she had made during her final years.

Chapter 5

Siiri had her work cut out coaxing Anna-Liisa to join her for a pointless tram ride. Of course Siiri could have ridden around gorgeous Helsinki on her own on such a bright autumn day, during that wondrous fleeting moment of the year when the leaves of the birches, lindens and horse chestnuts burned in various shades of yellow and orange but hadn't dropped yet. Anna-Liisa had been low for days now and downright glum as they sat at the card table this morning. Siiri decided a little joyride would be just the thing to cheer up her friend. Anna-Liisa simply didn't appear to be recovering from her husband's death, even though the couple's shared journey, which had commenced at Sunset Grove, had barely lasted two years.

'You can't measure it in time,' Anna-Liisa said. 'Those two years were the happiest of my long life. I don't particularly mourn the days we shared or what we did, nothing that concrete, but the man. My amazing Onni. I was so privileged to have him at my side, and at this age.' Her voice, typically so resonant, died as the tears welled up in her dark eyes.

From time to time Siiri and Irma wondered how long

they'd be forced to tolerate Anna-Liisa's grief. She repeated the same phrases, beautiful no doubt, every day as her tears fell. It had been touching for a while, but they had come to feel their friend should gradually be moving on. Her expressions of mourning had somehow taken on a flat tone. The same didn't go for Anna-Liisa's feelings, of course: the sorrow visibly weighed on her more and more heavily as the days passed. Her back was no longer as straight, her stride began to drag, and her face darkened in contemplation. More than once, Irma and Siiri had been tempted to remind Anna-Liisa of the amazing Ambassador's business affairs in the Helsinki underworld. Off-the-books rental units, bordellos and exploitation of immigrants, all of which had clearly played some role in their temporary commune in Hakaniemi, even though they had discreetly put the kibosh on investigating too closely.

'Yes. I suppose the sadness never goes away,' Siiri said, as the number 4 tram slowed to make the shift to the temporary tracks on Paciuksenkatu. The city had been building an underpass beneath the four-lane road just so a few joggers could run straight from Pikku-Huopalahti to Seurasaari; for as long as the project had been going on one would think they were erecting St Isaac's Cathedral. 'You just have to get used to it. That's what I did, little by little. Two days might pass now without me thinking about my husband.'

Anna-Liisa's eyes radiated disbelief. 'Really?'

'That's how it seems, although it might be that I think about him every day. But it's no longer as painful a memory as it once was. Now, my boys' deaths I've never been able to process. It seemed so impossible, having my children die of old age before I did.'

'They didn't die of old age. They killed themselves.'

'Anna-Liisa! How could you say such a thing? You know my sons—'

'One drank himself to death; the other ate himself to death. What is that, if not killing yourself?'

Anna-Liisa clamped her mouth into an impervious line and focused her gaze out of the window. At the Allergy Institute, a few immigrant women boarded the tram with their children, along with a troop of chattering Swedish-speaking schoolchildren. This drew their attention away from the unpleasant conversation and brightened the mood, since Siiri no longer needed to fear Anna-Liisa's brutal tongue-lashings.

Two girls sat down behind them and started squealing loudly. One of them was putting on her make-up, applying mascara and eye shadow with her mouth open; the other was engrossed in her phone.

'*Det är så* embarrassing!'

'Look, *hon ha* deleted *den*!'

'*Nej, va* being stupid.'

'*Helt* so fun.'

Siiri always enjoyed listening to how the Swedish dialect spoken in Helsinki grew more and more garbled by the day. First Russian was mixed in, then English, but now almost half of it was Finnish. One would have thought this would have cheered Anna-Liisa's profoundly Fennoman heart, but the more actively the girls behind them spoke, the more indifferent Anna-Liisa appeared to grow. '*Va ska vi gö me den där* private event? *Man måste* get *liksom* tickets.'

Suddenly one of the girls popped up and dashed out of the door. '*Ska du inte* coming?'

'*Jag ska käppä* to Kluuvi.'

'*Hejhej*, nähää!'

Siiri wondered whether 'nähää' was Finnish or Swedish. Did it mean *nähdään*, 'see you later?', or was it some youthful Swedish-language idiom for 'no'? The tram sped up Tukholmankatu, picking up fatigued nurses and confused alcoholics with bandaged heads at the Meilahti Hospital stop. The moment they sat down, the latter broke out the first aid they had bought at the state liquor store conveniently located right outside the hospital grounds and started administering it to themselves. The reek of stale and freshly opened booze settled over the other passengers.

'I went in for a shot. I haven't been drinking, I'm heading home. Might go for a run,' a rather intoxicated young fellow lied over the phone to his mother, wife or sister. He had gone in to get his publicly funded dose of narcotics, which were distributed to drug addicts so they'd be able to wean themselves off illicit drugs. Siiri had often listened to these detox patients as she sat in the number 4 and had been mystified to hear one relate she'd been receiving regular treatment for nine years. This didn't strike Siiri as particularly effective. But what did she know about illegal drugs? She did know something about the legal kind, as they were distributed by the fistful by the automated guided vehicles, or AGVs, that made the rounds of Sunset Grove.

Before they reached the stop at the new opera, Siiri suggested they change to a number 7 or number 8, as a dose of brisk autumn air would do them good after the alcohol-laden fug of the tram. But the gang of alcoholics disembarked there, and so Siiri and Anna-Liisa stayed put in the number 4.

'Maybe we should take this all the way to Katajanokka,' Anna-Liisa said. 'I'm not particularly interested in changing trams out of a sheer love for rail traffic. This line goes past that dreadful sugar cube designed by Alvar Aalto. Perhaps you aren't aware that the offices of the Awaken Now! Association are located there.'

The infamous Sugar Cube to which Anna-Liisa referred was the Enso-Gutzeit forestry company's former headquarters, a 1960s structure built on the site of the old Norrmén building designed by Theodor Höijer. The demolition of the Norrmén building had caused an uproar, even though Siiri had never found it particularly stylish or the least bit practical, since it only had one enormous flat on each storey. The fact that it had housed the Soviet Union's surveillance commission had done nothing to improve its reputation. And so it ended up in the dust heap of history, the gaudy old gewgaw. Siiri found Alvar Aalto's streamlined marble-faced replacement beautiful indeed, especially if you happened to catch it during a heavy snow – then it looked downright magical, glowing white against the golden onion domes of the Russian Orthodox Uspenski Cathedral. But how was it that the Sugar Cube had been taken over by charity organizations? She had had no idea.

'You don't keep up with the times, Siiri. I'll be happy to bring you up to date. Enso hasn't been Enso-Gutzeit for ages. It was simply Enso for a while, then it became Stora Enso, when a Swedish family, the Wallenbergs, and the Finnish government merged their failing forestry companies.'

Anna-Liisa was in fine form again. She launched into a thorough lecture on the reasons why no hope remained for the European forestry industry. No one used paper, plywood or cardboard any more. The only cellulose product for which there was still a demand was toilet tissue, and that was produced far from Finland's shores. Apparently the cheapest place to manufacture paper was in South America. Stora Enso had been chopped up, sold, and driven into receivership or something of the sort. The Wallenbergs got their money and the Finnish government got even poorer.

Now anyone who wanted to could lease space in Aalto's Sugar Cube.

'And if there's anyone who has money, it's these soul-savers, since they're running a flourishing caregiving business.'

Anna-Liisa was outraged by everything she had just explained, and Siiri felt that her friend's ire was partly directed at her, as if it were Siiri's fault that trees grew faster and taller in Brazil than in Finland, that eastern trade had collapsed along with the Soviet Union, and that these days people read the newspaper from annoying flickering screens built into the backs of tram seats.

'Put your money in caregiving! We guarantee the best possible ROI! Interest rates as high as 8.5%!' the screens screamed at this very moment. It was a paid advertisement, not financial news, although similar supposedly journalistic advice had appeared on Irma's green flaptop back when it still obeyed her. Irma claimed that her flaptop no longer understood her swipes, and so her beloved toy spent most of its time lolling at the bottom of her handbag.

'How is the settling of the estate going?' Siiri asked, trying to sound as nonchalant as Irma when she said something particularly tactless.

Anna-Liisa was a wealthy woman now, since the Ambassador had been opposed to drafting a prenuptial agreement, which meant half of his estate belonged to his widow. Unfortunately there had been a delay in disbursing the estate, as simply tracking down the Ambassador's heirs in the former Communist countries had proved extremely problematic. Once most of the beneficiaries had been identified, the greedy heirs started a ferocious battle over the money. None of them wanted Anna-Liisa to inherit half, because she had only been married to Onni for such a short time.

Siiri had followed these developments with concern, as Anna-Liisa was too frail to deal with such trivialities. Even now, her dark eyes went so black that Siiri could see herself in them: a worried face, wrinkled and creased, with a few silly strands of hair poking out from under her blue beret. She adjusted her hat and waited for Anna-Liisa to frame her thoughts.

'The fact of the matter is, the lawyers are still arguing over which of Onni's former family members are entitled to an inheritance.'

One man, apparently a retired dealer in bathroom tiles,

had popped up out of the blue somewhere in Yugoslavia and announced he was Onni's son. It had taken quite some time for the lawyers to successfully investigate the veracity of his claims. Then a Serb had asserted that his dearly departed older sister had also been sired by the Ambassador. The lawyers had been forced to root around Central Europe and Central America looking for this sister's five children from three marriages, and the more that turned up, the angrier the heirs in Finland had grown.

'Then we had to conduct DNA tests, which indicated that the man truly was Onni's offspring, but only two of this sister's children were, which was a strange outcome indeed. If the mother of the children is Onni's daughter, how could only two of her children carry his genes?'

'I don't believe that's possible,' Siiri said cautiously, without completely comprehending the landscape Anna-Liisa was cracking open for her.

Anna-Liisa laughed sourly. During her brief marriage she had learned enough about life's realities to realize that such genetic aberrations pointed to fraud. She lowered her voice and slowed her cadence as if Siiri were a slow learner who couldn't comprehend the difference between an adjective and a noun. 'The other three are not this woman's children. They're trying to swindle us. And that's not all. I'm being sued.'

Siiri squealed and was instantly ashamed of her reaction. An ice-cold stab pierced her head, and her heart started pounding more quickly than she would have liked. She clenched her fist to her breast and tried to breathe deeply, unsure of how long it would be before she was capable of thinking again. Sued! Was it possible that Anna-Liisa, as the recipient of property that had been acquired through illicit means, would be called to task for her husband's crimes? That did not bode well, not at all. But Siiri and Irma had never mustered the courage to confront Anna-Liisa about the Ambassador's affairs, and Siiri was incapable of asking anything useful now either. When it came down to it, she was far from certain that Anna-Liisa was aware of the type of criminal the Ambassador had been.

Anna-Liisa saw the boundless care in Siiri's face, took her hand and patted it soothingly.

'But they're all insane, so I have no cause for concern,' she said with such a carefree laugh that Siiri also convinced her heart to slow down again.

Chapter 6

Just as Siiri was rushing out of her flat to go down to play cards with her friends, she noticed a letter on her doormat: a proper, old-fashioned envelope, but no stamp or address. It didn't even have her name on it.

'How exciting,' she said to herself. Perhaps it was an invitation, or something else amusing.

She fetched the letter opener from her telephone table. It had belonged to her husband, who had always kept it on his desk, next to the paperweight and the hole-punch. She smiled for a moment at the thought of her husband at his desk and opened the envelope with one swift stroke.

The missive had been written with a tremulous but firm hand, the sort produced by her age-mates these days. It contained just a few lines separated without punctuation, as if the message were a poem:

> *I watch you from a distance*
> *Your smile, your eyes demure*
> *Could I overcome your resistance?*
> *Fear not, my heart is pure*

Yes, perhaps it really was a poem, as it had the requisite rhymes and other features. Siiri started to laugh. She re-read the spidery verses, shook her head, turned the paper over, but found no sign of the sender's name. That preacher couldn't be behind this silliness, could he? she reflected with a smile. She slipped the note back in its envelope and whisked the envelope into her bag. She would have to hurry; she didn't want to keep the others waiting.

'Going. Up.'

She spent an eternity in the corridor waiting for the elevator to go up and come back down. There weren't many floors above hers, but every stop took ages, as entering and exiting expeditiously was beyond the capacities of the building's elderly residents. Those capable of getting about on their own two feet would enter the elevator first, while those who hobbled about with walking frames were left nearest the doors. Every time someone needed to get out, those with walkers were first forced to march out into the corridor and then back in, the same tragicomic performance at every floor. The walkers bumped into each other, got caught in the gap, scraped at the legs of the independently mobile as they passed and escaped the control of their owners.

'Going. Down. Doors. Opening.'

The elevator was a youngish woman who sounded vaguely uncertain. Her daily announcements couldn't help but make Siiri yearn for the long-gone elevator girls at the Stockmann department store, with their blue uniforms, beautiful legs, efficient movements, bright voices and bilingual vocabularies. Siiri's daughter had dreamed of becoming an elevator girl when she grew up, until deciding to become a flight attendant and eventually ending up a translator and a nun. That's the sort of adventurer she was.

'Good morning, madam! Or should I say miss?' The strong scent of after-shave surged out of the elevator. A well-dressed man stood so awkwardly in the middle of the elevator that Siiri had a hard time deciding which side to squeeze herself into. The man stood tall and trim and seemed, in the manner of the composer Jean Sibelius, to be using his cane for nothing more than to put the finishing touch on his dandified presence. His hair was dark brown, certainly dyed, as at this age white and grey were the only genuine options for hair colour. Siiri had never encountered the fellow like this, one on one.

'I'm a widow. Siiri Kettunen, good morning.'

'Aatos Jännes, second floor, generous one-bedroom.'

'Doors. Closing. Going. Down.'

The man gave Siiri a handshake as firm as a soldier's, and her hand continued to ache for quite some time after he released it. Aatos Jännes didn't say another word during their brief sojourn in the elevator; he was humming something Siiri couldn't quite make out, but in all probability not classical music.

'First. Floor. Doors. Opening.'

'After you, Mrs Kettunen!'

'We generally use first names here at Sunset Grove. Just call me Siiri.'

Aatos Jännes drew his mouth into a smile and held his hand in front of the elevator's infrared eye, chivalrously protecting Siiri from the door and other perils. Siiri thanked him and turned towards the corner of the common room. Anna-Liisa already sat there glumly, along with the smiling Irma, who was busily shuffling two packs of cards. It took a moment before Irma noticed Siiri approach.

'Cock-a-doodle-doo!'

'I see you were privileged to ride the elevator with Aatos Jännes,' Anna-Liisa said, ignoring Irma's greeting. 'He's quite the topic of conversation around here these days.'

Now that the Ambassador is dead, Siiri thought, but managed to hold her tongue. Anna-Liisa reported many of the building's female residents were pining for Mr Jännes, although the widower had only taken up residence at Sunset Grove two weeks previously. He was known to attend afternoon dances in the city, occasionally requesting one of his co-residents from the retirement community to accompany him.

'Apparently he asks these women to chaperone him, despite being exceptionally active on the dance floor, with fancy footwork and fast moves.'

'To chaperone him?' Siiri asked, in an unnecessarily loud voice. Even Tauno heard her, despite sitting at some distance in his regular seat on the abandoned Jugendstil sofa.

'Well, well, isn't that something!' Irma exclaimed. 'You clearly sparked Siiri's interest. Do you want to start attending daytime dances with our new Don Juan?' She started painting visions of Siiri's and Aatos's afternoon assignations that bordered on the indelicate. 'That adorable little widow from our floor whose husband just died, is her name Eila, the widow's, I mean, I don't think I ever heard the husband's name, since Eila only refers to him as her husband, without using a name, although he must have had one. I always say "Veikko" when I talk about my husband, oh dear oh dear, my lovely old Veikko, but . . . What was I saying again?'

'Something about this Aatos Jännes,' Anna-Liisa said tiredly. She rapped the baize table top to reinforce her words, but the raps were listless. Her hands were visibly shaking; Siiri had never noticed anything of the sort in the past.

'Yes, she, I mean this petite Mrs Eila, had panicked when Aatos invited her to a daytime dance and so she accepted. She got very dizzy from the way Aatos whirled her around the floor. Her blood pressure is very low, you know, I mean Eila's, unlike the rest of us, and low blood pressure is a good thing, of course, since you don't suffer heart attacks so easily, although of course there's nothing I hope for as much as a merciful heart attack. I don't want you to misunderstand me, now; I don't find your company tedious, even though every day that passes at this religious observatory is so similar that it's impossible to know what season it is or even what time of day, since it's always the same grey, but . . . What was I talking about again?'

'It seemed as if you had some story to tell us about Aatos Jännes.'

'Oh yes, that's right. I certainly am a fuddy-duddy, but I always tell my darlings that they're not allowed to get upset with me, even though I'm such a forgetful old lady, seeing as how I'm already over the age of ninety, as a matter of fact so much over that I can no longer remember how much, but

I have no intention of turning one hundred, and I've told my darlings there's no point preparing any sort of big celebration, as I plan on kicking the bucket long before that.'

'Long before?' Siiri asked brightly.

But Anna-Liisa looked like a nervous wreck. 'Are you intending to tell us something about this new resident who has invented the surname Jännes for himself?'

'What do you mean, invented?' Tauno asked from the sofa. 'It sounds like a typical Fennoman name. Like Petäjä. Anna-Liisa Petäjä and Aatos Jännes, those are the kinds of names we all have.'

'Irma! Get to the point. Everyone else, silence!'

'You know, I can't remember what I was saying any more. Can you give me a little hint?'

Beads of sweat glistened at Anna-Liisa's pallid temples. 'According to you, this adorable woman with low blood pressure had been at a dance with Aatos Jännes. You never made it any further, despite the fact that you've been going on and on about your hundredth birthday.'

'But I have no intention of turning one hundred! Aren't you listening to a word I'm saying?' In her agitation, Irma began rummaging around in her bag and unpacked its contents onto the table, next to the packs of cards. The handbag disgorged a pair of bunched-up nylons, apparently snagged, as she generally carried an unopened package of spare hose in her bag for emergencies, a small bottle of whisky, a lace handkerchief, her oval fob, a box of pastilles without the attendant cigarettes and a colourful bag that crackled. She opened the bag and offered its contents to everyone.

'I have some snacks, help yourselves!'

They were little brown nibbles in a variety of shapes. Everyone eagerly partook, including Tauno, who hauled himself up from the sofa with difficulty and poured himself a fistful of Irma's treats from the bag. He decided returning to the sofa was too much trouble, so he stood there next to the women in his peculiar hunched stance. And who should happen to emerge from behind a pillar and make his way over to them at that very moment but Aatos Jännes himself.

'Well, look at that! Speak of the devil – I mean, what a devilish coincidence,' Irma said, with a tinkling laugh. 'Would you care for a snack, Mr Aatos? Have you noticed that everyone is always snacking these days? It's the latest craze, as they say. You have to be shoving something in your mouth all the time to stay lively. People can't even be bothered to sit through a movie without a bucket of food. Energy levels! That's the idiotic phrase you keep hearing everywhere. You have to keep your energy levels up, and that's why the supermarket shelves are jam-packed with temptations like this these days. Look at this bag! Partymix, it says, with a cute little cat smiling on it. That kitty-cat is the reason I grabbed this particular bag; there were miles of different kinds of snacks at the supermarket yesterday. Or was it the day before? These certainly are fresh—'

'Thank you, Irma.' Aatos Jännes's voice was a soupçon too high and delicate for his black-and-white matinee idol image, but he looked at Irma so intently that she stopped talking. There was a moment of awkward silence, as everyone was waiting for Aatos to say something more, since he had made such a dashing entrance into their little group.

'Ewww, goddammit!' Tauno spluttered and spat out Irma's little treats so they flew every which way, including the table top. Apparently in his greed he had crammed the entire fistful of titbits into his mouth at once. The ever-alert cleaning robot started up and moved towards them.

'Not to your taste?' Irma asked cheerfully, placing one of the dark brown nuggets in her mouth. The others looked on curiously. 'On the bland side. Not much to write home about. They must be very healthy, because one certainly wouldn't snack on these for pleasure.'

'Downright disgusting, if you ask me. And I've eaten everything from pine-bark bread to pebbles,' Tauno said, wiping his mouth on his sleeve. The robot cleaner was bustling at his feet, sucking up all the nibbles that had flown to the floor.

Now Siiri placed two of Irma's delicacies into her mouth, too. They were dry and hard and seemed very healthy indeed. She didn't dare bite, because her old teeth would have lost the battle against the crunchy morsels. She might break a tooth, or in the worst case, one might fall out. She tried sucking the little candies, but her mouth was so dry that she couldn't detect any taste. Anna-Liisa sucked on hers, too, and appeared satisfied.

'I can practically feel my energy levels rising,' she said. 'The flavour is really no different from our three-dimensional food waste. In other words, they have no flavour at all.'

'The smell is a little unusual,' Irma said, sniffing the bag in her hand.

Aatos Jännes watched them in amusement. He hadn't popped a single one of his own treats into his mouth; he just watched the others' reactions. Tauno started tottering off towards the drinking fountain to rinse his mouth. His cascade of curses echoed in the spacious lobby, above the elevator's announcements and the smartwall's sermon about the Holy Spirit manifesting in each of us. Aatos took the bag of snacks from Irma's hand, pulled his spectacles from his breast pocket and examined the ingredients.

'This is cat food,' he said matter-of-factly.

'Don't be silly!' Irma squawked, bursting out into her cheerful staccato laugh that started high and light and dropped from there. 'Do you think I want to poison us all?'

'That might not be such a bad idea,' Anna-Liisa said, trying to tidily expectorate the cat food she had been sucking on. Irma kindly handed her her lace handkerchief.

'I'm going to eat mine; they cost a mint. No one could be mad enough to make snacks for pussies. Fiddlesticks, is what I say!' She laughed so hard that her rotund body jiggled with joy.

Siiri couldn't get a word out. She had swallowed both nibbles without chewing. They caught nastily in her throat, but her stomach started feeling even nastier now that she knew she'd consumed cat food. At first she just experienced a slow rolling, but the waves of nausea gradually swelled and swelled until she was genuinely afraid she would vomit.

'Siiri, you look pale. Would you like some more fortification?' Irma handed the bag of cat food to her, and Aatos Jännes laughed out loud. He found the episode spectacularly funny, since he hadn't fallen for Irma's trick. Irma refused to admit she had pulled a prank and remained adamant that she had offered everyone a healthy energy boost. The text on the bag was in such tiny print that none of them could decipher what the nibbles were made of, but apparently Aatos was right. The big picture of the cat and the name, *Partymix Katzenfreude*, clearly indicated as much.

'Unless they're made from cats,' Irma laughed cheerfully, and was as unconcerned by this alternative as the notion that she had just fed her friends cat food. Siiri felt she was perspiring oddly and she wasn't feeling the tiniest relief, even though she sensibly tried to tell herself that cats were in all likelihood fed better food than they were back during the war or now in the retirement home, so it was unlikely any permanent damage had been done. It was simply the thought that was disgusting, that was all.

'They eat cats in China, so why not here?' Irma continued, and Anna-Liisa fainted. She was white as a sheet and went limp in an instant. Aatos Jännes leapt over surprisingly nimbly to catch Anna-Liisa before she could hit her head on anything. A volunteer staff member flew to their sides almost as quickly. None of the trained caregivers from the old retirement home days had ever offered assistance with such enthusiasm. But Sirkka the Saver of Souls' skills at administering first aid were slight. She lowered her hands to Anna-Liisa's head and started talking gibberish.

'How God anointed Jesus of Nazareth with the Holy Ghost and with power: who went about doing good, and healing all that were oppressed of the Devil; for God was with him. Acts of the Apostles, chapter ten, verse thirty-eight. I have been blessed with the Holy Spirit. I heal you, Anna-Liisa.'

A ray of sunlight fell upon Anna-Liisa's wan face, and a miracle occurred. She came to.

'How do you know my name, you godless creature?' she said weakly but angrily.

Sirkka the Saver of Souls looked at her hand as if doubting her own gifts. Aatos Jännes rose and released Anna-Liisa. He seemed very uncomfortable and surreptitiously disappeared to the left, whence he had come.

'Would you care for a snack? You can have the whole bag,' Irma said to Sirkka, who had been struck dumb by the ecstasy of the moment. Her hand was still on Anna-Liisa's head, and Anna-Liisa swatted it away in annoyance.

'Thank you, Lord, thank you,' Sirkka said before greedily snatching the bag of cat food from Irma's hand.

'You may leave,' Anna-Liisa ordered, as if she were a seventh-generation aristocrat addressing her lowliest servant on a British television series. Sirkka the Saver of Souls clacked off in her green high heels, and they could hear the bag of cat food crackle as she devoured the manna her miracle-working had earned her.

'She must have been hungry, the poor dear,' Siiri said, feeling rather recovered herself.

'Wasn't that a neat trick, giving her that dratted cat food?' Irma said, transferring the belongings from the table back into her handbag. In doing so, her hand struck on something the existence of which she had already forgotten.

'Look what I've found!'

She was holding an envelope. The same sort of envelope Siiri had nearly trod on on her welcome mat. Irma's letter didn't have a name, address or stamp either.

'What I have here is, my friends, a poem from an anonymous admirer. Isn't it sweet that I received a love letter in my last days.'

Irma opened the envelope, which contained the same sort of little card as Siiri's letter. But the poem wasn't the same. Irma read it in a vibrato, supporting her interpretation with gesticulations.

> *'I feed, ravenous, on pine and spruce*
> *Senses heightened, a bull moose*
> *But now that I've caught your scent*
> *My hunger will never relent'*

'Impudent!' Anna-Liisa cried in outrage. 'And clumsy to boot. Mine is better.'

Anna-Liisa had received a letter, too. She pulled hers out from the pocket of her black cardigan and recited the poem as if it were the handiwork of a skilled wordsmith.

'I yearn for darkest night
And bridge of sweet moonlight
That carrieth me to thee
Die, day, hear my plea!'

'I wouldn't call that much of a poem either,' Irma said, when Anna-Liisa's artistic pause had lingered embarrassingly long. 'I liked the bull moose in mine. Didn't you get any mail, Siiri?'

As she opened her letter, Siiri caught a whiff of Aatos's cologne, which still lingered at the card table. She drew the paper out of the envelope and for some reason sniffed it. A waft of the same powerful *kölnisch wasser*. Of course! Their mystery poet was the daytime dancer with dyed hair and erect bearing. They should have known from the start.

It all made sense, Aatos Jännes's demeanour, body language and cologne. Quite the showman.

'Now I remember what I was supposed to tell you about that adorable little widow and Aatos,' Irma said suddenly. 'He had asked her politely for a glass of whisky, and she had let him into her apartment.'

'She keeps whisky in her home? This petite widow?' Siiri asked in surprise.

'Why wouldn't she? Whisky is good for you. My doctor has ordered me to have a glass of whisky every night for my . . . all of this.' To Anna-Liisa's satisfaction, Irma cut the diversion short and returned to her original train of thought. As it turned out, Aatos Jännes's visit hadn't been particularly pleasant. The whisky had barely been poured into the tumblers before he had grown over-bold. Eila had not offered any details, but from the intensity of her indignation, Irma had deduced that Aatos had crossed the bounds of propriety.

'On the other hand, this Eila is a rather timid soul, so how do we know what sort of Sunday School girl she is.'

'It seems we have a real Don Giovanni in our midst,' Siiri said, and Irma smiled as if she wouldn't be at all disappointed to cross paths with a bull moose among the spruces.

Chapter 7

The young man's long, bounding strides were familiar to all of them. But he had otherwise *updated his look*, as they said. In place of the waxed hair he now had an even more remarkable coiffure: his hair had been shaved everywhere except the crown of his head, where it formed a blond strip and a small bun-like topknot: the precise opposite of an ageing man's hairstyle.

'Maybe he wants to communicate that his testosterone levels are still high, since he has so much hair growing on top of his head that he can afford to shave it bald everywhere else,' Irma said loudly to Siiri, who was sitting next to her.

Former Sunset Grove project manager, current Experience Director & Front-Line Support Jerry Siilinpää had slipped his feet into some sort of toddler slippers that had a separate pouch for every toe. It was as if he were barefoot, even though he wasn't. Combined with the suit that was too small and too tight, the slippers looked like gorilla feet. But in every other way, Jerry Siilinpää was the same. He vigorously bustled around at his laptop at the front of the room and eventually managed to connect it to the video projector, which started spitting out keywords and illustrative images on a screen that was far too large.

'GERONTECHNOLOGY: BRINGING JOY TO SENIORS'

The words formed gradually on the screen; at first they were a jumble and vibrated unpleasantly, but soon they found their place in time with breezy computerized music and formed the topic of today's Evenings at Sunset Grove presentation. A relatively small crowd had gathered in the auditorium, as Jerry's introduction to caregiving technology was too convoluted for most residents of Sunset Grove to comprehend. Anna-Liisa and Margit had taken their regular places in the middle of the front row, while Siiri and Irma sat a little further back, so they could whisper to each other without disturbing their gorilla-footed presenter.

'Hey, everyone, it's great to see all you guys here,' Jerry began, clicking a new graphic kaleidoscope onto the wide screen. 'I know you've all heard about gerontechnology, but it might seem a little dada.'

'. . . even though it's the latest,' Irma whispered in Siiri's ear so loudly that Anna-Liisa shot them an angry look.

'The latest, that's exactly right.'

Jerry wrote his favourite term on the flipchart and underlined it with a red marker. Then he started talking about humanized automation. A flood of arrows and huge numbers and fatigued sprites that were supposed to look chipper inundated the wall-sized screen. Siiri tried to make sense of the visual presentation, but the more she focused, the worse she felt.

'All right, gang, so we're all aware of the employment situation in Finland. The population structure is leading to a permanent cost deficit, and in the long run that's an impossible equation. Over the next twenty years, the ageing population will form an economic ball-and-chain that's just going to be far too heavy for Finland to carry. That being the case, the highly respected international credit-rating agency Goofy's has estimated that Finland is going to end up among the so-called super-ageing countries. Doesn't sound too good, does it?'

Jerry Siilinpää gave the audience a moment to consider their fatherland's fate as one of the world's most super-ageing countries. Each and every one of them felt guilty for this shameful state. When the mood started sinking from glum to black, Jerry once more took charge of the situation like an experienced monologue actor. 'But let me assure you: there's nothing to worry about, you can do something about this. And not just something, BTW, but quite a lot.'

'That means *by the way, btw*,' Ritva interpreted from the row behind Siiri and Irma.

'Exactly. Sustainable consumption and everyday technology, they're the solutions to everything that's bringing us down.'

Long words and spinning arrows flashed across the wall. Happy-looking sprites started pushing up from the bottom of the screen; one was sitting in a sailing boat and two were cycling aimlessly. Jerry spoke of the growing importance of free time, quality of life and everyday design.

'Encounters and meeting places are key.'

His presentation had advanced to cosiness, which he described as a factor that increased a human touch in one's life. It meant striving for an increasingly unique look by decorating with recycled furniture and introducing elements of rusticity alongside the traditional materials of the automated world, and in doing so steering the service experience in a direction that would generate the right sort of fermentation.

Siiri's head was thrumming and her stomach was churning; apparently some sort of fermentation was taking place there. Colours and strange words danced on the screen: acoustic listening chair, sensitive smart-tag, design-intensive product, interactive telemedicine, and stimulating multisensory auxiliary reality. She tried to focus on her fat ankles, but curiosity won out, and so she kept glancing up at Jerry Siilinpää's visually over-stimulating audit.

'What bugs you most when you guys think about automation and technology? People's attitudes. Exactly.'

Jerry was off and running. He paced the auditorium in long strides, waving his hands around. He pointed vigorously, alternating between the screen and some innocent resident who was trying to keep up with his vision.

'This is a digital revolution, the best ever, truly amazing. And you guys can help change the world, too.'

'Aren't we a little too old for this?'

It was Anna-Liisa. Her voice strove for friendliness, even though it was strained by fatigue and frustration. When Jerry didn't immediately parry this attack, the others took heart, too. A barrage of questions and random catcalls rained down on Jerry. Tauno demanded Sunset Grove's electronics be tossed in the lake and young women be brought in instead. Someone else wanted employees who were a bit older, as opposed to such inexperienced ones, no matter how sweet they might be. One insisted caregivers be Finnish, and the others got mad, because being old was no excuse for racism and many of their best caregiving experiences were with immigrants.

'But I'm going to keep saying "negro", it's not a bad word. And neither is Russki,' said an overweight woman sitting next to the resident with a Somali background. The Somali-Finn stared at the hands resting in her lap so expressionlessly that it was hard to tell if she understood the conversation surging around her, or if she was simply accustomed to not showing her feelings.

'If one of those coal-black men shows up one morning to wash me, it's going to terrify a feeble old woman like me.'

'There's nothing to be afraid of, Eila. No one is going to wash you. The toilet has an automatic rinse, one of those cosy humanized inventions. Haven't you noticed?' It was Tauno. He had advanced up the aisle and was now standing almost flush with the front row, fanning his hands furiously.

'How come there's no bingo any more?' asked the woman holding the seal pup in her lap. She still had a hair curler snarled at the back of her head.

'Bingo!' Siilinpaa exclaimed, dashed up to the flipchart and printed out the word in large, childish letters with a green marker. 'Let's not let things escalate too far. Bingo is a good point, I'll pick it up from here.' He pointed at the woman petting the seal pup, who didn't notice, because at that moment she was whispering something to her little robot that made its tail wag wildly.

Siilinpää felt that bingo didn't require expensive resources, by which he meant people. Why, anyone at all could play a fun game of bingo whenever they wanted by themselves with a computer; it was a cinch. Suddenly the screen was filled with a storm of websites shooting from different directions that vanished with a pop in the middle of the screen. Every website was an example of the world's easiest bingo game, and you could find them all from Sunset Grove's smartwalls, if you just bothered to search for them there.

'So we would play bingo alone?' Margit asked.

'Exactly. It doesn't take two to bingo, just to tango.'

Jerry started yodelling something in English and then laughed heartily to demonstrate to his grave-faced audience that he was lightening the mood.

'This is epic. Totally amazing!'

Then he compared bingo to a health centre and explained why they didn't need doctors any more either, any more than they needed a girl to call out the bingo numbers. Mobile appointments were the latest, and the integration of various electronic systems turned doctors from experts into service providers. And because all service was self-service, doctors also plummeted fast and hard on the digital service roller coaster.

In the middle of the whirlwind of terms, Siiri once more made out the word 'humanity'. Jerry pondered the deepest essence of humanity and rather speedily arrived at communication. He felt humankind had exceeded the limits of human communication. There was too much communication, and statistically that caused misunderstanding, generated unnecessary emotional reactions and was overrated.

'Misunderstandings always arise from emotions, am I right? And emotions bring in anger and irritation and that other negative stuff that makes life a drag. Who disagrees with me? No one.'

The presentation had grown almost psychedelic, so rapidly did the complicated words and animated presentations ricochet in and out. The adorable little woman complained she was feeling nauseous, and Tauno started cursing more and more emphatically. Siiri held her head and tried to force herself to obey: do not look at the wall. Irma looked pale, too, even though she claimed to find the presentation exciting.

'Computers never miscommunicate or cause misunderstandings. Computers don't interpret your tone of voice or mood; they just do what you tell them to and listen. It's that simple. Best ever.'

Jerry described humanized automation as if it were more miraculous than God. In this instance, humanity meant that some computers followed voice commands, recognized people and movements and reacted to changes in temperature or even the expressions on the user's face. And because they were computers, not people, they didn't cause confusion and stress, both of which were especially dangerous things for the panther crowd. He had used the term 'the panther crowd' to refer to them in the past, but no one was exactly sure what he meant.

'Silence is liberating! When humanized automation is your companion, you have the freedom to not communicate. You get to decide. And when we go further down this path, we come to gerontechnology and humanized automation increasing the end user's long-term independence, autonomy and freedom of choice. That means you decide what you're going to do. Is that epic or what? Such environments, like Sunset Grove here, are cost-efficient, customer-friendly, and it's both of those things 24/7. Exactly. This isn't dada; this is the latest. This is the solution to the ageing-induced welfare-deficit problem recessionary societies are facing, not some prehistoric HSS revamps, hey, get real, that stuff confuses normal folks like us.'

The adorable little woman threw up. A smooth brown porridge sprayed everywhere, because in her panic she clamped her hand to her mouth. Those sitting next to and in front of her got their share of the shower, but the majority of the gruel was in Eila's lap and on the floor. One of Eila's neighbours got upset, another one didn't understand what was happening, and a third vomited, too. More of the brown soup splattered to the floor and the back of the seal pup stroker. This was what the 3D-printed multicoloured food turned into in the stomach, of course, as when primary colours are mixed together, they create brown.

'It's that video. It's impossible to watch without getting sick,' Siiri remarked to Irma.

Tauno gave orders to the nearby troops, and the old

Somali-Finnish woman who had been sitting silently throughout the presentation led Eila from the room. Someone brought water, one looked for a cleaning robot, and the seal pup stroker tried to take off her clothes. Two robots woke up in their respective corners and hummed over to swab the deck. Anna-Liisa and Margit guided people out by an unsoiled path so they wouldn't track the mess all over the premises of the pilot project in monitored care. Siiri and Irma both felt so nauseous that they decided to go upstairs to rest. As she stood, Siiri spied two rats between the rows of seats, making their way to the scene of the vomiting. She was too exhausted to react; she just tiredly noted the rats' eagerness. Maybe the rats would be of some use cleaning up this mess.

Everyone did their part, either out of a desire to help or out of confusion. Only Jerry Siilinpää had frozen at the lectern in his gorilla slippers. He had never envisioned a turn of events like this in his worst nightmares, and he was at a complete loss as to what to do; nothing like this had been covered in his national defence courses or in his continuing education in innovative business strategies. At that moment, he secretly longed for staff, even Sinikka Sundström, former director of Sunset Grove, who knew how to dig into her positivity pouch for handfuls of good cheer and make problems disappear with two claps of her hands. But Sinikka Sundström and her positivity pouches were in Pakistan at the moment, volunteering at a children's hospital after having stepped onto the so-called pension pathway, which meant receiving full unemployment compensation until she reached retirement age. Jerry Siilinpää was Sunset Grove's sole employee. He shut his laptop, turned off the video projector, tore the topmost piece of paper from the flipchart, and packed his belongings into an orange satchel that in a previous existence had been a life raft. Then he flopped down at one of the desks and logged on to Facebook.

Chapter 8

Siiri tried to pick up the pace as she walked down her corridor, although this proved to be more effective at the level of intent than action. She knew she was late for the morning card game yet again, but her feet simply wouldn't move any faster. After all, she had to remain cognizant of her balance, as the most foolish thing a ninety-seven-year-old could do was to take a tumble because she was hurrying and break a hip.

As always, the corridor was deserted. Ghostly lights flickered on by themselves as her journey proceeded, but they reacted so slowly that she was constantly stepping into darkness and leaving oases of light in her wake. Just before she reached the elevator, she nearly crashed into a wheelchair in the gloom. It was a shock to the system: her heart started pounding nastily, she teetered dangerously, and she felt a stabbing pain in her head. A resident she didn't recognize, presumably a woman, was asleep in the wheelchair: the compact figure looked like a black lump with cropped hair that glowed white in the dark. And then the bright lights flashed on, illuminating the scene of their violent encounter. Siiri saw a motionless seal pup in the woman's lap and a hair curler on the floor.

'I beg your pardon, I'm so sorry. It was so dark I didn't see you. I didn't bump you too badly, did I? I'm sorry? Are you . . . are you all right?'

Neither the woman or her seal pup reacted. Perhaps she had fallen asleep; that happened all the time. And the seal pup's battery had apparently run out. Siiri decided to let the woman sleep in peace. As far as Siiri knew, Parliament hadn't yet interfered with an old person's right to sleep in her wheelchair in the corridor, only with the possibility of dying on the floor of her own home. Siiri continued on her way and hopped into the elevator, which was already calling to her invitingly.

'Going. Down.'

There was a robot in the elevator, one of those funny little cleaning gadgets. Siiri greeted it cheerfully and watched it bustle about. Apparently someone had thrown up in the elevator. The contraption whirred at the brown muck in the corner, but something must have been amiss, as instead of rinsing and scrubbing away the filth, it just spread it around.

'Look at what you've done!' Siiri cried to the robot. It stopped. 'Can you hear me? Can you understand me?' The machine continued whirring and smearing the liquid around. Siiri stamped her foot angrily and raised her voice: 'Stop! You're not cleaning, you're making a mess!' The robot stopped. It flashed a green light at Siiri and then a red one before retreating shamefacedly into the corner. 'Good robot.

You ought to think about what you just did,' Siiri said, bending down to pat the machine. It didn't react. 'I see, you're not as human as Jerry boasted you were. You don't react to touch.' The creature let out a little whimper and turned off. Maybe that was its way of saying goodbye to Siiri, as the elevator had reached the first floor.

'Doors. Opening. Please. Exit.'

So someone else had vomited. It had been going on for some time since Jerry Siilinpää's presentation, so it might well be an epidemic, not just a bout of general nausea brought on by Jerry's video.

'There's some virus going around,' Anna-Liisa said, sighing heavily. 'Norovirus, perhaps.'

Irma was playing solitaire because Anna-Liisa was afraid that the stomach flu would spread through the cards, which was perfectly possible, although Irma claimed to have washed the cards with her own two hands. It had been a terrifically time-consuming undertaking. She had wiped each of the cards individually with a hot rag and then dried them. Two times fifty-two cards plus the jokers. With surprising speed, she calculated that that added up to 110. With washing and drying, that meant 220 treatments.

'Are there three jokers in your packs? Usually there are only two,' Siiri mused.

'Hmm, maybe the third one is the spare card, but I always use all the jokers. They're my favourite card.'

'As far as I'm aware, jokers are not used in solitaire.'

'Pshaw, Anna-Liisa! You can do whatever you want in solitaire, because you play it by yourself. That's what makes it such fun. I use jokers, and then when it gets too difficult, I cheat a little. But just a little.'

'Let's get back to the topic at hand, please. We were discussing the virus.'

Irma believed it was all due to the computers. She had heard from her darlings that computers spread viruses, and now that Sunset Grove had been turned into a space station, the logical explanation was that the electronics were spreading viruses to the residents.

'Perhaps that's the whole point, for us to die of machine-induced lorovirus!' Irma laughed heartily, wiping the tears from her eyes with a lace handkerchief. '*Döden, döden, döden.*' She rolled her eyes to look as scary as possible.

'What do you make of our little Jerry?' Siiri asked, when it felt like an appropriate moment to move on from microbes and conspiracies. She knew nothing about viruses, but she washed her hands five times a day and had been healthy for decades. In retrospect far too healthy, of course, seeing as how she was still alive.

'We could stop washing our hands,' Irma proposed. 'You're the one who said it.'

'We've already covered viruses; now we're talking about Jerry Siilinpää.'

To Siiri's surprise, Anna-Liisa took an extremely positive view of the young man. She admitted Jerry's use of Finnish was peculiar, but felt he was a good person at heart and a product of his environment. Siiri thought back to the photograph Irma had found somewhere on the Internet with her flaptop, the one of the Ambassador and Jerry together taken during the retrofit of Sunset Grove. Could it be possible that Anna-Liisa was defending the lad out of loyalty to her husband?

'It's not as if he can help it, the fact that people speak like children irrespective of setting, even in Parliament: hey guys, best ever, what's the vibe and what have you. Jerry is adapting to his surroundings, unlike us, who speak an ancient dialect, especially Irma. Language is constantly changing, which is what makes it such a fascinating reflection of the times. Of course I personally mourn the disappearance of the possessive suffix, as evidenced in the speech of our previous prime minister, but then again he appeared at official events in knee-breeches and summer shoes, so it's not as if we need to take him very seriously.'

'The prime minister? If we don't take the prime minister seriously, then who?' Siiri cried. Just the day before, she and Irma had watched a parliamentary session and been very satisfied with all of the ministers' behaviour and attire. But she had to admit that she had not, perhaps, paid sufficient attention to possessive suffixes.

'I'm not following this conversation at all. Aren't we talking about Jerry? I think he's a very nice boy,' Irma said, cheating herself at solitaire and trying to cover it up so Siiri and Anna-Liisa wouldn't notice.

They swiftly came to the unanimous conclusion that, despite his incomprehensible jargon and whirling arrows, Jerry had their best interests at heart. He sincerely believed in modern technology. He had probably gone through a lot of trouble to acquire so many backers for the pilot project in monitored caregiving, and perhaps all this foolishness would actually lead to Finland becoming an international lodestar in elder-care. A spiralling cost would turn into a source of wealth: what could be more gratifying?

'And these volunteers? Did Jerry procure them? Or come up with the whole idea?' asked Anna-Liisa. She viewed them with a deep suspicion.

'I doubt it. Jerry doesn't seem . . . charismatic that way,' Siiri said. 'My understanding is that it's very difficult to attract volunteers to unpleasant places like this. I mean retirement homes.'

'Has anyone seen Margit lately?' Anna-Liisa suddenly asked, uncharacteristically leaping from one topic to a third. The tremor in her hands was more marked than ever, and Siiri suspected this was one reason she had refused to play cards, in addition to the viruses. Perhaps her shaking hands could no longer hold cards.

No one knew anything about Margit. She hadn't been seen in the communal area for days, even in her automatic black artificial-leather massage chair, and it had been ages since she'd made an appearance in the dining room. Then Irma remarked that Ritva hadn't asked any of them to join her for a pint at the Ukko-Munkki for quite some time, either.

'Should we be worried about them?'

'Yes, perhaps they also caught a stomach virus from these dratted contraptions,' Irma suggested, but Anna-Liisa had her own theory.

'I suspect Margit has joined the ranks of these volunteers.'

'That's nice,' Irma said casually, exchanging a nasty king for a smiling joker and slipping the king under her behind. In her view, it was a purely positive, if rather surprising, development if Margit, whom she considered a rather selfish individual, had taken up volunteer work and would be helping more severely incapacitated residents, now that the primary source of assistance at Sunset Grove was a smartwall. Anna-Liisa feebly protested, but Irma didn't let her get a word in edgeways. She launched into a long-winded reflection as to whether they should have a bad conscience for gossiping at the baize-covered table instead of helping the robots assist their sickly neighbours. 'Was Jerry referring to our old card table with all that talk about rusticity? What do you suppose? I certainly have no use for rustic furniture; I'm a city girl, not some bumpkin from the suburbs.'

Then Siiri remembered the seal pup lover sleeping outside the elevators on the fourth floor. She had left the poor woman alone in the corridor. Perhaps she should go back and check on her? Surely they could voluntarily do that much to help the volunteers?

'Why bother,' Irma said. 'Sleeping in the corridor isn't dangerous. Play a round of double solitaire with me.'

And so they played, with Siiri losing badly to Irma. She was unable to concentrate, and her thoughts meandered down unpleasant paths. She thought about Jerry Siilinpää in his funny footwear, glanced in concern at Anna-Liisa, who sat in silence for the duration of their prolonged game, and pondered the viruses lurking about Sunset Grove before her thoughts circled back round to Margit's mysterious disappearance. She found it impossible to bring order to her reflections and shifted the cards mechanically around the table. By the time they finished the third round and Irma exulted in her victory by singing the prelude to Charpentier's *Te Deum,* Anna-Liisa had drifted off in her chair.

Chapter 9

Siiri and Irma decided to take a tram to go grocery shopping; it was more exciting than walking to the nearest Low Price Market. The tram took them to a bigger supermarket on Mannerheimintie practically door to door, and the trip was as fun as riding the roller coaster at Linnanmäki theme park back in the 1950s.

Navigating your way around a new store was always difficult at first. It was impossible to find what you were looking for, especially when the store was larger than the old Seutula airport back when they had last had occasion to set foot in it, perhaps in the 1970s, before their husbands retired and still travelled abroad on business from time to time. Irma remembered that her lovely Veikko always brought her expensive perfume from his travels, but for the life of her Siiri couldn't remember having ever been given any gifts by her husband.

'Maybe he didn't bring you anything,' Irma said. 'If he was a tightwad.'

Siiri almost took offence, because her husband hadn't been the least bit stingy, just a sensible, responsible individual, and in the 1970s such people didn't splurge on luxuries. One had to be thrifty and carefully consider what was necessary. Back then, there was no talk of consumer overspending or a citizen's obligation to put money into circulation; instead, headlines discussed the oil crisis that meant frivolities like leisure flying and motorboat races were forbidden. But Siiri decided there was no point getting upset with Irma, because she couldn't see Irma. Instead, Siiri was confronted by the shelves in front of her, which held more varieties of salad dressing than her husband's study had books. And that was a lot.

'What on earth was I supposed to buy?' Siiri thought out loud, paralysed by the sight of the bottles. She turned around and saw twenty yards of potato chip bags.

'Cock-a-doodle-doo!' Irma's cheerful voice was echoing from the north-east. Siiri headed for the familiar sound, passing the handmade chocolates and endless rows of pasta in various shapes and varieties. Irma had discovered the free samples, where a friendly-looking Asian woman was offering insect-based foods to interested shoppers. A young man who smelled powerfully of alcohol and claimed he was going fishing was waiting in line with Irma to try the mealworms.

'Try one, Siiri! It doesn't taste nearly as bad as it looks and sounds.' Irma crunched the worms in satisfaction and then selected a grasshopper. The consultant explained to her how to prepare a delicious and nutritious meal from insects. 'Oh, I know it's ecological and healthy, but all we eat at our retirement home is mashed food waste from the dispenser and cat nibbles,' Irma said, and to Siiri's relief her friend didn't buy any insects.

They dragged plastic buckets around behind them, miniature shopping trolleys of some sort for smaller purchases. The other customers were pushing around gargantuan wagons they shovelled food into as if preparing for months-long stays in a bomb shelter. Irma started relating a younger cousin's account of the bombing of Helsinki and how he had climbed out of the Tiilimäki bomb shelter during an air raid to watch the searchlights criss-cross the skies of Helsinki. When two beams caught a Soviet plane in their crosshairs, it was shot down and the sky exploded in a shower of colours.

'My cousin always told the story so vividly, how it had made an indelible effect on him, and then years later, meaning just recently, he had got his hands on the diaries of his brother who had died at the front, and this story was in there. In other words, it wasn't his own memory, even though that's what he'd believed all these years.'

'That's what memory is like,' Siiri said. 'My husband used to tell my dreams as if they were his own.'

'Yes! And now they're keeping tabs on our memories. If you don't instantly remember your social security number or the maiden name of the minister of internal affairs, they prescribe you Alzheimer's medication. It's insanity. Now what on earth where we buying?'

They both decided to buy half a litre of milk, blood pancakes that were about to expire, rye crisps, eggs and instant coffee. Irma intended on also fishing around for some pound cake and other goodsies. But they couldn't find any of the items they were looking for. They wandered and wandered, without ever seeing a salesperson they could ask. Even the insect consultant had packed up her bits and bobs and fled by the time they returned to the intersection near the pasta aisle thirty minutes later.

They persisted in their hunt. They decided to start from the western edge of the supermarket and systematically walk down every aisle from end to end. It couldn't be a more laborious undertaking than slogging through snowfields on wooden skis in barely above freezing temperatures, which they successfully survived in their middle age. The soda section was immense, and they gladly left it unexplored. At its eastern edge they entered an unpleasantly cold pocket, and just as Siiri suspected, they were approaching the freezers and dairy products. Somewhere among the ice cream chests and shrimp towers, they found a corner jam-packed with various milk products, milk-like products and light margarine.

As they walked south down the fifth aisle, they stumbled across the prepared foods, which they had to scour for some time before discovering traditional blood pancakes. There weren't any that had just expired, and so they took full-price packages. Occasionally they lost their plastic baskets, and Irma realized she was hauling the wrong basket behind her, as she hadn't been shopping for chaga mushroom powder and twenty-two bottles of beer. They desperately hawked the beer and dehydrated health-food to oncomers to no avail. In the end, they came upon their baskets in the orange department, which they couldn't remember having set foot in. Three enormous Ugli fruits had appeared in Siiri's basket, which she hid among the biscuit packages in mortification. But since serendipity had led them to this oasis of fruit, they decided to buy bananas and apples. Weighing them was difficult, as they couldn't remember the right codes, and when they did the apples tumbled from the bag to the floor and the machine weighed them incorrectly. Just before giving up, they finally got the machine to weigh them accurately, but then discovered it was out of pricing labels.

'I'll manage without apples,' Siiri said with a huff, abandoning the apples and rustling plastic bags on the automatic scale. After scrounging together a random collection of items, they reached their limit. They wanted to pay but couldn't find the cash registers anywhere. They spun around between the candy shelves and the deodorants, until a friendly lad with metal spikes in his face told them that the automatic cash registers were immediately to the right, next to the pornographic magazines and artificial flowers.

'Aha, so we get to try communication without emotions and misunderstandings,' Siiri said as they fearlessly approached the cashierless cash register. All they found was an uncomfortably low machine that had a limited ability to read the prices of their purchases. First they had to open a plastic bag and stretch it across a rack; their own shopping bags were not acceptable. After that, they waved their purchases at the device like they waved their fobs at their doors at Sunset Grove. Occasionally the machine would whine and flash, at which point they were allowed to transfer the purchase into the plastic bag. Even though Jerry Siilinpää had specifically said machines didn't have feelings, theirs got upset seven times, at which point it made an unpleasant noise and refused to cooperate, just like a poorly raised three-year-old. When this happened, a schoolboy wearing clothes that were too large for him would appear, turn off the machine, turn it on again, and start the process over again from the beginning, without saying a word. Seven times.

Once Irma got her purchases into the mandatory plastic bag, it was time to pay. The machine offered options, and Irma shoved her debit card into the slot that looked like the right one. It wasn't the right one, though, because the machine spat the card angrily to the floor. Irma tried to pick it up, but couldn't reach it no matter how hard she stretched.

Then a pair of garish green high heels appeared before them, and a familiar woman with black hair bent down, retrieved the card, and handed it to Irma.

'Sirkka the Saver of Souls!' Irma cried thoughtlessly, because that wasn't really the volunteer staff member's name. Sirkka looked at them suspiciously, clearly not recognizing Irma and Siiri as acquaintances from Sunset Grove. She simply introduced herself as Sirkka, and when she and Siiri shook hands, Siiri's purchases tumbled from the flimsy plastic bag to the floor. Once again, Sirkka bent down politely to gather up their belongings.

'How kind of you. Buying food this way is quite a challenge for us,' Siiri said apologetically.

'I didn't catch your last name. Do you use it?' Irma asked amiably. 'Not everyone does these days.'

'I'm Sirkka Nieminen,' the woman said. 'And now I remember you from Sunset Grove. You were present when I was blessed with the gift of the spirit and the Holy Ghost entered me.'

'Yes, it was that rat.'

'I haven't seen you for a while. Have you been busy else-where?' Siiri asked, hoping to move past any misconceptions involving the rat and the Holy Spirit.

'I don't have anything in my life other than Awaken Now! I do what the Holy Ghost obligates me to. It's a gift that has been given to me. It's that simple.'

'Aha, well then. Do you suppose you could help us pay for these purchases? You see, it isn't that simple for us.'

Sirkka the Saver of Souls gave them a disconcerted smile, flashed blood pancakes and milk cartons at the infra-red eye and paid for the purchases with Irma's fob, which to Irma's surprise served as a payment method. Siiri and Irma took their plastic bags and thanked Sirkka, whose sacrificial mindset had been of concrete service to them both this time.

'Jesus said: "For my flesh is meat indeed, and my blood is drink indeed." John, chapter six, verse fifty-five.'

'Is that so? We'll be on our way now, to go and warm up some blood pancakes. Eating printed food every day gets a little tedious.'

'I'll bless your food.' Sirkka lowered her hand to their bags. '"This is that bread which came down from heaven:

not as your fathers did eat manna, and are dead: he that eateth of this bread shall live for ever." John, chapter six, verse fifty-eight.'

'And so the blood pancakes became wafers,' Irma said, yanking her bag away. Then she cast herself and Siiri out of the consumer's paradise.

Chapter 10

An announcement glowed on the lobby smartwall:

'Good morning! Died today: Suoma Marketta Leppänen. Awaken Now! offers its condolences!'

Siiri wouldn't have known who Suoma Marketta Leppänen was without the accompanying photograph of the deceased. The petite white-haired woman was sitting in a wheelchair with a seal robot in her lap. The only thing missing was the curler.

'Death shall destroy both the young man and the virgin, the suckling also with the man with grey hairs. Deut. 32:25.'

A picture of a candle next to a bouquet of white roses flickered beneath this meditation. In the bottom corner, a little garden gnome cried its eyes out. Siiri stared at the image and felt the thrum in her head grow stronger and herself get dizzy. She had to sit down. The only free seat in the vicinity was Margit's beloved massage chair, which Siiri collapsed into before she passed out. Had she passed a corpse in the corridor as she was rushing downstairs to play cards? How was it that she hadn't noticed that the woman in her wheelchair was dead? Or had the white-haired old lady genuinely been asleep at the time, with death not reaping her until later? And did any of this matter in the end? The woman was ancient and tired, and barely spoke two words to anyone, just cuddled with her toy. Perhaps dying in a wheelchair wasn't the worst alternative. Despite the logic of her explanations, Siiri couldn't rid herself of the unpleasant notion that she had neglected another human being. What action should she have taken if she had realized the seal pup owner was dead? Where in this e-chip merry-go-round did one report a cadaver one had stumbled across in the hallway? Who came to collect those who succumbed in their smartpants, the elderly who died on their own, and in their own time?

'That's the idea behind smartpants: they can tell if the person wearing them is alive or dead,' Irma said consolingly. Irma had forced Anna-Liisa out for a little walk to the seashore, and now the rain-dampened duo were recuperating in massage chairs at Siiri's side. None of them started up the chairs, since they knew how horrible that felt.

'They're not just trousers; they're overalls. They also have models with trousers and a separate wrap top, but I have no idea which model this Mrs Leppänen was wearing when she died,' Anna-Liisa said, letting it be understood that she was as well versed in this sphere of life as she was in many others. According to her, smartclothes were woven with smartstrands that weren't the least bit smart but were capable of performing simple mechanical measurements. 'This is what passes for intelligence in our society these days. So be it.' Anna-Liisa held a reflective pause before continuing.

There were two types of smartclothes: those for healthy people, and those for the elderly. Healthy people wanted to continually monitor their body function and for that reason used smartclothes to collect various observations about themselves. 'This monitoring doesn't make them any more healthy, so it's all utterly pointless, especially since so much of this so-called information is gathered that even the most long-suffering soul wouldn't have time to process it all during one incarnation.' She allowed her gaze to wander to the ceiling as she took a moment to ponder the content of her lecture, which at this point might have slipped into dealing with life after death. Then she sighed twice and pulled herself together. 'I'd be happy to tell you more, but our topic proper would seem to be the smartwear of the elderly. Its primary purpose is to monitor the heart and circulatory functions. The clothing reports the results to a computer, from which a doctor can then, if desired, substantiate whether or not the wearer is dead. I presume this was what occurred with Mrs Leppänen. It's another matter entirely how the doctor reacts to the information he or she has received.'

'You're saying information zips from a blouse directly to the doctor?' Irma had to confirm this, because it sounded so incredible.

'But we don't have any doctors here,' Siiri said. Sunset Grove had let go of all of its dedicated doctors the previous year, as national statistics had shown that, for all practical purposes, no one in Finland had a personal physician any more. Health-care districts had been expanded to the point where one doctor was responsible for half of the country; it was completely natural that no one wanted to do that much work, and that's why there was a shortage of doctors. Statistically there were sufficient numbers of them, but because each one worked an average of three days a week, that meant there weren't enough to go round. Anna-Liisa had seen this somewhere, too – not in the newspaper of course, because she didn't have the requisite device for reading it, but some publication she deemed credible regardless.

'That's the crux of the problem,' Anna-Liisa said, looking satisfied, as she had led her audience onto the desired path without unnecessary offshoots or circumlocutions.

'*Des Pudels Kern*!' Irma cried. It was one of her favourite sayings. 'Goethe's *Faust*, you know.'

'Doctors? Those virtual beings who have been transformed from experts into mobile services?'

'I must say I'm impressed by how contemporary your vocabulary is, Siiri. The crux of the problem is that no one is doing anything with all this constant flood of information being generated about us and everyone else: for instance, the fact that an old woman has died in her electric wheelchair.'

They all paused to reflect on Anna-Liisa's ruminations. For a long time, no one said anything.

'For we must needs die, and are as water spilt on the ground, which cannot be gathered up again. 2 Sam. 14:14.'

The smartwall offered a constant barrage of Bible verses for the angst a naturally approaching death aroused in old people. Oh, smartwall! How little it knew of Sunset Grove's residents and their concerns. Probably nothing was anticipated with such longing in this incubator of gerontechnological caregiving as a beautiful, gentle death.

Siiri felt like climbing out of the massage chair but couldn't. She had sunk into its depths and couldn't find anywhere to take hold and dislodge herself. How did Margit manage this? She was, of course, vastly fatter than the slender Siiri. Irma couldn't get out of her chair, either, and practically choked on her laughter.

'Verily I say unto you, I am like water spilt into the massage chair!'

'Has a robot been invented for this? Some clever hoist? What would its mating call be?' Siiri said, and got Irma to sing passages from opera arias. Anna-Liisa looked impatient and didn't say anything.

'I am the resurrection, and the life: he that believeth in me, though he were dead, yet shall he live. John 11:25.'

Just as they had given up crying for help, Aatos Jännes stepped out of the elevator. He rushed right over to his tercet, as he called them, and offered aid with both hands. He tugged the women out of the chairs one by one, uttered vaguely inappropriate sentiments, and whirled Irma, who was the last to be resurrected, around the lobby in a waltz. Irma broke out in a high, tinkling laugh and would have been happy to continue dancing, but didn't dare when she saw her friends' grim faces.

'Would you care to chaperone me to the dance tomorrow afternoon?' Aatos whispered in Irma's ear, and Irma nodded, giddy as a teenage girl. If there was anything she loved and missed from her earlier life, it was waltzing.

Siiri couldn't believe her eyes; after all, Irma had been the one to tell them about the adorable little Eila's unpleasant surprises in Aatos's company. On the other hand, Don Giovanni managed to seduce 2065 women before getting his just deserts.

'There's always a Zerlina in the crowd,' she muttered to herself, hoping Irma would hear.

Chapter 11

While Irma was making eyes at her dancing partner, Anna-Liisa and Siiri went for a tram ride. Irma and Aatos had made a conspicuous departure by taxicab, which Aatos had paid for with invalid coupons, even though he walked and danced on two feet with no trouble. Siiri remembered that Anna-Liisa's Ambassador had used similar coupons despite not being disabled, and for that reason refrained from remarking on the matter. Apparently it wasn't uncommon for elderly men to arrange small perks for themselves at the expense of those who genuinely needed them.

It was a snow-free November and pitch-black by 5 p.m. Riding the familiar routes in the darkness had an ambience of its own, as one could see into people's flats. The homes glowed cheerfully into the gloom, creating a cosy mood. Siiri was eagerly anticipating the handsome chandelier on the third floor of Mannerheimintie 45, but when the tram drove past, the chandelier had disappeared. In its place was a depressing contemporary hardware-store find.

'Perhaps the owner of the chandelier died,' Siiri remarked matter-of-factly.

'Or else they came to their senses and rid themselves of an impractical lighting fixture that collected dust,' Anna-Liisa countered.

They gazed out at the apartments on Mannerheimintie and wondered why they didn't spy bookshelves in any of them; all they saw were blank white walls and the occasional television that took up half the room. They didn't see a single bookshelf during the entire ride from Töölö to Stockmann. At Aleksanterinkatu they switched to a number 2, which turned into a number 3 at the southern harbour. They were curious to see if the situation improved with regard to bookshelves and chandeliers in southernmost Helsinki. But no luck. Not a single book on the walls of the high-ceilinged, generous rooms. At least some inherited art flashed past behind the irregularly shaped windowpanes. Tehtaankatu 12 was one of Siiri's favourite buildings: a regal yellow building from the 1920s, a little younger than her, in other words. She would have recognized it in her sleep from its bay windows, where on this evening ecologically responsible Ikea lamps glowed in competition with the televisions. One measly bookshelf appeared in the next building over, on the first floor of Bertel Gripenberg's dreadful concrete monstrosity. Some old-fashioned humanities student must have been holed up in there.

'I'm not being taken to court after all,' Anna-Liisa suddenly blurted out. She looked relieved and wanted to report on the most recent developments in detail. One of the Ambassador's offspring had been convinced that Anna-Liisa had disposed of the Ambassador's property during their brief marriage, but when they had sought legal recourse, a settlement had been reached. As a result, Anna-Liisa had to pay some cumbersome compensation to several of the Ambassador's children and grandchildren.

'Can you afford it?' Siiri asked in surprise, as it appeared as if the Ambassador's greedy heirs were sweeping the entire estate into their own pockets, leaving Anna-Liisa nothing but expenses. But Anna-Liisa put Siiri's mind at ease. She had been wise enough to prepare for the worst, or rather Onni had, and so she had a little extra money stashed away. Nor was there any way the Ambassador's most brazen relations could cut her completely out of her husband's estate.

'Are you still keeping the money in the jewellery box?' Siiri asked, at which point Anna-Liisa laughed bitterly and then said that was a private matter. She was right, of course. Siiri was ashamed of having been tactless enough to say what was on her mind.

'But can you imagine, one of his former wives, this Yugoslav, insists she's an heir now, too.' Anna-Liisa was almost excited by this turn of events, as she found it unprecedented but absolutely legal. When her daughter, who was sired by Onni, had died, the daughter's share of Onni's estate had transferred to her. 'And she's older than I am!' Anna-Liisa laughed heartily, as she had during the happiest days of her engagement. Siiri didn't know what was so funny, but Anna-Liisa hadn't been this carefree in ages, and so Siiri relished it. 'There you have it, money is nothing but a headache,' Anna-Liisa continued, after her laughter died. 'It's all the same to me how much of this mess I inherit. I'm not going to live much longer regardless, and I don't have any children. Which brings me to my biggest headache.'

The tram trundled down Fredrikinkatu, the most enchanting of Helsinki's longer streets. It was full of little boutiques, and they were kept lit in the November murk even though the shops were closed. Anna-Liisa said that she had received an unusual phone call from a stranger, a man who had claimed to be representing the Awaken Now! Association, the very one that recruited the volunteers who worked at Sunset Grove. The fellow had asked peculiar questions about Anna-Liisa's life as a widow. The phone call had left her feeling disconcerted; she had grown sceptical when the caller offered to help her in any potential problems, free of charge.

'That was kind of him. I'm sure he has your best interests at heart. Haven't you decided what will happen to your estate when you die? If you don't make a will, everything will go to the state. That's not what you want, is it?'

'I know. But I'm afraid this man has something else on his mind,' Anna-Liisa said glumly. Siiri tried to dispel her concerns and started musing on how Anna-Liisa could use her money wisely. What if she set up a fund at the Finnish Cultural Foundation to support the literary activities of female Finnish teachers?

'Sure! Or I can establish an association for cat lovers and pour my money into that!'

In the end, they had quite a jolly ride home, planning the most effective way to burn through Anna-Liisa's wealth, as it was much wiser to use the money up than pass it on and be a bother to someone else. But when the tram fearlessly raced down Paciuksenkatu towards Munkkiniemi and Sunset Grove, Anna-Liisa grew serious again.

'Have you happened to notice how much we're paying for the privilege of serving as test subjects for automated data processing?'

That Siiri had not done, as her great-granddaughter's former boyfriend Tuukka continued to manage her banking. She hadn't heard a peep from Tuukka in months, which meant things were going fine. But Anna-Liisa had heard from her own banking representative that payments had skyrocketed since the renovation. 'At this rate we'll all be penniless if we live to see one hundred,' Anna-Liisa said.

'Luckily, we won't!' Siiri remarked blithely as they stepped out of the tram on Munkkiniemi Allée.

Chapter 12

'Shameless cad! Degenerate! Take that, and that, you would-be Casanova!'

Siiri and Anna-Liisa were approaching Sunset Grove after their tram ride when they suddenly heard a curious commotion. A large taxi van purred outside the building, and shrill shrieks could be heard from the vehicle. They recognized Irma from the high notes.

The driver was still in his seat, as nowadays taxi-van doors opened at the touch of a button and drivers no longer needed to budge to feign courtesy. But as the volume of the exchange escalated, he decided to haul himself up from his seat. Hearts hammering, Anna-Liisa and Siiri exchanged glances as the African driver yanked an enraged Irma from the van, followed by a bleeding Aatos.

'Lord have mercy! What have you two been up to?' Siiri cried in horror.

'Dancing our hearts out!' Irma cried angrily and marched inside, dragging her cane behind her.

The taxi driver demanded Aatos pay the fare, but Aatos looked confused and didn't understand what was going on.

As the foreigner yelled at him rudely in poor English, Aatos pulled crumpled coupons out of his pocket, which the driver grabbed before speeding off. Siiri and Anna-Liisa quickly followed Irma inside and helped her sit down at the card table. Aatos remained standing outside, which was probably a wise decision under the circumstances.

Irma huffed and puffed, but was otherwise in extraordinarily good form. She explained that everything had gone well as long as they were dancing at the Kinapori senior centre. There had been a nice crowd and a fine orchestra, and Aatos had been a spectacular dancer.

'Besides, I was a tremendous *succès*! So popular, as a matter of fact, that when seventy-year-olds kept asking me to dance, Aatos started getting a little jealous. Perhaps that's what made him so indecent on the ride home.'

Irma and Aatos had barely made it into the back seat of the taxi van before Aatos had started pawing at Irma.

'It was awful, animalistic and compulsive.' Irma looked at them in shame. It was no doubt embarrassing for her to have thrown herself so recklessly into the company of such a suspect character. 'Imagine, at this age! But I do so love dancing! I never would have thought the first time a man tried to force himself on me would happen at the age of ninety-five. If the driver hadn't come to my aid, who knows what might have happened?'

'Aatos's nose was bleeding. Did you hit him?' Anna-Liisa asked, demonstrating her experience as an interrogator.

'I certainly did! And I didn't just hit; I kicked and bit. What would you have done if you had been in my shoes?'

They saw the manhandled Aatos Jännes wander unsteadily into the lobby and off in completely the wrong direction. He didn't look like himself; blood was still dripping from his nose. The little lobby robot was on the alert; it smelled the blood and started whirring in Aatos's footsteps, cleaning the red droplets from the floor. Siiri felt it was her responsibility to help the hapless Casanova, as he didn't even know where he was going.

'Home . . . back to Karelia,' he muttered in a weak voice. 'To my mummy's house.'

'Let's stop for a moment and see where the blood is coming from.'

When they halted, the diligent cleaning creature bumped into them and started whining unpleasantly. Siiri kicked the robot out from under her feet, at which point it produced some sort of alarm, a high siren wail. A nearby smartwall was immediately on the case.

'Technical malfunction detected! 1) Turn off the device 2) Clear the area 3) Contact the maintenance company. The righteousness of the upright shall deliver them: but transgressors shall be taken in their own naughtiness. Prov. 11:6.'

'Transgressors and naughtiness! Even the smartwall knows what sort of man you are,' Siiri said and looked at Aatos, the wall and the robot with equal disdain. She was about to switch off the howling cleaner when she realized the bleeding Aatos was the more pressing issue, despite making less noise. She pushed him down in a walker someone had left in the middle of the floor, and Aatos obeyed, docile as a child. His left eye was swollen, and his nose was still bleeding. But Siiri's practised scan, seasoned during wartime, could detect no wounds or serious contusions.

'Wait here, I'll get some paper.'

She had no idea where to look for paper or tissues – except of course Irma's handbag. But it felt inappropriate to turn Irma's sacred talisman over to the man whose indecent assault would demand substantial recovery time. Out of the corner of her eye, Siiri saw Anna-Liisa trying to calm the ever-more agitated Irma at the card table.

'What if we tried to name the Finnish market towns from the 1970s? Do you remember how it begins, Irma? Alavus, Anjalankoski, Espoo, Forssa . . . Clap your hands rhythmically like this, it serves as a mnemonic device.'

Suddenly Siiri noticed a sign on the first door in the corridor. It read 'Self-Service First Aid'. It was Director Sinikka Sundström's now-redundant former office that had been converted into a storage room. Strange that Siiri had never paid attention to it before; one would think that she would have made a note of such a spectacular Words in a Word term. She knocked on the door and opened it. The lights inside the room came on automatically. Self-Service First Aid turned out not to be a cache of bandages and gauze, as Siiri had assumed, but stocked with computers. The largest screen in the room greeted those seeking emergency assistance:

'Tomorrow, by that time the sun be hot, ye shall have help. 1 Sam. 11:9.'

'That's not going to do us any good. The sun doesn't shine here in November, and it won't be hot for some time.

Maybe in June,' Siiri said sourly to the screen, and started studying the device. It must have been one of the humanized gadgets Jerry Siilinpää had been advertising, which meant she was supposed to talk to it.

'I. Didn't. Catch. That. Please. Speak. More. Slowly.'

Siiri couldn't think of how to explain to the machine that a confused daytime dancer was sitting on an abandoned walker in the middle of the lobby, bleeding from his nose. The machine needed clear, simple instructions stripped of emotion. She decided to try one word. She bent in closer to the gadget, felt stupid, and hoped that not too many people were watching her foolishness through the surveillance camera. She loudly stated:

'Blood.'

'Donate. Blood. Go. To. Station. Two.'

'Oh, for goodness' sake, what a blockhead. Who would want blood donated by a ninety-seven-year-old?'

'I. Didn't. Catch. That. Please. Speak. More. Slowly.'

'NOSEBLEED!' Siiri shouted while looking around to see if there was even a sink in this purgatory.

The machine had been struck dumb, but text appeared on the screen: 'They have ears, but they hear not: noses have they, but they smell not. Psalms 115:6.'

The next kiosk would have allowed her to conduct an electronic health check, and the next helped you fill a tooth or insert an implant, complete with instructions and all the necessary equipment. In the corner of the room stood a blood pressure gauge and scales, along with a blood-sugar-level detector. A stack of tiny cotton pads for wiping the blood from needle-jabbed fingertips stood on the table. Siiri snatched a fistful, turned back to the first kiosk and thanked it for the edifying chat.

'Thanks. Be. To. God. In. The. Name. Of. Our. Lord. Jesus. Christ.'

The machine had found its voice again: a low baritone whose phrasing lacked both legato and aspiration. Siiri slammed the door to the Self-Service First Aid behind her and rushed back to Aatos's side, but apart from the abandoned walker, the lobby was as unpopulated as it was dim. Only the offended cleaner sobbed faintly in the corner, as the smartwall at the heart of the space tried to calm it.

'Grace be with you, mercy, and peace, from God the Father, and from the Lord Jesus Christ, the Son of the Father, in truth and love. 2 John 1:3.'

Siiri looked at the little flashing device, whose work she had so callously interrupted. She felt disconsolate, as if the simplest task had grown overwhelmingly difficult. There was no help to be found anywhere, and the latest craze to strike these screens, the ever-changing Bible phrases, made her more disoriented than ever. She bent down to the cleaning robot, looked at the controls, and found a big round power button at the back. She pressed the button, patted the robot, and said:

'Why don't I show you a little mercy.'

Chapter 13

On a dark, seemingly endless November day, Siiri and Irma had settled into Siiri's armchairs for a peaceful lunch. It was a little uncomfortable, but because change was supposed to be invigorating, they wanted to eat somewhere other than the dining table from time to time. Siiri dropped a dollop of lingonberry jam next to her liver casserole, and Irma spread butter on hers. Neither one spoke. The moment was a little awkward, as Irma clearly had no interest in discussing her dancing excursion with Aatos, but Siiri felt a brief exchange regarding the previous afternoon's episode would have been appropriate.

'Oh dear, real butter certainly is goodsies. No low-fat margarine for me; I want butter. And no health nut is going to tell me butter will kill me at this age. What if we had a baguette for dessert, with a thick layer of butter and some sugar sprinkled on it? I love the way it crunches. Did you and your children ever satisfy your sweet tooths with that back in *anno dazumal*?'

They sat in silence again. The lack of chatter stopped bothering Siiri, because Irma appeared to have wholly recovered from Aatos's assault. It was good to eat together. The prosaic presence of a beloved friend was soothing, and Siiri was happy again, so happy that she felt a little hum in her upper abdomen, even though they hadn't exchanged any words. A glance out of the window did nothing to clarify whether it was night or early morning, but they had no doubt it was the perfect moment for lunch. One of the glazed balconies at the end of the building blazed like a beacon; the resident had left all the lights on, and anyone who cared to could see the empty wine bottles stored on the balcony, heaps of plastic bags stuffed with them, and, as a cherry on top, a stack of beer crates, the old-fashioned kind one no longer saw at the supermarket. The resident had also arrayed the balcony with generously sized pants and bras she was presumably airing. Siiri wondered whether the apartment belonged to Ritva Lehtinen, but then recalled the horror shows from the previous summer and realized Ritva lived in the apartment opposite, one floor up.

Suddenly a young woman in a white lab coat appeared on Siiri's wall and said: 'Aha, it looks like we lost the connection. Wait a second . . .'

The image disappeared. There was some faint buzzing and humming, and Siiri caught a glimpse of a fragmentary Bible phrase, but before she could even begin to decipher it, the woman in the lab coat returned in unnaturally large scale. She looked straight into Siiri's room and frowned.

'For some reason I can't see or hear you, and no one's answering at VirtuDoc mobile chat. So let's just continue; the important thing is that you can see and hear me. If for some reason you can't, just end the session. I see there at the bottom of the screen that we still have a connection . . . So we were discussing some symptoms that are in all likelihood side effects of the medication . . .'

'Oh, this is exciting! I wonder whose doctor's appointment we're participating in? What do you think, are we here realistically or virtuosically?' Irma said, remarkably restored.

'In real time or virtually, you mean. I don't have the foggiest idea.'

They were whispering just to be sure, but the mobile remote doctor clearly couldn't see or hear them any more than she could see or hear the poor soul whose appointment they had involuntarily invaded.

'Is that how you contact a doctor here?' Siiri whispered. She had never tried VirtuDoc, because she had no interest in visiting a doctor to hear how she should change her lifestyle and install pointless accessories in her heart. Such things were for the middle-aged. Only once had she and Irma amused themselves by pressing the buttons at the MeDoc kiosk in the lobby, but Irma suspected that was something different.

'You don't see anyone's face at the MeDoc kiosk. You just talk with a computer. You tap in your questions and symptoms and the machine picks an answer at random. Don't you remember? You entered constipation, and it suggested a laxative, which was sensible of course. A lot faster than begging for the same information from a health centre.'

'These sorts of . . . I mean this, what you were talking about, a certain sexual overactivity and even . . . hypersensitivity that expresses itself in, for example . . . prolific or . . . prolonged erections, are . . . very common among men who take these medications, unfortunately.'

'It's some man who has a perpetual erection!'

'Shh, Irma, we can't let ourselves get caught.'

'In your case, I see several suspect prescriptions . . . or their combined effect . . . this mood stabilizer for one, hmm . . . and risperidone treatment or . . . this Alzheimer's medication, it's hard to say . . .'

'The poor man has Alzheimer's, too!'

'Irma!'

The doctor glanced down to look for some piece of patient information she was lacking. She stalwartly maintained her position in front of the camera, head upright but a little tilted, even though she could have easily bent down over her papers. They could see a fat, green pharmacopoeia from 2010, folders in various colours and a row of photographs of smiling children. Siiri counted three children, but it was hard to say if one of them appeared in more than one photo.

'Terribly young to be a mother,' she said.

'Or a doctor,' Irma added.

'I'm most liable to think it's the Alzheimer's medication . . .' the doctor muttered. Her words tumbled out slowly and almost inaudibly: cholinergic and neural pathways, probably not priapism, possibly relaxation of the iliac artery. They pricked up their ears and leaned in, as if that would help them to hear more clearly. 'Have you experienced dizziness, exhaustion, trouble with your vision, diarrhoea, nausea? Agitation, aggression? Anything in addition to these constant and prolonged . . . umm . . . erections?'

'The poor thing! All those symptoms from a medication!' Irma bellowed so loudly in Siiri's ear that it hurt.

Then the doctor abruptly disappeared from the wall. Siiri and Irma didn't make a peep, as they were sure that they were being watched. Irma slowly lowered the plate she had licked clean to the coffee table and stared guiltily at the smartwall, as if she'd been caught doing something very naughty indeed. They heard a faint thunk. Then Siiri dared to breathe again, too, as she believed the unpleasant episode had come to an end. But she had barely got her thumping heart to steady before Aatos Jännes's face was staring at them from the wall. Irma squealed and Siiri thought she would faint. She rested her head against the back of the armchair, closed her eyes and slowly counted to ten. She hoped that when she raised her head, Aatos Jännes would have disappeared from her life for good.

'Can he see us?' Irma asked, frozen on the spot, dropping the words from the left corner of her mouth so only Siiri would be privy to her fearful question.

'Can you see me now?' Aatos's voice was less confident than normal, and he stared straight at Irma and Siiri from under his luxuriant eyebrows. He had been to the barber since the last time they had seen him; they could tell because his eyebrows had been trimmed to an even length.

'No,' Irma said seriously.

'Yes, I can see you,' the doctor's voice said.

This time they didn't see the VirtuDoc, just the patient.

The doctor sounded agitated and fed up. She clearly didn't know how to use the device and was eager to move on to something more challenging than conversing over a satellite connection with a sexually over-active World War 2 veteran who was suffering from dementia. The doctor said she could adjust the dosage of Aatos's prescriptions to reduce the harmful side effects, but that would decrease the medications' effectiveness as well.

'So, doctor, you'd like me to choose between a constant erection and losing my memory?' Aatos smiled flirtatiously, and they knew which alternative he would choose.

'I'm not . . . wouldn't exactly put it that way. This medication slows . . . the advance of Alzheimer's and . . . for you the symptoms have appeared to have stabilized . . . considering your age. But we're talking about a . . . progressive . . . terminal illness . . . what I mean to say is, it's incurable.'

'No need to take my age into consideration. Any thirty-year-old would be proud of this. I've got a raging hard-on right now. Would you like to see?'

Irma squealed again and covered her eyes. Siiri lost the fifth-octave A and grabbed her friend's arm.

'How do we exit this appointment?'

'We can't. Let's just suffer through to the end,' Irma whispered, pulling her lace handkerchief from her sleeve. She blew her nose so forcefully they were afraid they'd be detected, but to their misfortune the scene on the wall continued to unfold undisturbed.

Aatos had risen and was fumbling at something in a way that prompted the doctor to raise her voice.

'There is no need to take off your clothes. We are remote!'

We are remote, if only Anna-Liisa had been around to witness that. The doctor ordered Aatos to sit down immediately and bravely held forth on various forms of mental and physical sexual function. They heard the terms 'frontal area' and 'diminished control', 'impulsivity' and 'involuntary vulgarity', 'improperly folded proteins' but also 'virility', 'frustration', 'risk of stroke' and, finally, a list of peculiar abbreviations.

'You could do an online . . . ADSC-ADL interview, a series of CERAD tasks and an MMSE test, so we could get the status . . . an understanding of the disease's . . . current manifestation. You do have . . . your login information, don't you?'

Aatos was silent and looked straight ahead without moving, as if he were deaf.

'I'm going to send you . . . your login information, it should appear on your smartwall . . . now. Can you see it? As I said, this priapism . . . these symptoms, the prolonged erection . . . is very . . . typical with Alzheimer's medication and could . . . intensify. In your case . . . considering your age . . . we could gradually wean you off the medication.'

'Does it make women more active, too? There's no sign of that around here. Or else none of these goddamned cock-teasers take Alzheimer's medication. Could you prescribe something for, say, Irma Lännenloimi, she's one good-looking filly.' Irma blushed in pleasure and was immediately taken aback by her reaction, remembered the scene in the taxi and dived into her bag to rummage around for something she might have lost.

'His brains have clearly moved to his privates. Can't even remember my name. Lännenloimi! What a ridiculous name, don't you think?'

Siiri smiled. She had absolutely no interest in being tormented by Aatos Jännes's dementia-driven sexual fantasies in her final retirement years. By now the doctor's tone was curt. She told Aatos she would decrease his dosage substantially, because she didn't view its benefits as meaningful at this stage of the disease. She disagreeably reiterated the incurable nature of Alzheimer's and Aatos's advanced age. The only thing missing was a prognosis of the patient's imminent death delivered in medical jargon. Siiri started feeling sorry for Aatos Jännes, who was staring at her from the smartwall in a state of discombobulation as he tried to grasp why the young female doctor wanted to strip him of his one last source of joy.

'You're saying no more hard-ons?' Aatos desperately repeated the rhetorical question while gripping some ambiguous clump of fabric, apparently a foot rag or the like that served as a security blanket.

'It won't be long before he's asking for his mummy again,' Irma whispered, clearly not feeling the slightest sympathy for her dancing partner.

And then the image vanished as unexpectedly as it had appeared during their lunchtime tête-à-tête. To brighten the mood, an aphorism appeared in its place:

'For the child shall die an hundred years old; but the sinner being an hundred years old shall be accursed. Isaiah 65:20.'

They stared at the smartwall without speaking. Siiri thought about Aatos Jännes, his inappropriate behaviour, crude groping, illness and treatment. She tried to picture what Aatos was doing in his apartment at that very moment. Was he reading the same Bible passage they were, without understanding its applicability to his life? She doubted he had started testing his memory electronically, as the doctor had ordered.

The pin-drop silence continued for quite some time, until they caught a faint scratching from the kitchen. Siiri and Irma remained motionless in their armchairs, like unwilling participants on some unpleasant group tour. Surprise after surprise kept appearing before their eyes while they just sat there. Not that this last one was exactly unanticipated; they both gathered that their old friend was scrabbling about the rubbish receptacle in the kitchen, the fat rat who, whiskers covered in fruit soup, bolted lightning-fast into invisibility when Siiri finally pulled herself out of her chair and opened up the door to the cabinet under the sink.

'At least you're a living, breathing rat in the flesh, not some remote virtual creature,' Siiri said, without feeling the slightest repugnance for her uninvited guest. She set out a bit of hardened cheese on a plate and left it next to the bin.

Chapter 14

Anna-Liisa and Irma, model rehabilitation-group students from the old stick-exercise days, had, through the guidance of a few biblical phrases, discovered the fitness console centre on one of the first-floor corridors. They wanted to show it to Siiri too, even though they knew she felt moving for the sake of moving was silly. Siiri simply couldn't grasp that people ran on the spot in display windows to become healthier and live longer. Picture-window athletics were a relatively recent phenomenon; before, gyms were in basements or otherwise hidden from view, but now people wanted to be permanently on display. Gyms and glazed balconies had become stages, street-level storefronts had become attorneys' and account- ants' offices, with white-collar workers gawping at their phones for the whole world to admire.

Siiri had only ever run when she was in a hurry, or when she saw the pedestrian light turning green — then it was always worth taking a couple of quick steps. She felt no great need to get into shape to die as healthy as possible, and had no intention of sweating on a treadmill.

'But this is fun, and nothing fun is pointless,' Irma said,

theatrically opening the door to the mysterious room by waving her fob in a grand arc at the blob on the wall.

Inside they found surreally bright light and seven large screens, the sort that were just a moment ago called flat-screen TVs and at some point merely televisions. A red mat stood on the floor in front of each of these screens. Only one of the machines was in use: a shaky old woman stood at it, clutching her walker with one hand and brandishing a small white baton in the other. She swatted it around as if she were being attacked by winged demons. The severity of her dementia was hard to judge.

'She's playing tennis,' Anna-Liisa said, politely lowering her voice so as not to disturb the woman's athletic interlude.

'I don't see a ball. Is it air tennis of some sort?'

'Blockhead! The ball is there on the screen. Her opponent is there, too, that young man with a beautiful tan,' Irma explained, as she grabbed another baton. She wanted to play tennis too, because she had been rather good at it when she was young, back when the rackets were wooden and tennis was played in July on private courts at seaside villas. Her cousin Kalervo had taught her before the war, and their shared pastime had continued passionately for years until they had abruptly been forced to quit by Kalervo's vaguely unpleasant and very unathletic wife Ingalilli. 'She was such a fine lady she couldn't even hold the racket properly. But if you don't care for tennis, Siiri, you can choose something else. There are all sorts of choices. They have badminton too; it's a little less demanding than tennis. And you don't have to be afraid that some gust of wind is going to carry off your ball. Or is it a ball, the thing you play badminton with . . . what is it?'

'A shuttlecock, Irma.'

'Yes, exactly, thank you, Anna-Liisa. But, Siiri, you could pick slalom and pretend you're in Lapland or the Alps. Just imagine!'

Irma whacked backhands and forehands like an old pro. Siiri still couldn't see a ball anywhere and couldn't see what Irma's flailing and competitive whooping had to do with the images moving across the screen. Anna-Liisa looked on with interest and claimed the game was based on motion capture technology. 'A little like burglar alarms or other home appliances.' She boldly grabbed two batons and pretended to use a skipping rope. Nothing came of it, of course, because Anna-Liisa would have actually needed to skip, and she was incapable of doing so, so she just waved the batons about, confusing the screen. 'Perhaps I should switch to something simpler. What else do they have here . . . boxing, zumba, meditative jogging, balance tests . . .' She gazed at the screen in bafflement and selected the balance tests. It posed no problem for the seasoned seated-exercise enthusiast, and a flush of vigour coloured Anna-Liisa's pale cheeks. 'For goodness' sake, Siiri, you try too!'

Siiri stepped onto the mat in front of one of the machines, and her height and weight appeared for the whole world to see, after which the machine offered a plethora of options. Siiri pressed what she understood, but her hand didn't always hit what she meant it to, and so at first she ended up in yoga class, which was relaxing and pleasant, not that she had any intention of lying on the floor, because she would have never got up, and then playing golf, which she didn't know how to play and had no interest in learning. She accidentally swiped the screen with her elbow, and the machine selected something called fitnessbeat. At first she had to think of an alias for the figure on the screen (she chose 'Siiri Kettunen') and a country ('Finland'), after which she apparently started walking around the world, because there were endless continents, mountain ranges and cities on offer.

'Maybe I'll go to the Great Wall of China,' she said, by now rather excited. She started walking on the spot along the Wall in a stunning springtime landscape: 'This is wonderful!' After going quite some distance, she decided to learn a jiggling disco dance that was unbelievably comical and laughed so hard she wet herself. After getting the machine to stop, she cautiously looked around, as she had been so focused on her own world that she didn't know what the others were doing. Perhaps they were all gaping at her, mortified on her behalf. But no, Anna-Liisa was throwing non-existent darts at the dartboard on the screen with a look of intense concentration, and Irma was whirling around on her mat, swaying her hips wildly.

'I'm doing the hula hula! With a virtuosic hoop! Isn't this more fun than you ever could have imagined?'

'Can't you two take anything seriously?' Anna-Liisa asked, a tinge of disapproval in her voice as Siiri and Irma spun, swayed and laughed on either side of her dart game.

'Oh, Anna-Liisa!' Irma laughed, and then stopped rocking. 'I'm so old I want to have a good time.'

Anna-Liisa stopped throwing her invisible darts, looked at Irma, and gradually a merry, irresistibly beautiful smile spread across her face. 'Actually, Irma, you're very wise.'

'Nonsense,' Irma said, then lowered her voice: '*Döden, döden, döden.*' She knew Anna-Liisa found her habit of repeating funny phrases over and over the opposite of wise. 'Why don't we take a break? I have a little whisky in my bag, if anyone wants a nip.'

They sat along the back wall, where Jerry Siilinpää or some other expert in cosiness had placed a rustic bench: an ugly old object one could rest on when the console-led exertions proved too fatiguing and one felt faint. The old woman playing tennis was still swatting in exactly the same way as when they had entered. Her face was alarmingly pale, and sweat was dripping down her cheeks.

'Do you suppose that's still healthy?' Siiri asked Anna-Liisa. They all panted rather heavily, squeezed right up against each other on the hard bench, which was not only uncomfortable but cramped. Irma took a swig from her tiny whisky bottle, and when Anna-Liisa also wet her whistle, Siiri decided she would partake of the post-athletic medication too. But the marathon tennis player continued at her game. They watched the old woman with increasing concern but didn't comment. In the end, she sensed their gazes on her back and called to them without turning round:

'How do I get out of this? I can't get this to stop!'

She swatted and swatted, gasped, staggered and swatted, as if the virtual balls were bombs she needed to repel to stay alive. Siiri rose and went over to the woman, took her by the elbow and felt her trembling from the physical strain, and perhaps fear and anxiety. Her arm was cold and clammy, streams of sweat percolated down her deathly white cheeks and her heaving breathing wheezed and rattled alarmingly. Siiri led her off the red mat and turned the woman's petrified face in her direction.

'That's how. That's how you get out of it. It's a machine you control, not the other way around,' Siiri said, even though she was no longer so sure. As she wrenched the woman out of the machine's sphere of influence, the game ended, and an aphorism appeared on the screen as a reward for the woman's athletic exploits.

'But this thing commanded I them, saying, Obey my voice, and I will be your God, and ye shall be my people: and walk ye in all the ways that I have commanded you, that it may be well unto you! Jerem. 7:23.'

The woman looked at Siiri without seeing her, went limp and collapsed, dragging Siiri down with her. Siiri felt the woman's frail bird-bones beneath her and was afraid she would crush them despite her slight weight, which had just been broadcast on the screen: 56 kilograms. She didn't hurt herself in the fall, because the tennis player gallantly offered herself as a human shield. But the crash was substantial, and she couldn't tell if an eye-blink or an hour had passed before things started happening again. She was lying on her back next to the dainty woman, whom she couldn't hear breathing. Her own breath was steady, but her heart was pounding wildly. Irma and Anna-Liisa were studying them from somewhere in the stratosphere, and Siiri couldn't make out what they were saying. Irma looked horrified; Anna-Liisa inquisitive. Slowly Siiri understood that someone new, possibly one of the volunteer staff members, had entered the room and was crouching down next to the old woman sprawled on the floor – the other one, that is – anxiously probing her throat and wrist for a pulse. Evidently they unanimously agreed Siiri was alive, as they allowed her to lie there in peace.

'Lord have mercy, Holy Spirit hear my prayer,' the volunteer staff member babbled, without the slightest idea how to do anything sensible. Siiri didn't remember ever having seen this woman before. She had grey hair and a face so furrowed that she had to be a retiree. Or a fellow Sunset Grove resident.

'Is that garment she's wearing under her dress a pair of smartoveralls?' Anna-Liisa asked, articulating clearly. The volunteer looked at the old people, more addled than ever.

'If it is a smart garment, her physical condition has been archived in the catacombs of the health centre. It's possible the alarm was sounded automatically and we'll be seeing some young medics appear before we know it.'

'Lord have mercy, Lord have mercy. Holy Spirit, hear my prayer.'

Irma opened the door and yoo-hooed out into the corridor in her high falsetto. 'Cock-a-doodle-doo! Are there any young medics out there? We need help down here! In the Console Cemetery!' And would you know it, two young men were wandering around the lobby of Sunset Grove with a trolley, and they were greatly relieved to have Irma's crowing direct them to the right place. Siiri tried to pick herself up from the floor so she wouldn't end up in the ambulance by accident, but doing so was difficult. Anna-Liisa tried to lend a hand, in vain. It was only when the volunteer interrupted her prayer and came over to contribute to the tugging that Siiri finally rose. Her head momentarily went dark, but she relied calmly on Anna-Liisa's iron grip and her vision gradually returned and the thrum faded.

'Would you like some whisky?' Irma whispered, turning her back on the volunteer and the medics, who were securing the tennis player to the stretcher with cable ties. Siiri grabbed the flask and took a big swig. The alcohol flowed through her numb body. She could feel her mind growing clearer and the blood starting to circulate in her calcified veins.

'Thank you, Irma. That did me good.'

The medics raised the stretcher onto the trolley, looking ready to leave. Now the volunteer grew alert; apparently she felt her moment had come. It was her turn to participate in administering first aid.

'You are the Lord's little lamb,' she said to the patient, who was white as a ghost. 'And that is enough. It is enough for thee, who have suffered the agonies of thy paltry life. The shepherd will carry his lamb across the great stream to the green pastures of paradise. All sinners, even the worst blasphemers among us, make this journey on the shoulders of the good shepherd. It's that simple.'

The medics observed the woman's blathering in disbelief, unsure whether she was a patient, a resident or a disturbed bystander.

'We have to get going,' the fellow at the back said, pushing the trolley so hard that his partner at the front stumbled into the corridor and onto the path laid out by the good shepherd.

Chapter 15

'Friends, may I present Oiva!'

Tauno was standing in front of the card table, clearly a little nervous, fanning his hands and gazing brightly and happily at the rather short man standing at his side, who truly did have lush whiskers and the same sort of glasses as President Paasikivi. Siiri, Irma and Anna-Liisa studied Oiva curiously, feeling like favourite aunts, so proudly was Tauno introducing his friend to them. Siiri was the first to rise to greet Oiva, whose handshake was a little squishy, his eyes enlarged by his high-strength spectacles.

'And I'm Mrs Anna-Liisa Petäjä, MA.'

'My name is Irma Lännenleimu and I'm just a grand-mother. I have six children and over fifteen grandchildren and five great-grandchildren, even though I've only met some of them, these great-grandchildren, as my darlings are too busy to come and visit me, which I understand perfectly well, as what's there to see in a silly old fuddy-duddy like me, and besides, they have much more important things to be doing. They live all over the globe. My granddaughter, whom we'd all written off as an old maid years ago, just got married in Peru, imagine, as if she couldn't have found a man any nearer. One of my darlings is gay, and he has registered both his dog and his relationship, and they are all adorable—'

Irma's nervous babbling stopped as abruptly as if she had hit a brick wall. An awkward silence ensued, as suddenly she and everyone else understood what was going on and why Oiva and Tauno hadn't been allowed a shared unit at Sunset Grove. Gay couples were not permitted in retirement homes. Even cohabitation was forbidden; that was why the Ambassador and Anna-Liisa had rushed to get married, in order to be able to live together in the flat they owned.

'Why don't you . . . please, join us,' Anna-Liisa said listlessly, after the silence had continued far too long and Irma was still buried in the bottom of her handbag, cheeks burning.

'What was I looking for again . . . was it my pastilles or my spare nylons . . .'

'Would you like to play cards?' Siiri suggested, but Oiva and Tauno didn't even know what canasta was. Siiri suggested Russian whist, bridge and Liverpool rummy, but the boys weren't familiar with these diversions either.

'All I know how to play is shit your shorts,' Oiva finally said, with a hearty laugh.

'But that's perfect for a retirement home!' Irma said, shuffling the pack. 'How many packs? Just one? And five cards a player, I see, so that's how we soil ourselves.'

As she dealt, she began to reminisce how they had all laughed when Sunset Grove had shown the American film

Baby Geniuses at movie night. 'But that was when we still had an activity director.'

They had a grand time, even though Anna-Liisa and Siiri felt that the game they were playing was childish and too simple. But it was a superb way of breaking the ice. By the time they had played several rounds and Irma had been condemned the potty-pants in every one, the conversation had imperceptibly grown comfortable and natural. Only Anna-Liisa had fallen silent as she slumped, pale-faced, in her chair. Siiri and Irma asked about Oiva's retirement home, and it turned out to be very old-fashioned, as they had several caregivers for every ten residents and permanent kitchen staff, too.

'Not a single robot?' Siiri asked in surprise, and Oiva assured them that they didn't even have a drinking fountain.

At that moment, they heard a tenor voice cry out: 'Emergency! Sodomites in the vicinity!'

Swinging his walking stick, Aatos Jännes strode briskly past their table and stopped a short distance away. 'Who let that psychologically disturbed hermaphrodite in here?' he demanded, pointing his stick theatrically at Oiva, who had turned his back.

Anna-Liisa's wrath was magnificent. There was no sign of frailty as she blazed bright red and sprang up more nimbly than Siiri had seen in many moons.

'Stop right there! Aatos Jännes, you are . . . a barbaric . . . barbaric bushman . . . a base . . . grand inquisitor!'

'Verdi's *Don Carlos*!' Irma cried, but her attempt at lightening the mood came to an abrupt end, as Anna-Liisa was more than serious. She rapped her cane dully against the floor, and now that she had worked herself up shouted so stridently that her coiffure started to come undone. Her dark eyes flashed mercilessly, and she let fly a seemingly endless flow of insults directed at Aatos, announced he was Carl von Linné's short-skulled prince regent, the forefather of eugenics, a useless flatfooted proto-Indo-European, philosophically obnoxious and less human than a robot. 'What makes you think you have any say in who does or doesn't visit here? Do you, perhaps, consider yourself some pseudo-schooled practitioner of advanced phrenology?'

Aatos Jännes gazed at Anna-Liisa, his eyes glowing with admiration. Siiri knew the type, the sort of man who believed he could extinguish a woman's outrage by making things erotic, as if a little feminine fury just added to a woman's charms. But Anna-Liisa paid no heed; she continued her browbeating in a quivering voice until Aatos grabbed her by both hands.

'My dear Anna-Liisa, calm down. You are adorable, and I will leave you to enjoy the company of these eunuchs. But you'd come to your senses if you only felt what I have standing in my trousers.'

He kissed Anna-Liisa on the check so loudly that the smack echoed through the room, then looked at Oiva and Tauno and said: 'This loveliness is wasted on you Uranians!' Then he spun on his heels and made his escape via the elevator.

'Doors. Closing. Going. Up.'

They were extremely shocked. They had never experienced

anything of the sort. Anna-Liisa was so upset that her hands were shaking and tears were streaming from her eyes. She frantically tried to rub her cheek, as if it were permanently tainted by Aatos's brazen smooch. Irma's lace handkerchief came to the rescue yet again. Siiri couldn't really hear anything, not even the fifth-octave A, the thrumming and rushing in her head were so loud. Only Oiva and Tauno remained tranquil. They thanked Anna-Liisa profusely for her idiosyncratic harangue and said Aatos's behaviour was downright polite compared to the things they'd been forced to experience during their long lives.

'When you take into account, ladies, that at the age of fifty we were still considered criminals and it wasn't until we were retirees that we were no longer classified as mentally ill. Attitudes have been slower to change than statutes.'

'And then AIDS came, too,' Oiva said.

'AIDS? Isn't that some memory test?' Irma said.

'The human immunodeficiency virus causes a disease known as AIDS,' Anna-Liisa said wearily. 'It's an abbreviation for . . . something.'

'Yes! There are all sorts of viruses going around Sunset Grove, too. You catch them from these gadgets you're supposed to pet and paw at.'

'Petting and pawing can indeed prove fatal,' Oiva chuckled.

Chapter 16

Siiri could see the AGV, a perpetual presence in Sunset Grove's corridors, approach from a distance. It was a trolley originally designed for industrial use, a large, gleaming unmanned cabinet that independently traversed the hallways, distributing medicine to residents. Siiri didn't take any pills, not a single one, so she willingly made room for the dosing device as it ploughed down the deserted corridor towards its next patient. The AGV knew to stop at the correct door, which would open with a mutual exchange of flashing lights, and then enter to administer the appropriate medication. A similar trolley, slightly larger, wandered around gathering laundry and distributing clean clothes for those residents prepared to pay for this service. Irma called the trolleys ICan'tSees and always gave them an even wider berth than Siiri.

Siiri was convinced the trolley made mistakes. How could it be so certain about who lived where and what pills it was supposed to give them? But Anna-Liisa had explained that the reason caregiving technology was such an immensely successful business was because, unlike people, machines never make mistakes. They never tired and were never careless, unable to speak the resident's language properly or even bad-tempered. This AGV hummed good-naturedly down the corridor, played a simple melody when it arrived at an apartment like the ice cream vans children loved, and treated all of its victims with a consistent mechanical equanimity.

The corridors were empty. Aside from the singing medicine trolley, there was no sign of life or even a glimmer of light.

'Or does a robot count as a sign of life?' Siiri asked herself, then laughed out loud. She had been talking to herself more and more often lately, but she wasn't the least bit worried. There was always some smartwall or plump rat around listening to her ruminations.

False windows had been installed along Sunset Grove's vista-free passageways. In the summer they had brightened the space, but in early December, with Helsinki as dark as it was rainy around the clock, it seemed the height of absurdity to have sun-drenched Tuscan landscapes blazing on the walls. Nevertheless, Siiri stopped for a moment at one of the artificial panes to soak in the billowing fields of grain and the skies of unbroken blue.

'Beautiful. Landscape.'

The unfamiliar voice came from behind Siiri. It wasn't the hesitant woman from the lift, the confident man from the smartwall or any other of the machines Siiri recognized. She turned and saw the most nonsensical creature she could imagine, a stunted white frame with feet and hands and a head, a screen for a stomach, a clunking jaw and idiotically gawping eyeballs with eyebrows that danced in the air. They rose and moved as it spoke, reinforcing the creature's attempts to be simultaneously human and infallible.

'Hello. How. Are. You.'

There was a little resonance to the voice, and the cadence was even more monotone than usual. Upon closer examination, the constantly moving eyebrows proved to be nothing more than beams of light; remarkable how they could move in the air in time to the creature's voice.

'This is my caregiving robot, Ahaba. It's ancient Hebrew and means "love".'

Delicate little Mrs Eila was standing next to her new friend, looking abashed. She was just getting used to Ahaba, who was the third robot specializing in social needs to move into Sunset Grove. 'I'm a bit like a guinea pig. They say I'm perfect for this, because there's nothing wrong with my head but I need assistance. That way I can give them feedback while they develop Ahaba. He helps me with everything, even going to the toilet.'

The three of them stepped into the elevator, with Ahaba leading the way and the ladies following. Siiri had always considered people who called animals 'he' or 'she' a bit barmy. But to hear Eila calling this robot dwarf 'he' was simply comical. Eila was in such poor shape she would have been incapable of getting out of bed without Ahaba's help. Ahaba rose, alert, at Eila's command, then lifted her out of bed and helped her wash and dress herself. Probably fed her, too, if Eila wanted him to.

'My hands are so stiff I can barely put on a blouse any more, not to mention nylons or shoes. Can you dress yourself?'

'Yes, for now, but it's slow going. So do you have to live with that creature day and night now? Where does it sleep, in your bed?'

Eila laughed at Siiri's question, and Ahaba guffawed, too. They stepped out of the elevator and proceeded slowly towards the card table. Ahaba offered Eila one arm and supported her as they made their way to the corner.

'See how sweetly my escort assists me?' Eila said proudly. Since Ahaba had appeared in her life, she hadn't needed her walker. As they sat down at the baize-covered table, Ahaba stood behind Eila like one of the president's bodyguards. 'It's rather remarkable, actually,' Eila continued, lowering her voice so as not to offend her manservant's sensibilities. During her brief orientation to the robot, the trainer, a volunteer, had explained that Ahaba was not simply a technological support, he also entertained, soothed, consoled and delighted. 'But so far I haven't got anything out of him but Bible passages and trivia questions. Does anyone know why the Bible is quoted everywhere here?'

Siiri did not know, although many suspected Sunset Grove's owners now included a religious cult. Anna-Liisa in particular was extremely suspicious in this regard, but there had been no official confirmation of the connection.

'Isn't it also a little strange they don't let visitors in here any more? I mean anyone except these preachers,' Eila continued. Ahaba clearly didn't offer her conversational companionship of a sufficiently intelligent nature, despite the humility he showed as a partner. She began explaining at length how her sole grandchild had tried to visit her at Sunset Grove, but because he didn't have the requisite fob, he had been foiled at the door.

'Couldn't you let him in?' Siiri asked.

'I had no idea he was coming! I didn't hear about it until afterwards. Since then, I've started paying more attention to what's going on around me, and I've noticed there's no one around here but residents and robots. And the occasional volunteer.'

'Or rat!' Siiri cried, making Eila titter again.

'I don't even have a phone since they removed all the old landlines,' Eila said.

Residents desiring contact with the outside world had to establish it through the digital network, but few had succeeded in their fumbling attempts to connect to their kin via smartwall. Siiri's great-granddaughter's former boyfriend Tuukka, who was extraordinarily clever with buttons and gadgets, was the only outsider who had appeared on Siiri's wall, and he only rarely, because they had no other business to conduct than Siiri's banking transactions. Most recently Tuukka had been a little concerned about the rising costs at Sunset Grove, which was strange, as the residents had been under the impression that the reason for exchanging the staff for machines had been to cut back on expenses. But Tuukka had said that machines were always expensive, and three ministries wanted to support the digital elder-care operations primarily because health technology was the hottest thing on the market. Those were his exact words: 'the hottest thing on the market'. Siiri remembered remarking that she thought 'being hot' meant something was stolen, and received an arrogant huff from Tuukka in response.

Ahaba helped Eila blow her nose and decided to revive the lagging conversation.

'How. Many. Sons. Did. Leah. Bear. Jacob. A) 12 B) 3 C) 6.'

Three alternatives flashed in the skeletal robot's belly, and Eila was supposed to pick the right one. She wearily pressed the C with a knobby finger, and the humanoid rewarded her with a fanfare played on an artificial horn and clumsily clapped its clanking hands. These appendages had five fingers and joints, just like real hands. It clearly had an intelligent grip and must have belonged to the highest caste of robots. The AGV was the lowest caste, a static crawler. Siiri silently listed the names of Leah's sons, Reuben, Simeon, Levi, Judah, Isacchar and Zebulun, and decided Eila was right. Sunset Grove had never been inundated by visitors, but this autumn there hadn't been a single one. Even Irma's darlings had completely forgotten her among the surveillance cameras. Irma firmly believed her darlings peeked in on her from their computers, but even if they did, what joy did that bring her?

'Can. You. Name. The. Sons. Leah. Bore. Jacob. Press. Reply. First.'

Eila pressed the reply button and, out of a sense of obligation, listed the names Siiri had just recited to herself, to another rousing fanfare, and just to be sure added Rachel's sons and the sons of Jacob's handmaid as well as her only daughter, but couldn't remember the daughter's mother. Ahaba was dumbfounded.

'I. Didn't. Ask. For. That. Information. I. Didn't. Ask. For. That. Information. Press. Question.'

Eila addressed the caregiving machine as if it were a child: 'Oh dear, oh dear. I'd like to speak with Siiri Kettunen now, Ahaba.'

'That. Is. That. I. May. Be. Comforted. Together. With. You. By. The. Mutual. Faith. Both. Of. You. And. Me. Romans. Chapter. One. Verse. Twelve.'

'Does that mean it approves of our conversation and will wait before it continues the trivia quiz?' Siiri whispered to Eila, and Eila giggled like a silly teenager. It was a relief to laugh together at Ahaba, who was really a machine, not a human; it wouldn't be offended even though they were openly mocking it.

'Did you hear about the death in the Fitness Console Centre?' Eila suddenly asked, and Siiri felt the A note in her left ear intensify to a stabbing pain. 'A couple of days ago, a woman got stuck on the game machine and died. I wonder how they found her; no one ever goes in there.'

'I was there with a few of my girlfriends just then,' Siiri heard herself saying in a monotone voice reminiscent of a robot's. This was the second resident of Sunset Grove to die on her hands. How was it they hadn't intervened in the old woman's life-threatening exertions in time, instead of gazing on and sipping whisky? She didn't have the nerve to mention this to Eila, who was gaping at her in disbelief.

'Christ's blood almighty! What happened?'

Ahaba joined in the conversation. 'Whoso. Eateth. My. Flesh. And. Drinketh. My. Blood. Hath. Eternal. Life.' The robot stared right at Siiri with its spherical eyes and quizzically raised a light-beam eyebrow. Siiri felt incredibly guilty and was afraid she would faint.

'She . . . we . . . she was playing tennis and fell into my arms, and we both ended up on the floor.'

Stumbling on a primary source visibly revived Eila. According to her, all sorts of rumours had been going around among the residents of Sunset Grove about the fitness console death, and the stories had grown wilder by the day. In the latest version, the old woman had supposedly lain in the gym for weeks and mummified before a cleaning robot had stumbled across her and moved her into the corridor, where one of the volunteers had discovered her. Siiri shook her head. Eila was a little disappointed when Siiri discredited the most incredible reports and said the old woman had been trundled off into an ambulance with astonishing speed. 'The incident proved that these cameras and smartclothes really can be useful in an emergency,' she said to Eila, at the moment herself believing there were concrete advantages to living in a residential laboratory. Eila thought for a moment. Then she shot Siiri a sly look and said:

'In this case, the concrete advantage being that a dead body was carted off before it had time to mummify. Is that it?'

'Yes, I suppose so,' Siiri said, and they both broke out in smiles. 'And I learned I'll never be going back to exercise in that Console Centre!'

'Eila. It's. Time. To. Eat.' Ahaba held out an arm for Eila, and they all headed to the dining room together, to order red triangles and green balls for lunch.

Chapter 17

'Art is important not only for the able-bodied, but for the elderly, the severely disabled, and the incarcerated,' said the curly-haired man, who had donned a screaming electric blue bow tie on a normal Thursday and taken off his shoes as he stepped inside Sunset Grove. He looked vaguely familiar, but Siiri wasn't sure where she had met him before.

'Maybe he appeared in your dreams virtuosically through your smart-alec wall,' Irma suggested with a tinkling laugh.

Anna-Liisa's 'Shhh!' came with a confidence and immediacy only accessible to an adult who had spent her entire career shepherding restless schoolchildren to sit silently in rows. If the 'Shhh!' didn't work, it was followed by a stern, penetrating gaze, which Siiri and Irma had learned to feel in their bones.

The man explained in a soft voice that art was neither elitist nor a pointless diversion, but rather a preventive health measure that conserved societal resources. That's why art belonged to everyone, even the elderly, whose lives would otherwise be so limited.

'A beautiful painting, moving music, a beloved book. Each one generates individual happiness and well-being. And the happier individuals are, the healthier society is. Fewer onerous health care costs accumulate, and unpleasant consequences such as alcoholism, violence, divorces and drug abuse are minimized. A beautiful painting, moving music, a beloved book. It's that simple.'

'It's the preacher!' Irma whispered, and suddenly Siiri also remembered having seen him collecting funds from Margit. They had barely seen Margit since, so thoroughly had she been enjoying her own company or that of the volunteer-led prayer circle. But now she was sitting in the front row, enraptured by their ringletted speaker. At her side were Eila and Ahaba, both equally alert.

The man had to be from the Awaken Now! Association. He continued his lecture about the benefits of art before suddenly leaping over to Satan and demons. Art was an incomparable weapon for repelling them.

'Art serves at the pleasure of the Holy Spirit,' he said in his soft, velvety voice.

Behind him stood a woman who was for all practical purposes naked and a man in dirty dungarees and one of those flaccid articles of clothing termed a 'hoodie'. They must have been artists. The event had been advertised on their smartwalls as the 'Thursday Art Experiment'. Siiri had feared residents would be called on to paint and act themselves, but Irma knew what lay in store: improvised poetic dance performed by professionals. The auditorium was unusually full, as the simple fact that multiple visitors had been allowed on the premises was sufficient to spark the residents' curiosity. Of course some were also interested in art. Tauno had invited Oiva, and as Siiri and her friends waited for the art to begin, Oiva had confessed his passion for theatre and literature to them. Anna-Liisa had engaged him in a fascinating discussion regarding the short stories of Thomas Mann, which always seemed to include either a violin or a lonely homosexual if not both, enquiring as to whether the violin was, perhaps, a symbol of homosexuality in some subcultures. Oiva had just laughed, and Siiri never learned the truth of the matter, because just then the man with the bow tie had shepherded them to their seats.

Now he was sustaining a brief, effective pause at the lectern.

'Before Taija and Sergei begin their performance, let us come together in prayer.' The man raised his arms to the side as if he were the pastor of a large congregation – either that, or about to take off in flight. He closed his eyes. 'Lord, let your Holy Spirit fall on these people to serve as a source of strength in their lives. Let it revivify their souls so Satan will no longer have dominion over them, so they will say no to the lusts of the flesh and earthly temptations and yes to the Holy Spirit.' The warm voice paused for a moment, then the man opened his eyes, lowered his hands and gazed out at the flock of dozing, grey-haired sheep and the one alert robot. The time for frank speech had come.

'You must let the Holy Spirit into your hearts. Only then can you partake of the divine order of things. And then you shall turn away from impurity and dishonesty. Harlotry and lust. All that sin entails.'

The man held another pause, and everyone noticed who he was looking at. Sitting was uncomfortable for Tauno, so he was standing in the aisle next to Oiva. He supported himself on the back of Oiva's chair, back hunched more prominently than usual and eyes nailed to the ground, but Siiri could see the pulsing at his temple. Oiva was calm. He squeezed Tauno's hand and looked right back at the preacher.

'I also had a devil as my bedmate, but I chose the Holy Ghost. You can do as well, if you so choose. It's that simple. Taija and Sergei, please.'

The man turned his back on the audience and called out his stone-faced artists. The apparently naked woman wasn't naked after all. She was wearing a nude leotard that did little for her bony frame. She stalked across the lectern in long strides, arced her hands in big movements and tossed her head back and forth. When she approached Sergei, she wrapped herself erotically around his dirty dungarees, but he just stared at the rear wall before shouting in a raw voice:

'Moon, my friend, sun, my mother, stars, my children. Space, that great infinity.'

The woman whirled at the front of the auditorium in increasingly frenetic movements and produced all manner of noise that should have been drowned out by music. Her feet clomped, her hands slapped against her body, she wheezed and panted. She intermittently lunged into the audience, between the rows of seats, and Siiri was terrified she would drag her or some other victim onstage.

'Darkness, silence. SILENCE!' The man shouted so loudly his neck veins bulged. 'A frozen heart inside your soul. YOUR SOUL!' He pointed directly at Siiri. 'Where is the moon, where is the sun? You have lost everything as a result of your sins, a black void, infinite emptiness in SATAN'S GRIP!'

'This is loonier than eurhythmics,' Irma said to Siiri unnecessarily loudly, as after his satanic bellowing Sergei held a long pause. Tauno and Oiva started laughing, and Siiri saw that even Anna-Liisa was holding back a smile. Only Margit followed the performance, entranced.

'The emptiness of your soul, the hardness of your heart. The Lord saw fit to afflict Christ and condemn the sin in him, as in you.'

'This isn't art,' Siiri whispered to Irma. Margit had raised her hands to her temples and was shaking her head in a strange fashion. Was she feeling ill? It would be no wonder, considering the experimental nature of the health-art being offered. A gust of pungent sweat from the stage wafted deeper and deeper into the audience.

The woman, was it Taija?, turned out uncontrolled pirouettes while Sergei stood solid as a pillar. When Sergei eventually got to the Garden of Gethsemane and the Cross of Golgotha, Taija started moaning and screeching, a happy, lunatic smile on her face, but a blank stare in her eyes.

Sergei looked up at the auditorium ceiling and muttered in a barely audible voice:

'Even in this room, there are those guided by Satan. Satan is using them to lead them to perdition.' He lowered his eyes to the row where Siiri, Irma and Anna-Liisa sat and roared out the concluding words, spit spraying: 'THE HOLY SPIRIT SENT BY GOD PURIFIES JESUS CHRIST, WHO BECAME MAN!'

After an uncomfortable silence, the audience clapped politely. Sergei's cheeks were glowing, sweat was streaming down his brow and he was trembling, even though he had done nothing but mumble and bark without moving. Taija rose from the floor and panted nearly as alarmingly as the poor woman whose final act in this life had been a bit of exercise in the Console Centre.

'This time we're not getting involved. She can keep gasping for air, for all I care,' Irma said, reading Siiri's thoughts. 'But a shot of whisky would do her wonders.'

Suddenly Taija shrieked. A rat was scampering across the lectern. The audience stopped clapping, assuming that the performance was continuing. Those who had already stood sat back down, and those who had fallen asleep awoke, like in authentic tent revivals. But Taija had frozen on the spot and Sergei couldn't get a word out. The rat assumed the role of a lump of dried moss on the middle of the stage, and Siiri relished the aesthetic pleasure of the moment, as the trio formed a beautiful still life.

'I don't believe that's the rat you've been feeding,' Irma said. Siiri agreed. This was clearly greyer, and its tail had been severed or was otherwise stunted. Siiri's rat had a long, handsome tail.

'There's another one!'

It was Tauno's voice. He pointed at the corner of the stage. Siiri caught a flash of a tail, as this second rat wasn't as interested in improvisation as the one still cowering on the stage. After a pause that seemed to last an eternity, Taija rushed into Sergei's arms. Then Sergei came out of his stupor or was frightened, it was hard to say which, but he started stomping his feet and braying verses about Satan so frantically that the rodent came out of character and skittered back into the hole whence it had miraculously emerged. The audience was mesmerized and clapped wildly for the performance, perhaps most of all because it was over and because the vermin had been chased from the room. Only Margit sat silently, unable to discern what was performance and what was something else. Sergei and Taija stood on the stage, bewildered by the excessive applause. Eventually the audience started gathering up their canes, handbags, hearing aids and walkers, intent on making their exit. But then the man in the bow tie stepped out and raised his shepherd hands into flight mode.

'Not again,' Irma said, shuffling towards the exit even more quickly.

'We'd like to thank Taija and Sergei for that moving piece of poetry and dance. Perhaps it gave you food for thought regarding the lusts of the flesh and the Devil. Remember: all you have to do is open your hearts and ask to be filled by the Holy Spirit and freed from sin. If you'd like to make a donation to Awaken Now!, the boxes you all know are at the doors; all you need to do is flash your fob at them. I can also accept cash. It's that simple. After all, you weren't asked to pay for the performance, am I right?'

The curly-haired man walked to the door intolerably slowly and shifted his pleading gaze from elderly resident to elderly resident like a beggar, which is what he was, of course. When he reached Anna-Liisa, he stopped. A flush rose to Anna-Liisa's cheeks, her facial muscles tautened, and she refused to return his gaze.

'Have you prepared a will, my dear widow?'

The man's voice was still velvety, and he smiled at Anna-Liisa benevolently with the wet pools of his eyes. But when he took Anna-Liisa's hand in both of his own, she yanked it back angrily.

'My will is none of your business.'

'Making a will is no simple matter. We want to help, and we have the necessary expertise. After all, we don't want your money to be scattered to the four winds, do we? You decide what happens to it. We just help. It's that simple.'

'You just said it wasn't simple,' Anna-Liisa snapped, standing up. Siiri was surprised to realize her friend was taller than the curly-locked shepherd, who must have been short indeed for a man. She hadn't got this impression as she watched him praying at the altar. 'Irma and Siiri, let's go to my apartment to drink whisky and play cards.'

Irma immediately caught on.

'That's right! It's time for our daily dose of sin. Come on, Siiri! Maybe we can look at some pornography, too. The Internet is full of it. Open Sesame, and we can watch all sorts of disgusting things.'

The man's expectant hand remained extended, but he was unable to come up with a fitting Bible passage for this moment. He gazed on in silence as the three nonagenarians marched out of the room, laughing gleefully.

Chapter 18

Siiri woke up later than normal; she could tell because the sun was shining in through the window. Seeing as how it was late December and the room was so bright, the hour might have been who knows what. She marvelled at the motes of dust dancing in the sunlight, unable to recall when she'd last been surrounded by such glory. After sitting up and sliding into her slippers, she paused in front of the smartwall. To her shock, it was dark. Not a single report about the previous night or the quality of her sleep, not even a teeny-tiny biblical passage or review of the residents who had died over the week.

'The age of miracles hasn't come to an end after all,' she said to herself, her stiff legs carrying her tentatively into the kitchen.

The kitchen light didn't come on automatically the way it normally did, and she didn't know how to turn it on. She poked at the stove for a while, but it didn't react in the least, not even a whine. At least the radio still obeyed her; it was an ancient contraption she had bought back when her husband was still alive. One changed stations by rotating the knob, but Siiri had never done so during her lengthy sojourn at Sunset Grove, because YLE Radio 1 was her most faithful companion. It was from this radio, a bit grimy now, that she and her husband had listened to the Pearl Fishers concerts while reading the morning paper at the big table in the kitchen. Their children had thought it strange, but to them it had been a pleasant way to start the day.

'No newspaper, and no Pearl Fishers, either,' Siiri said. 'And of course, no husband. Oh dear, oh dear.'

She tried to infer the time from the radio programme. A young woman was just wrapping up a talk show about the everyday challenges of parenthood, and then the overture to Rossini's *The Thieving Magpie* started up. It instantly filled the morning with a bright, delicious joy, although apparently the morning was no longer morning. She must have slept until nearly noon.

'Siiri! Warning! I'm breaking in!'

It was Irma making a racket out in the corridor. Before Siiri could reach the door, Irma had yanked it open and strode in, brandishing a weapon.

'Good Lord, what's got into you?' Siiri asked in astonishment.

'This is a mechanical handle,' Irma said, displaying the object in her hand. 'I used it to break into your home. It's an emergency. There are boxes in the corridor that say to break the glass in case of emergency. So that's what I did, and here I am!'

Siiri smiled. Irma had a very dramatic temperament and apparently didn't remember she could step into Siiri's and

Anna-Liisa's homes as easily as her own with a flash of her fob. In her other hand, Irma held a burning candle.

'Who named you Santa Lucia?' Siiri asked.

'I'm no saint; I'm Lucifer. *Döden, döden, döden!*'

Irma sat down in Siiri's armchair and launched into her morning news report. The electricity was out, and no one knew why or how to fix it. Sunset Grove had been thrown into turmoil. The residents didn't know what time it was, the smartwalls had gone black, the dining room wasn't working and neither were the elevators, medication hadn't been distributed and the heating may have shut down, which meant the building would gradually begin to grow cool. Some residents were locked in their rooms, the least fortunate strapped to their beds.

'They can't get up without apparati and androids. Anna-Liisa told me the robots need electricity to work. Without it, it's as if they lose their brains. That means the motorized caregivers and doodads don't work and seal pups can't soothe the elderly. Do you see, we're in grave danger!'

Irma was genuinely terrified, on the brink of hysteria, even though she had clearly got a boost of energy from the possibility of an exciting adventure. Only now did Siiri realize that a hunting knife dangled from the belt of her friend's dress.

'What on earth are you doing with that?'

'Anna-Liisa gave it to me. She has everything one might need for a rainy day. Where is that Rossini coming from? Your radio? How did you get it to work? Ahh, of course it's a portable radio and runs on batteries; you're a genius. This is the overture to something. I read that during this mechanized golden age the only reliable mass media during an emergency is the radio, because it works even when all the computers and the Internet have fallen. Can you say that about computers, or only about those who die in war? The wartime euphemism came from wanting to avoid the word "death", or so I've understood: falling was more beautiful than dying, but I suppose it would take more than one blackout to kill the Internet. Why, the entire world is in there! Anna-Liisa is waiting downstairs and is very agitated. I promised to make sure you weren't dead. Do you have food? The refrigerators aren't working, so you need to gobble down anything that might spoil and rescue the ice cream from your freezer compartment. I ate three ice cream cones for breakfast and half a litre of slightly sour milk, and now I've got a terrible case of flatulence.'

'What else is new? Are there any staff members downstairs . . . or anywhere? Someone who could help, at least during an electricity outage?'

Irma laughed her high, tinkling laugh and shook her head as if Siiri had proposed some awfully amusing thought experiment.

'There aren't even any of those preachers around! Demented residents are bartering a handful of oats for a cup of buttermilk. It's like being in the Helsinki bomb shelters during a Soviet air raid. Some people don't even have food, can you imagine?'

Siiri hurried to throw something on and then explored her fridge, retrieving a yogurt for herself and Irma and making them both a sandwich. Thus fortified, they would be able to keep going for some time, despite the fact they couldn't boil eggs. And Irma was already in fine fettle. The Rossini was followed by an overly romantic piano piece, but Siiri didn't dare turn off the radio, because they might miss an important bulletin. She used to get extremely annoyed when, in the middle of a Mozart string quartet, someone with a poor command of Swedish would suddenly butt in to report that a wolf had been spotted somewhere in the hinterlands beyond Lieksa and as a result the entire nation needed to be on alert. Emergency bulletins were always read in Finnish and Swedish.

'That's what makes them such fun! The way this current crop of radio announcers speaks Swedish is very strange. It must be the mandatory Swedish they're taught in schools.'

They wolfed down their meagre fare and prepared to make their way downstairs to discover what sort of chaos reigned there. As she searched for her bag, Siiri reflected how almost everything these days was dependent on electricity, even the doors to their apartments. Without Irma's emergency key, she would have been locked in her cubbyhole for God knows how long.

'Do you know what electricity is?' Siiri asked.

'Not really. But I harbour a deep suspicion of anything that runs on it.'

'Me too,' Siiri said, in relief. 'It's like we're on a desert island without something we need and we don't even know what it is!'

Irma laughed so hard the candle went out. But then they

noticed that it was no longer dark in the kitchen and the hallway. The lights had come back on! Just to be sure, Siiri tried the stove. It was working, too. Irma had already rushed over to the smartwall.

'For when they shall say, peace and safety 1 Thess. 5:3. No name days today! Nevertheless the Kenite shall be wasted Num. 24:22. Awaken Now! would like to wish happy birthday to: Sleep efficiency 0.2! And there came against Gibeah ten thousand chosen men out of all Israel. Warning! Error! They meet with darkness in the day time, and grope in the noonday as in the night. Job 5:14.'

'That smart-alec wall is as comforting as one of Job's friends. Do you believe it really knows how to think?' Siiri asked.

'Of course not. It's a machine,' Irma replied. 'Besides, spewing Bible phrases from memory with no regard for the circumstances would seem the opposite of smart to me.'

'I think the Bible contains a lot of wise and beautiful thoughts. But this last quote is of absolutely no consolation, despite its accidental appropriateness.'

They poked about Siiri's home for a moment and grew convinced that the electricity outage had passed. Irma set the television blaring to a barrage of local news from around Finland. A storm was raging in south-eastern Finland, and in Häme snowfall had caught drivers off guard. She and Siiri decided it would be best to head out into the world, at least as far as the ATM. The more uncertain the world grew, the more important it was to keep a little cash stashed away in one's purse. Irma set off to fetch her overcoat, and they agreed to meet at the elevators.

To their surprise, the elevator wasn't working yet. They had to make their descent via the deserted stairwell, its corners festooned with frightful cobwebs and dust bunnies.

It was dreadfully deserted down below. Anna-Liisa wasn't sitting in the common room, and they heard no voices from the dining room. One skeletal Ahaba-like robot had keeled over on the sofa, two rats were sleeping under a smartwall, and the long-abandoned walker stood sentry in its familiar place in the middle of the floor. The lights were beaming brightly, even though the sun was doing its best to banish the deep December gloom, which meant electricity and energy were surging into the building once more.

'Perhaps they all went back to their flats since they had to wait so long without food and light. Not many were clever enough to deal with the circumstances as resourcefully as you did, Siiri, by sleeping until noon.'

Chapter 19

Siiri and Irma tried to withdraw cash from the ATM on Munkkiniemi Allée with little success. Two female and one male employee sat inside the bank, looking unoccupied, but the door wouldn't budge. A sign on the door announced that one could only enter by appointment. Irma had to crow for quite some time before one of the women came over to crack the door, but it made little difference. She informed them that the ATMs had been outsourced, and the branch employees had no control over them.

'There's some temporary technical disturbance.'

'But can't you just give us cash from our accounts?'

'No. We don't have any money here. If you have a bonus chip for the supermarket, you can withdraw cash while you're doing your daily shopping.'

'Are you insane?' Irma looked as if she were on the verge of seriously losing her temper, but she calmed down when the woman took their contact information to forward a complaint to the bank's customer relations department. They liberated the bank employee from her chilly spot and allowed her to resume her repose.

Siiri and Irma decided to take the number 4 tram to Kata-janokka, where the nearest safe ATM was located. With-drawing money downtown was risky. The talk at Sunset Grove was that thieves lurked in the vicinity of the down-town ATMs, ready to knock over the elderly and make off with their money.

'They could turn Katajanokka into a museum,' Irma exclaimed. 'Look at all the beautiful old buildings; there's a grocery store, an ATM and a phone booth, perhaps even a few live-in maintenance men still around. It's like being in a Swedish children's movie.'

The former headquarters of Enso was lit up like a Christ-mas tree and beamed beautifully, even from a distance. The marble Sugar Cube took perfect command of its site across from the Uspenski Cathedral, which was no easy architec-tonic neighbour. It looked downright gorgeous in the fading light, with two candles burning in each window, like at the Presidential Palace and the Ministry of Finance. It created just the right amount of Christmas spirit, a blend of festive and cosy, unlike the gigantic flashing illuminated advertise-ments at the city's shopping centres. One time Siiri had made the mistake of standing outside the Kamppi Mall staring at a continuously changing wall-sized Christmas ad and felt nearly as nauseous as at Jerry Siilinpää's resident event. Behind the Sugar Cube, a Ferris wheel, someone's bizarre brainstorm for luring Russian tourists, stood empty and motionless in its red holiday lighting. From the tram window, they had seen adults waiting for the brightly lit carousel among the handcrafts stands at Senate Square, and on Aleksanterinkatu they had spotted a Santa Claus dancing on a tightrope. Helsinki was clearly turning into an amusement park, and Siiri and Irma viewed this as a happy development.

They climbed off the tram at the first stop in Katajanokka. From there, it was just a walk across the street to the ATM. Siiri let Irma lead the charge at the machine, but this proved a mistake. Irma was a little fuddled. She pulled her fob out of her handbag and started flashing it at the screen as if she were trying to pay the automated cashier at the supermarket.

'Wait a minute, what am I doing?' Irma suddenly squealed and started laughing. 'How silly of me.'

'Select. The. Desired. Amount.'

'Goodness gracious! It's talking to me like my refrigerator.' The ATM had retrieved the necessary information from Irma's fob and now it couldn't wait to give her money. Irma wanted to make sure the cash wouldn't be withdrawn from some poor student's account, and so she dug around in her bag for the big slip of paper where she had written down her important codes. She clearly and audibly enunciated her birthdate, social security number, phone number, blood type, the phone numbers of a few of her children and a couple of her previous addresses as well as her PIN code for the ATM. Unfortunately, they weren't sure what part of the ATM they were supposed to speak to. After Irma had listed all of her vital personal information for a third time, the ATM went dark.

'Another electricity outage! Now the trams will stop running and we'll be stuck in Katajanokka forever,' Irma cried in alarm. 'And that scamp ate my card! No, wait a minute, I didn't use my card. But now I'll never get my money; this contraption robbed my account. What on earth will we do?'

'May I help you?'

The voice was familiar, and so were the shoes.

'Sirkka the Saver of Souls! I mean, Sirkka . . . you have a last name, too, but I can't remember it any more. Lehtinen?'

'Nieminen,' Sirkka said, glancing nervously from side to side without the tiniest trace of a smile. 'And you two ladies are from Sunset Grove.'

As if by miracle, Sirkka the Saver of Souls had appeared for a second time to succour them in their time of need, but she didn't feel like a guardian angel the way the motorcycle-loving Mika Korhonen had, so long ago. There was a coldness to her, a mysteriousness, as if she were hiding something. Was it possible she had a connection to some all-seeing central surveillance that gave the command to come and save them whenever necessary?

'How much cash do you want to withdraw?' Sirkka asked, without so much as a glance Irma's way.

'Well . . . why don't I take out, say, two hundred euros.'

'Two hundred euros?' Sirkka repeated, raising her eyebrows like Ahaba the caregiving robot.

'Is that too much? Or too little? Maybe I should take three hundred.'

Sirkka seized Irma's fob, which was still hanging round her neck over her winter coat. She flashed it once at the ATM and the money appeared in the tray.

'Well, that was handy. Just a flick of the wrist!' Irma said in satisfaction as she retrieved the stack of notes. 'How can I ever repay you?'

Sirkka the Saver of Souls temporarily lost command of her face. She smiled, then grew serious, grimaced and in the end appeared to be laughing to herself. Her eyes were glued to the wad of notes in Irma's hand, which seemed an irresistible temptation for the volunteer staff member. Siiri remembered how greedily Sirkka had grabbed at Irma's bag of cat food and started pitying the poor woman, who must have been desperately short of cash. She was always wearing the same clothes.

'Maybe you can help me, too,' Siiri said briskly. 'Is it really true that I have to use my Sunset Grove key-fob to withdraw cash from my account? Doesn't my debit card do anything any more?'

Sirkka rapidly descended to earth and was herself again. She explained in brusque main clauses that the key-fob wasn't a key-fob. It was an *active chip*.

'Aha,' Irma said.

While Sirkka withdrew a hundred and fifty euros with Siiri's active thingy, she explained that the chip contained all the essential information about its bearer, including his or her medical records, and it replaced one's social security card, debit card, key, identification, everything – even driving licence, if she had a valid one. And of course passport, if they still wanted to travel out of the country.

'Oh, that would be fun! I've only been abroad a few times in my life,' Irma said, staring in admiration at her fob, which had suddenly transformed into a magical talisman. 'Last time I had a passport must have been in the 1970s. Or was it the 1960s when Veikko and I went to Hamburg and saw some terribly long Wagner opera? *Die Meistersinger von Nürnberg*, doesn't it last five hours, even though it's purported to be a comedy? Veikko slept through the first two acts, but I stayed awake, it was such an incredibly gorgeous performance; we didn't have anything like that at the old Helsinki opera house in the 1960s. Or was it the 1970s?'

'What do we do if we lose the chip? Or it breaks?'

'It won't break. It's made of nanomaterial.'

'Beg pardon?'

'Nanomaterial. Silicon-based fibrils. But you mustn't lose it, of course.'

'Did you know we had an electricity outage at Sunset Grove today that lasted hours? We're all wholly dependent on electricity. Don't you think it's downright dangerous that the electricity can be cut off just like that?'

Irma looked at Sirkka the Saver of Souls demandingly, intent on getting a meaningful response out of her. But Sirkka didn't know anything about the outage. Nor was she clearly particularly interested in what sort of harm or accidents the temporary loss of electricity might have caused in the retirement home.

'But . . . isn't our research station under constant surveillance? Is it really possible that a serious accident could take place there without a camera somewhere waking up and sounding the alarm? There must be some Beelzebub watching us all the time, as if we were baboons at the zoo.'

'The alarm systems work automatically . . . and of course they require electricity.'

Sirkka told them she was a volunteer staff member and not actually responsible for anything. She started looking increasingly harried and would have surely rushed off on to more important things, if her gaze hadn't been so fixated on the bundles of cash in the old women's hands.

'If you'd like to make a donation, I can be of assistance,' she finally said.

'Are you short of cash?' Siiri asked.

'In a pickle, that's what we call it in our family. My mother always withdrew her entire pension at once from the bank and splurged on oranges, taxicabs, and other foolishness until she was in a pickle. For the rest of the month she ate oatmeal at the Primula Cafe and was satisfied with that. The cafe doesn't exist any more; it was the one on Munkkiniemi Allée and it's an estate agent's or nail studio now. One day I tried to go into that little accessories boutique on the Allée, it's always been there next to what used to be the lamp shop in the building with Mauno Oittinen's statue of a little boy and three swans at the top, painted swans, they're not statues, you see, but can you imagine, there was a note on the door to the boutique that said they were moving online. How stupid. Now some hair salon is going to move in there too, of course.'

'And all the tithe of the land, whether of the seed of the land, or of the fruit of the tree, is the Lord's: it is holy unto the Lord,' Sirkka said, still ogling the money. 'Leviticus, chapter twenty-seven, verse thirty. I'm not asking for myself. I'm in the service of the Holy Ghost, and all donations go in full to the Awaken Now! Association.'

Siiri and Irma started vocally calculating how much one-tenth of their recent withdrawals would be. At the same time, they pondered whether they should check their account balances and give a tenth of all they owned or if the Association would make do with just a small cash gift. They were teasing Sirkka, of course, which she didn't grasp; she kept holding out her hand insistently to receive her share of the old women's money.

'You're saying you want fifteen euros from me and thirty from Irma? A total of forty-five euros? Oh dear, we don't have exact change.'

'A man's gift maketh room for him, and bringeth him before great men. Proverbs, chapter eighteen, verse sixteen.' With every moment that passed, Sirkka Nieminen appeared to be more machine than human. But they couldn't flash a smartfob at her or give her simple commands. Suddenly a sly look flickered in Irma's eyes and she said as proudly as a child who has just learned her multiplication tables:

'And also that every man should eat and drink, and enjoy the good of all his labour, it is the gift of God! Got you! That's from the Bible, too. I bet you didn't guess that an old secular lady like me could recite relevant verses off the top of her head. That was from Ecclesiastes. Let's say chapter three, verse thirteen.'

Sirkka the Saver of Souls gaped at Irma and still didn't understand that the elderly women had no intention of participating in supporting the mission of Awaken Now!

Association, despite partaking of its bounty every day at their monitored caregiving pilot project. She grabbed at Irma's money and tried to take one fifty-euro note, but Irma clenched her fist tightly and repelled the attack.

'And if thou refuse to let them go, behold, I will smite all thy borders with frogs,' Sirkka hissed, her eyes slits. 'Exodus, chapter eight, verse two.'

Irma upped her one: 'There's your money, take it and be gone! Genesis, chapter twelve, verse abracadabra.' She let go, and Sirkka the Saver of Souls nearly toppled on her behind, as she was gripping the involuntary alms for all she was worth. After realizing that she had earned the Awaken Now! Association fifty euros as a result of her heated struggle, she pulled herself together and raised a hand. In the other, she clutched her take, knuckles white.

'Blessed shall be thy basket and thy store. Blessed shalt thou be when thou comest in, and blessed shalt thou be when thou goest out. Deuteronomy . . .'

But Irma and Siiri didn't stick around to listen to chapter and verse. They were in a hurry to catch the number 4 tram, whose bright lights gleamed at the corner of Kruunuvuoren-katu more invitingly than any holiday display. The driver saw the elderly pair hustling over and patiently waited for them. Siiri suspected he recognized her; so often had she ridden in his steady hands.

'Thanks ever so much!' Siiri said to the driver, and he nodded at them with a cheerful smile. They sat in Siiri's favourite place, the first row of two seats side by side, and simply panted for a moment, shocked as they were by Sirkka's behaviour. Religious people were always grasping, of course, but for an adult woman to steal money out of their hands, well, that was unprecedented.

'I had no idea you could recite the Bible at the drop of a hat,' Siiri finally said, once the tram had snaked slowly down Mariankatu and onto Aleksanterinkatu.

'You have to speak to an enemy in their language, otherwise they won't understand. I studied my Bible, but I modified it slightly. There's no mention of money in Genesis, people are just commanded to take a wife or rise up and go. But my God understands ancient texts need to be adapted to the situation.'

Chapter 20

Siiri and Irma tried to spend Christmas with Anna-Liisa. Their friend had been so debilitated by the entanglements surrounding the estate that she wanted to stay in bed, and so they had brought her a bit of swede casserole and some sliced ham. They didn't have much else in the way of holiday cheer except Irma's green flaptop, which she had regained interest in when she heard it made it possible to celebrate a multi-reality Christmas.

'What in God's name does that mean?' Anna-Liisa barked from the depths of her bed. She was very wan and had lost even more weight, despite having always been thin, a real 'skinned flint', to use one of Irma's idioms. She had a copy of Thomas Mann's *The Magic Mountain* on her nightstand, as well as a little notebook and a pencil stub no more than a couple of centimetres long. She was frugal when it came to pencils, sharpening them down to the nub.

'Are you reading *The Magic Mountain*?' Siiri was delighted, as she had read it at least three if not four times and never tired of the novel's narrative, reflections and humour.

'It's stupendous,' Anna-Liisa said with a sigh. 'I'm taking

notes, as it's full of ingenuous little insights. Major ones, too, of course, but one can't exactly write those down. Has it ever occurred to you that Sunset Grove is the same sort of isolated hospice for anaemic shut-ins as Berghof Sanatorium is in *The Magic Mountain*?'

Anna-Liisa hadn't got very far in her present read, although she already knew the work by heart. She was making slow progress, and the book's pages were littered with her underlinings, exclamation marks and comments. Siiri felt it wasn't strictly kosher to deface a book with one's own commentary, and in the past Anna-Liisa had been resolutely of the same mind, but now had come to the conclusion that no one else would read *The Magic Mountain* once she was finished with it, so it made no difference what she scribbled in the margins.

She read them a few select quotes to support her claims. At the beginning of the book, the young Hans Castorp journeys by train to Davos to pay a short visit to his cousin at the Berghof Sanatorium. His tubercular cousin tells him he will have to spend at least six months recuperating, and the notion strikes Hans Castorp as horrific, as six months is a long time, longer than anyone has.

'But time held no meaning for the sanatorium's patients. Three weeks was like one day. Note that Hans Castorp's supposedly brief visit extends to seven years. He arrives a healthy man and gradually adapts to Berghof's customs, identifying so completely with them that he eventually discerns a rattling in his lungs, and that's the beginning of the end. We never learn if his illness is imagined or real.

Company makes the man, if you'll allow the cliché. As in asylums like Sunset Grove, where we languish with no concept of the passage of time.'

'I'm as healthy as an ox. And not the tiniest hint of a rattle anywhere,' Irma said, swiping at her tablet with swooping arcs in an attempt to force it into obeisance. 'Nor are there any mountains in the vicinity.'

'Yes, well. One passage that struck me was the one stating that life at the sanatorium was not real life, nor was it real time. Isn't that distressingly similar to our own lives?'

'They also drank red wine in the middle of the day, as far as I can recall. Apropos, I brought along a box of nice red that's nearly full. It's Italian, soft, and supple, the kind that used to be sold in the bottle with the funny crooked neck, do you remember? But why won't this contraption find the apps now that would let us celebrate a supernatural Christmas? Abracadabra and voilà – there it is, have a look.'

Anna-Liisa sighed deeply, closed *The Magic Mountain* and lowered it to the nightstand as if it were her most precious treasure. Irma stood and spun around in the room with the tablet in front of her face. The screen displayed what they would be seeing without it: Anna-Liisa's sparsely furnished flat. Upon the death of the Ambassador, Anna-Liisa had given away his gorgeous antiques to his avaricious heirs and moved into a studio. The sole remaining reminder of their brief union was the vast bed where the poor widow was drowning in pillows and blankets.

'Look! This is our real reality, can you see?'

They looked at Irma in concern, as neither Siiri nor Anna-Liisa understood why Irma was so elated.

'I believe you have a camera in that gadget of yours,' Anna-Liisa said, as if addressing a five-year-old who had drawn an incomprehensible mess and was asking the viewers to interpret the work.

'Of course. But the mind-boggling bit will appear in just a minute, wait.'

Irma sat down on Anna-Liisa's wooden kitchen chair and executed commands on the flaptop with a jangle of her gold bracelets. She told them she learned about the multi-reality Christmas app from her darlings, a few of whom had appeared on her smart-alec wall the day before last. They'd been so thrilled by the app that they had actually deigned to meet Irma briefly at the Fazer Cafe, eaten mounds of shrimp sandwiches and Christmas tarts on her tab and uploaded everything necessary for the game to her computer.

'Then they were in a terrible rush to get going, as all my darlings are spending Christmas together on the other side of the world this year, too. Was it Vietnam, I wonder? Is it safe to travel there? All I remember about Vietnam is that endless war between Nixon and the Soviet Union, and for what? Utterly in vain. *Einerlei*, they all flew off somewhere and in consolation, my sweet darlings set up this game for me. Now! There we go! It's working. Look!'

A video of Anna-Liisa's studio was still playing on the flaptop, but Siiri, Irma and Anna-Liisa had been joined by a dark-haired young man in military uniform. He was sitting on a chair at Irma's side, looking perfectly natural. Siiri didn't recognize him, but before she could ask who it was, all sorts of people started emerging from Anna-Liisa's kitchen onto Irma's screen. In the meantime, no one emerged from the real kitchen, not even a rat. Two handsome young men posed hand in hand on the flaptop screen, in all likelihood Irma's gay darlings that she always spoke of in such loving terms, as well as a few young women with babes in their arms. Irma turned the flaptop camera towards the balcony, and Irma's retired doctor daughter Tuula appeared there, as if conjured up to have a smoke.

Anna-Liisa was flabbergasted. 'What is this, pray tell?'

'This is a multi-reality Christmas game. This way I get to celebrate Christmas here in your apartment with all my beloved darlings, including Veikko, even though he died ages ago. He's here as a young soldier, because that's what he was like when I fell in love with him. Oh, he was so handsome, so manly. And he's sitting right there next to me.'

'Isn't this a little . . . macabre?'

'Not at all! My darling Jeremias is a computer genius and he makes games like this for a living. Apparently you can do quite well for yourself with such things these days, since he always has an expensive new car and lots of money.'

'Except when it's time to pay for shrimp sandwiches and Christmas tarts,' Siiri said, unable to restrain herself. But Irma ignored the sally. She had made careful note of Jeremias's instructions regarding her new game, which made one's everyday reality multi-dimensional, as something Jeremias called 'enhanced reality' inserted itself between the real world and the virtuosic world.

'Jeremias said I could talk to Veikko through this game, but I'm not that silly.'

Irma rotated her flaptop and squealed whenever she came across one of her darlings in the image. It was a parallel reality, that's what she called it, and was pleased to have remembered such a fancy term. According to Jeremias, enhanced reality was the hottest thing and allowed intimate devices, like one's phone or tablet, to become magical objects one could use to see into the future and the past. Belongings acquired new layers, and phenomena difficult to perceive with one's senses became perceptible.

'For goodness' sake, you're talking like someone who has found religion. I for one don't grasp the sublimeness of your artificial reality in the least,' Anna-Liisa said.

Irma's darlings had also told her about a game where one took tram rides both in the real world and virtuosically at the same time.

'All I have to do is hold the tablet up and with a flick of the wrist I can look out at a view from the 1930s, while the tram itself transforms into a 1980s model. Do you see? Then I'm in this time, the 1930s, and the 1980s all at once!'

Anna-Liisa shot down Irma's fanciful notions. 'No, you're not. You're in the present day, Irma, regardless of whether you're surrounded by a dozen gadgets and screens muddling your thoughts. If time even exists, that is. If you had had the patience to sit still and listen while I read you select excerpts from a novel written in the 1920s and set in the 1910s, you would have understood this concept. Would you like me to read more?'

Irma was stunned, and witnessing her friend's profound disappointment made Siiri feel bad. After all, Irma had gone through a lot of trouble to learn her wondrous new way of spending Christmas, with her beloved children and grand-children and dead husband joining her from Vietnam and beyond the grave.

'Maybe we . . . Why don't we revive our book club?' Siiri suggested. 'We could read together the way we used to.'

'But not on Christmas Eve, I hope,' Irma huffed, flinging her tablet into her bag. 'It's like casting pearls before swine.' She pulled out the swede casserole and the ham and marched demonstratively into the kitchen to heat up their modest Christmas supper.

The moment they were alone, Anna-Liisa grabbed Siiri's hand, squeezed it hard, and looked at her friend in anguish.

'Help me, Siiri. I'm too tired to fight over Onni's estate. The affair has taken on such bizarre dimensions.'

As Irma clattered needlessly loudly in the kitchen, Anna-Liisa unravelled the tangled mess for Siiri. Half of the heirs were suing the other half, and Anna-Liisa could no longer keep up with whether or not the suit involved her too. She had refused to hire a lawyer and appear in court. Her deepest wish was to rid herself of the entire estate, and in this the Awaken Now! Association had assumed a dismayingly active role. Any number of men in suits who took off their shoes at the door had been running in and out of her apart-ment, explaining how simple it was to transfer wealth in donation form to a not-for-profit charitable organization.

'That curly-haired fellow with the bow tie is the worst of

the lot. The other day he sat here so long that in the end I was forced to threaten him with the Day of Judgment and the fires of hell before he would leave. I haven't been out of bed since, I've been so exhausted. Like Hans Castorp, even though I entered this place a healthy woman.'

'How can I help?' Siiri asked haplessly, as the rushing in her ears and aching in her head intensified.

'I'm not certain myself. I just can't do this alone any more. At first I thought I wouldn't bother you with the matter, but during recent weeks everything has got so out of hand that it's too much; it's simply too much. You just sitting there and listening is a great help. Many things become clearer when you unburden yourself to someone else, don't you agree?'

'Yes, of course, but I have to say I understand nothing about quarrels among heirs. What I do understand is that this revivalist organization's attempts to seize your property sounds immoral. Should we report them somewhere?'

'Yes, but where? Don't you think I've considered that already? This is a trap that has been carefully laid, this marvellous new Sunset Grove.'

Anna-Liisa had survived any number of travails during her lifetime. Sunset Grove did not have a single, clearly identifiable owner, as it was initially established with innovation funding from three ministries and then sold to an international conglomerate. But Awaken Now! wasn't among the owners, and its link to the practical operations of the retirement home was ambiguous in the extreme. Both Siiri and Anna-Liisa knew it was highly unlikely that an international investment company and the other shareholders would be interested in the concerns of an elderly Finnish woman.

'I suppose the only thing you can do is take each day as it comes. But let's do it together, my friend.'

Anna-Liisa rewarded Siiri with a beautiful smile and continued to squeeze her hand. Her eyes grew a little moist, and Siiri felt a lovely warmth surge through her stomach. Just then, Irma came out of the kitchen carrying a tray she had laid prettily with three plates, three glasses of red wine, and two candles. Each plate held a serving of swede casserole and two slices of ham.

'A bit of swede and a slice of slam, as I always say. Merry Christmas, you lovely dears!' Irma's eyes twinkled, and she raised her wine glass high like the Statue of Liberty and toasted Christmas. '*Döden, döden, döden!*'

Chapter 21

The pre-Christmas electricity outage proved to be more than just a scare for Sunset Grove. Many devices were addled afterwards and exhibited strange behaviour. No one was shocked to discover that the food mash appeared in random lumps instead of triangles and cones, that the daily religious sentiment didn't suit the tenor of the day, or that the fridge spewed whatever silliness happened to pop into its head. But the fact that the caregiving robot Ahaba had strangled Eila shocked everyone. It beggared belief. How could such a thing even be possible? There was no way a machine could have been programmed to act in such a human manner.

'Robots are God's handiwork, too,' Margit said. She no longer dyed her hair jet-black, but allowed the white to thrust forth from the roots. Her new appearance reminded Siiri of a character from an animated children's movie, an evil woman who hated dogs and drove too fast in her convertible.

'How could you make such a preposterous claim? Humans are the ones who built the robots and assigned them their tasks. And it is humans who are responsible for this murder, even though it would be nice to blame God and pray for mercy on the robots' souls,' Anna-Liisa said in a voice that had lost its characteristic vim and vigour.

They were sitting in Anna-Liisa's cramped apartment, meeting for their book club. But nothing came of reading, as Eila's death had thrown their thoughts into turmoil. Just as they were getting somewhere, they reached a long conversation between the humanist Settembrini and the engineer Hans Castorp that also touched on religion, and this discussion about the balance between technology and humanity inevitably led to reflections on the murder committed by the caregiving robot.

It was equally shocking that Eila had lain dead in her robot's embrace for quite some time before being discovered. The psychopathic Ahaba was incapable of reporting the death to the patient registry at the health centre, and not a single one of the sensors in Eila's flat had sounded the alarm the way they should have during an emergency. The pharmaceutical AGV had even delivered its daily doses to the dead woman for over a week despite the extraordinary circumstances. It was only when the municipal health inspector had arrived at Sunset Grove in January to survey the rat population that the body had been detected.

'Of course that inspector didn't find a single rat,' Irma huffed. She didn't find the rats as stimulating a presence as Siiri did. Their numbers had started to increase, and in the end Irma had written a letter to the city's Department of the Environment demanding an investigation. Their jaws had collectively dropped when her handwritten missive had actually reached its intended recipient and a health inspector came knocking at Sunset Grove's doors the following week. Aatos Jännes had let him in, but not before conducting a thorough inquisition, as if he'd enjoyed a lifelong career at the Security Police or as a bouncer at a Helsinki bar. More than anything, Aatos wanted to know whether the inspector was one of Tauno's fairy friends, and when he wasn't, the inspector had been allowed to go about his business.

'Ahaba probably lost power at the fatal moment,' Siiri pondered. Unlike most residents, she didn't believe the robot had been programmed to kill its wards. 'All it would take would be for the power to go out and the robot to collapse on top of Eila. She couldn't get out from under it and died in her own bed.'

'Luckily she didn't die on the floor. That would have caused a scandal, and Sunset Grove would have been in the news again.'

'It must have been a dreadful end to a long life,' Anna-Liisa said sombrely.

Suddenly Margit burst into tears. They looked on in astonishment as she tried to calm herself by mechanically reciting prayers to Jesus Christ. Anna-Liisa found the praying irritating, but even she understood that interfering at such a delicate moment was not fitting. It was dreadful that a third resident had died in the clutches of the machines. These were not the sort of happy deaths they'd been lulled into accepting and, in their own cases, anticipating. In the past, death had been a mundane occurrence at Sunset Grove, good news rather than bad, but these recent incidents had turned everything topsy-turvy. There was no honour to dying in a robot's embrace or by over-exertion from an exercise game console. Even though the seal pup owner may have died happily mid-caress, Siiri saw something unpleasant in it, propped up alone in an electric wheelchair in a retirement home, clenching a robotic toy at the moment of one's death. What if the death had been caused by the electric wheelchair after all, if it had broken down and left the old woman to starve to death in the corridor in her smart-diapers? Or if the seal pup had short-circuited and given the poor woman an electric shock? Nevertheless, Eila's demise in Ahaba's embrace was the most anxiety-provoking of the deaths, since she was the one who had so meekly subjected herself to the companionship of the caregiving robot and demonstrated its skills to Siiri just a couple of days before the fateful moment.

'Yes, well, I assume Eila just rested there before losing consciousness. She probably didn't suffer dreadfully. Nor did she have to die alone, as her beloved personal caregiver was there,' Irma said, trying to lighten the mood. Anna-Liisa shot her an exhausted look and, to Siiri's surprise, smiled. She had imagined the others would find Irma's japes offensive. But Anna-Liisa just shook her head and wryly said: 'What are we ever going to do with you, Irma. *Döden, döden, döden.*'

Then she hoisted herself up into a sitting position and made sure the front of her flannel nightshirt was buttoned. Her bun had flattened into a straggly mass, and her reading glasses were sticky. Siiri wasn't used to seeing her friend so deflated; Anna-Liisa was always so well groomed and firm of mien. But the nightmarish battle over the estate and the helping hands of the Awaken Now! Association had driven Anna-Liisa into such a tight corner that she appeared to have decided to solve her problems by sinking into her bed. Siiri let out a deep, tremulous sigh, and tears welled up in her eyes. It was disconcerting, reacting so strongly in the presence of others. But the others thought she was mourning Eila and paid her no heed.

Anna-Liisa listlessly reached for the book and started reading in a weak voice: 'At noon the patient will be brought the same broth as was brought yesterday and will be brought tomorrow. At the same time—'

'Broth! I do love my boullion, especially with, say, cabbage pie. Such delicacies aren't served in our rest home, and if they were, no one would . . .' Irma's flight of fancy was cut short by the appearance of a familiar curly-haired man marching into the flat, an electric-blue bow tie at his throat. He was accompanied by two laddish galumphs in suits, barely of age, who also removed their shoes at the door. The boys gawped and tried to hide behind the curly-haired man's short but broad back.

'The Lord's blessings on you,' he said, casting a gentle eye over his flock. 'Aha, I see our numbers have grown. And Margit is here, too. It's lovely to see you, Margit. Are we interrupting a prayer circle, perhaps?'

Siiri and Irma stared, dumbfounded, at this troika standing in front of Anna-Liisa's bookshelf, looking as if they'd been forced to come and pay their respects to their ailing grandmother. Impatience washed across Anna-Liisa's face, but she didn't say anything, simply frowned in irritation and closed her eyes like a child who wanted an unpleasant situation to just go away. But Margit smiled and bounced up with an unusual agility to bury the curly-haired man in an embrace.

'The Lord's blessings on you, Pertti!'

The adjutants opened their satchels and spread various papers, presumably testament-related, across Anna-Liisa's desk. The grifters clearly hadn't given up on the idea of having Anna-Liisa's property transferred over to the Awaken Now! Association. Or was it possible their visit pertained to Anna-Liisa's diminished condition? Had things progressed to the point that they would be transferring her to the dementia unit or some other place of perpetual bed-rest?

Pertti eyed the boys' papers in satisfaction, soothed Margit with a few apt Bible passages and pressed her into her seat with a hand of blessing. Then he bypassed Siiri and Irma without a word of greeting, perched on the edge of Anna-Liisa's bed and tried to take her hand with the customary lack of success. One did not just touch Anna-Liisa without her leave.

'Anna-Liisa. Dear Anna-Liisa.'

'I'm not your dear. I'm Mrs Petäjä, MA.'

'All right, let's just calm down.'

Pertti shot a quick glance at the young men standing at attention, took strength from Margit's admiring gaze and switched strategies. Now he spoke in a loud voice, as if Anna-Liisa were an imbecile who was hard of hearing. The familiar velvety tone had utterly vanished and the main

clauses now were modified by dependent clauses and parti-
cipial phrases. He informed her that he had prepared all the
requisite paperwork as agreed, giving his audience the un-
equivocal impression that he was working in seamless concert with Anna-Liisa and in accordance with previous
arrived-at arrangements.

'In reference to our earlier conversations, I'd like to re-
iterate that all that's required of you is your signature on a
few documents, the contents of which remain no doubt clear
to you based on said conversations. It's that simple.'

Anna-Liisa looked at the man with faded brown eyes that
in their prime had been jet-black. Now a flickering flame
ignited in them; Siiri had experienced it on more than one
occasion when unconscionable behaviour had forced Anna-
Liisa's hand.

'If I hear that idiocy from your lips one more time, I will
go insane. It's that simple!' Anna-Liisa had suddenly got her
strength and her commanding voice back and now projected
boundless disdain for the volunteer intruder. 'Nothing is that
simple! Not life, not death, and certainly not religion. If
something is simple, it's you. You think you can pull the
wool over the eyes of the elderly with your vapid Bible passages and phony recitations. You think we don't realize what
lies behind your simplistic aphorisms? Money. That's right,
money! You are a greedy and immoral man, presumably a
criminal as well, perhaps even an atheist, and hell will freeze
over before I become so demented as to donate anything I
own, even my old woollen knickers, to any of the organizations represented by you and your inane experts. And if you

don't stop hounding me, I'm going to report you to the police. I will ask for a restraining order if I can't think of anything else. It's that simple!'

'And that's that. Brava, Anna-Liisa!' Irma applauded enthusiastically, and Siiri felt enormous pride in her courageous friend. The adjutants looked at the tips of their socks, and Margit was horrified. She rose and wrapped her arm around Pertti's shoulders as if protecting a tormented schoolchild from the class bully.

'She's very old and gets in a state from time to time,' Margit explained to Pertti. 'We can't take what she says seriously. Don't feel bad. I know all the good work you do, and above all, God knows. That's what's important, right?'

'God schmod,' Pertti said with a startling worldliness, before wrenching himself out of Margit's arms and to his feet. He jangled the keys in his pocket antsily. 'Let's go, guys. Bring the papers, don't leave any of them behind.' Those mute assistants, those panicky paladins, packed their documents into their satchels and marched to the door, socks slipping against the floor. Pertti turned once more towards Anna-Liisa and said in his former velvety voice: 'Anna-Liisa, you need rest. I won't abandon you. You resist in vain. You're not seeing the big picture. You're afraid, that's only natural. But we'll help you. Good day to you. A very good day to you, Anna-Liisa.'

Chapter 22

There was a momentary silence after the men left. No rat scrabbled at the waste bin; the smartwall didn't come up with some germane Bible phrase. Anna-Liisa had gone ashen as a result of her exertions, and Siiri went into the kitchen to fetch her something to drink. Irma offered to retrieve a box of red wine from her apartment, but Anna-Liisa firmly declined. She took a few sips of water from the glass Siiri brought, and then they sat silently again, each of them lost in her own thoughts. It was pitch black outside, a normal January afternoon in Helsinki. Anna-Liisa's ancient wall clock ticked tirelessly, swinging its pendulum and demonstrating its unshakable faith in that credo questioned in *The Magic Mountain*: that time is a stable and objective measure of life. In the end, Margit wanted to speak.

'Pertti is a good man,' she said, then paused as if to consider how this claim would be received. They all looked at her expectantly, and so she continued cautiously, recounting how she had made Pertti's acquaintance at resident events and found him to be an intelligent and empathetic individual. 'I've never been particularly religious,' she said, now a little more confidently. 'A nominal Christian. But the pain involved in Eino's illness and passing, thinking about euthanasia and death as a relief, threw me into a state of uncertainty and angst. That's why I felt safe at Pertti's prayer circles. And then, all of a sudden, it happened. I found religion, just the way they describe it in books.'

'Did you speak in tongues? Or did you fall to the floor?' Irma asked inappropriately, but Margit just smiled. She was getting up to speed and described in detail how Pertti had asked God's lambs to stand and Margit had instinctively stood, the only one, boldly. She had known with an astonishing certainty that she was doing the right thing. She had felt an incredible warmth throughout her body, momentarily lost consciousness and fallen into Pertti's strong arms. When she came to, she had known without asking that the Holy Spirit had touched her. 'I'm blameless for my sins and I bare my heart to my Saviour. He knows me better than I know myself, and that's why I'm at peace. The power in Pertti's hands made me feel so safe that I started to cry and laugh out loud.'

'When you put it that way, it sounds nice,' Siiri said, as she had genuinely felt Margit could use something of the sort in her life. They, the random band of friends Margit had left to her, had not been able to provide the security and the meaning Margit craved from life.

But Anna-Liisa was not softened by Margit's revelations. 'How much have you donated to this security network of yours?'

'That doesn't matter,' Margit said. Donations were voluntary, and if someone did as much good for Margit as the Awaken Now! Association had, she was happy to support its valuable work. 'As you know, I don't have any children and I can use what little money I have left as I see fit. I can't take anything to heaven with me, and I don't need anything. My deeds will be rewarded in heaven.'

An awkward silence fell. Siiri sensed that Anna-Liisa had a tart remark on the tip of her tongue about channelling money straight to heaven, but Margit's pious sincerity staved off any jibes. She herself was curious to hear more about Awaken Now!, and the relieved Margit gladly shared the little that she knew.

'I'm not actively involved in the association itself. I've been a little selfish in simply seeking their help. But this lovely woman that you might have met, Sirkka, has told me a bit about their work. Pertti is rather discreet, you see; he doesn't like discussing anything but matters of religion during prayer circle, which I like.'

'All he's spouted about in my presence is inheritance law; he hasn't quoted a single word from the Bible,' Anna-Liisa remarked coolly.

'Yes, he has an eye for what interests people,' Margit said. She had heard from Sirkka that Awaken Now! was originally an American congregation that had come to Finland in the 1980s. The association was active in charity work and did an exemplary job carrying out the congregation's social responsibility work. Elder-care was dear to its heart, as were dogs and whales, and even though Sunset Grove was the first retirement home it was monitoring in Finland, Margit had heard that several others around the country were in the works.

'Yes, I understand elder-care is the most profitable business sector in the Nordic countries at the moment,' Anna-Liisa interjected.

'I think it's lovely that Awake Now! is fiscally responsible as well. When you donate them money, you can be sure it will be used wisely.' Margit was still unable to explain where the association's funds were actually directed and the nature of its involvement in Sunset Grove's operations, other than foisting Bible phrases and prayer circles on residents in hopes of extracting eventual alms. In the end, Margit grew upset in the cold cross-fire of Anna-Liisa's arguments and burst into tears yet again. It was very distressing. Irma, who had followed the conversation with uncharacteristic restraint, felt bad enough to offer Margit her lace handkerchief and tender consolation. Siiri felt utterly helpless and couldn't get a word out.

'All right, I believe that's it for our book club today,' Irma said, drowning out the prayer Margit was muttering to herself. 'I must say I enjoy re-reading old books, because I can't remember anything I've read any more. Oddly enough, the same doesn't apply to music. Have you noticed? Music sinks in somewhere so deep that Mozart's compositions are an integral part of me now. I'm positive that even if I grew so demented I were nothing but an unconscious carcass planted in my smartbed, I'd recognize Mozart's Clarinet Concerto, so remember to play it for me when I'm incapable of asking for it. Now I'm babbling again, forgive me. Perhaps you could come to my place, Margit, for a glass of wine and some liver casserole? You'll feel better. Would you like to come too, Siiri? We can leave Anna-Liisa to rest here, you look so tired, and it's no wonder with bow-tied imps like that skating in and out with their brazen papers. Excuse me, Margit, I don't mean to offend you, but this Pertti of yours hasn't treated Anna-Liisa as lovingly as he has you. Or would you like me to bring you some wine and liver casserole, Anna-Liisa? I'd be more than happy to. Could you please hand me back my handkerchief, Margit? It's my mother's and very dear to me.'

Margit was just slipping Irma's beloved memento into her handbag, but she handed the damp linen back to Irma. She declined the offer of wine, as upon her enlightenment she had turned her back on alcohol, although no one had specifically urged her to. It had just seemed like the right thing to do. Margit glanced at her gold watch from Spain, which Eino had given her at the onset of their blissful retirement years, and noticed she was late for her afternoon prayer circle. She scurried out, leaving her friends to jointly ponder the day's adventures that had invaded their lives, even though their intention had been to quietly read a German novel about life in a sanatorium on the cusp of the First World War.

'You know,' Anna-Liisa finally said. 'You know, another reason *The Magic Mountain* is an appropriate work for our lives is that it depicts the moment before catastrophe strikes.'

Chapter 23

Experience Director & Front-Line Support Jerry Siilinpää had invited the residents of Sunset Grove to an informational session titled 'Rats Among Us?' All able-bodied were present; even one straight-A student from the dementia unit had hauled herself to the back of the auditorium in her electric bed. She had oxygen whiskers in her nose that kept slipping out, despite Tauno's best efforts to hold them in place.

As always, Jerry enthusiastically jumped right in. 'Yeah, so hi everyone, great to see such a big crowd here today!' He appeared agitated, punched one hand into the pocket of his overly snug sports jacket, took it out, tugged the jacket straight with his other hand, swivelled his head as if it had got stuck in the jugular notch, and got down to business. 'Rats. That's right, rats have been seen here at Sunset Grove. Someone had even reported them to the city. But no worries. Let's just say that rats are pretty innocuous animals.'

'Innocuous? They carry all sorts of diseases, from the plague to Ebola,' Ritva shouted in a raspy voice from the back row. Siiri thought Ritva had decamped for the more efficient environs of manual caregiving units, as it had been ages since there had been any sign of the coroner. But here she was among them, the same as ever – with the exception of the sun visor, which had been replaced by the kind of cap one used to see on working stiffs at service station bars, in observation of winter.

Ritva continued: 'There was a nasty stomach virus going around here; I had to go to the hospital for IV hydration. Couldn't it have come from the rats?'

The room erupted. Everyone had something to say about diarrhoea and the stomach flu; someone claimed that someone else had died from the most recent virus, and many remembered their experiences with rats from decades past, from a time when Jerry Siilinpää's grandparents were still attending grammar school in the countryside.

'Hey, guys, come on, hey, can I get you guys to pay attention for a sec?' Jerry shouted from the front. 'OK, so there have been some sightings of rats. The inspector didn't find any, BTW. But let's say someone has seen a couple of rats, that doesn't make this some epic nightmare, like, worst ever or anything. And the stomach flu is totally normal in places like this.'

The audience rejected this perspective as well. Suddenly every other resident had seen several rats, and Margit managed to project her voice above the others', as she hauled her massive carcass to a standing position in the front row and described at length how a large, filthy rat had attacked her when she was taking out the rubbish.

'It jumped out at me when I opened the bin lid. I still don't understand how I didn't have a heart attack then and there. God was with me.'

Aatos Jännes wanted to speak briefly on the reproductive capacity of rats and substantiated his claims with statistical information that was initially quite convincing, until he meandered into a comparison of the rutting periods of various mammals and started fantasizing about how, of all species, only man mated continuously and for pleasure.

'That's not true!' Tauno brayed, fanning his arms furiously. He launched into a verbal volley against Aatos in retaliation for past offences, and reminded the audience that the lions of the savannah mated with any lioness who happened to walk past without reproductive intent.

'I've also read that, as a matter of fact, quite a few of our local mammalian species mate for the sheer joy of it, too,' Anna-Liisa said, catching Siiri and Irma completely off guard. They had never imagined their friend would have the energy to come down to the auditorium, let alone get caught up in a debate regarding the mating habits of animals. But Anna-Liisa seemed like her old self in her black mourning garb, with her hair nicely combed. She was sitting at the rear of the room in an otherwise empty row, and her voice was once again audible and authoritative. 'Fidelity to a mate has not been observed in most species, which is yet another indicator that our notions of animal sexuality have been profoundly romanticized to comply with Christian conceptions of the family. I have understood, for instance, that it is not unheard of among willow tits for two males to mate with each other. Assuredly something other than reproductive urges is involved in that instance.'

'Exactly! Which brings us to the matter at hand!' Tauno bawled. Jerry Siilinpää was engrossed in the world of his smartphone and didn't appear to hear. 'We've been locked up with robots and religious fanatics in an artificial environment where diversity commands less respect than it did in the military during the 1960s. Robots is what they are, every last one, the food printers, the sweeping machines and the volunteers who heal through the power of the Holy Spirit. They even recite their scriptures like robots.'

'Yup, point notated,' Jerry said. He had been paying attention to what was going on in the room after all.

'Notating is documentation according to a system of notation. A composer notates, but you note,' Anna-Liisa observed.

'That's what they're like,' Irma whispered to Siiri. 'My darlings can be having five different conversations on the Internet, watching television, eating and talking with me on my smart-alec screen. Sometimes they're even more absent-minded than I am, but I don't like to criticize them, because they're so patient with me, even though I'm such a . . . a . . . for Pete's sake, a . . .'

Siiri stepped in to help: 'Forgetful old lady.'

'Yes. A forgetful old lady. Now how did that slip my mind?'

'Exactly. So you guys know a ton about rats. Let's brainstorm this case a little and start by zooming in on the real problem. Here.' Jerry drew a shapeless lump on the flipchart, which might have been a rat or some other action point. 'What do we see here?'

He looked at his audience, undismayed by the reception his brainteaser had received. The dementia unit's valedictorian had fallen asleep, and Tauno couldn't get her oxygen whiskers to stay in place. He had to prop himself up next to the hospital bed in his peculiar hunched-over stance and hold the tube to the snoring woman's face with one hand. Siiri felt Tauno could have freed the sleeping dementia patient, because she could hear her breathing perfectly well without any extraneous apparatus. Margit had dozed off in the front row, and Anna-Liisa's vigilance had waned; she was getting tired and suddenly looked rather pallid. Smiling mysteriously, Aatos Jännes scratched out something into a pad of paper he pulled from his breast pocket, tore off a corner of the sheet, folded it, and told his neighbour, a dotty old man with Type II diabetes, to pass the note on.

'Just like a naughty schoolboy!' Irma huffed.

'Or Count Almaviva,' Siiri said, as the note made its threatening approach.

'Nonsense. The Count doesn't write a single letter in the *Marriage of Figaro* — although he receives plenty, of course. One from Figaro and another from Susanna, but that one was dictated by his wife.'

Jerry Siilinpää tried to rouse his audience: 'Why don't I make this a little easier for all of us. So there are a few rats. What's the big deal?'

The note had reached Siiri, who to her great relief read Irma's name on it. She wouldn't have known what to do if

Aatos Jännes had tried to woo her with one of his salacious rhymes. Irma took the note and blushed, but didn't open it.

'Oh, for goodness' sake,' she sighed, clutching the folded note to her breast. Siiri thought she could sense Jännes's greedy gaze on the back of her neck.

'Exactly, rats are kinda gross, even though we don't have any reason to feel that way. I mean, come on, some people keep rats as pets. It's the latest. But I'm getting the vibe that our pilot cohort in monitored caregiving isn't so stoked about welcoming our little friends. So let's open a case. What do you say, guys?'

'Stop yakking, for crying out loud,' Tauno shouted so loudly that the snoring dementia patient stirred in her bed. 'Kill them and be done with it.' The oxygen-whiskered valedictorian whimpered.

'Right. I'll draw a cross here, so we can all get a handle on our veteran's approach. And now if I pick it up from Tauno's item, I'd say: why not.'

'You'd say or you're saying?'

This was Anna-Liisa's voice, by now fatigued but still emphatic. Irma tried to unfold the note in a way that would keep its contents private from Siiri. Siiri followed along as Jerry unravelled the case and inevitably advanced towards killing the rats, which one would think would have been obvious with a less rigorous audit. Out of the corner of her eye, Siiri monitored Irma, who read the message hidden in her palm, blushed even more deeply, smiled girlishly, glanced over her shoulder and nodded in Aatos Jännes's direction, in a sign of either submission or gratitude. Lord help us, Siiri thought and felt the blood rush in her ears until it completely drowned out the fifth-octave A. Had Irma completely forgotten the sort of man Aatos Jännes was?

'Why the hell are you wasting our time with this gibberish when you could have just called the city sanitation department and brought in a professional exterminator to take care of the problem?' By now Tauno was roaring so violently that saliva sprayed to the floor.

Jerry Siilinpää thanked Tauno again for the valuable comment, took it from there and started talking about participatory decision-making. This meant that even minor decisions were no longer made using common sense, but as many people as possible were gathered together to throw out spontaneous cogitations, which were then drawn on a flip-chart in arrow and lump form.

'I mean, it's not like this is the Soviet Union, right? Community is the key word, and experiential expertise is what matters,' Jerry explained, looking genuinely interested. An experiential expert was anyone impacted by the matter at hand; in this case, the residents of Sunset Grove. 'In other words, the primary experiencers. Which means you.'

'You want me to tell you where your focus is?' Ritva blurted out.

'What about the rats? Wouldn't it be a good idea to survey their experiences, too?' Tauno asked, to rousing applause and an explosion of laughter.

'Exactly. Right, right.' Jerry started pulling himself and his belongings together on the lectern. 'Let's just say that commitment is at the core of participatory decision-making. The experiential experts commit to the decision, and every phase of the decision-making process is documented in open data. Transparent management without any organizational charts, the latest. But why don't we gradually start wrapping things up here?'

Jerry seemed even more agitated than at the beginning of the session. He paced back and forth in his gorilla feet before announcing the rats would be exterminated, the rubbish bins would be removed to make way for automated waste collection and the topic of the next resident evening would be a small survey of the future of health and caregiving technology. He gave a friendly wave, called out bye now, and left. Then Sirkka the Saver of Souls appeared out of nowhere and suggested they all pray together and afterwards collect donations.

The majority of the audience felt their limbs miraculously invigorated when Sirkka launched into an intercession on behalf of the alcoholic son of someone she knew. Siiri and Irma caught up with Anna-Liisa at the door, but Margit remained planted in the front row, collection box in hand, inviting uncertain sheep to join her flock.

'Would you prefer to join me for the poetry club rather than stay here and pray?' Aatos Jännes asked, eyeing Irma lustfully. He was standing outside the doors to the auditorium, handing out slips of paper to passers-by. Siiri took one, read the clumsy attempt at verse printed on it and gathered that Jännes was serving as the leader of the poetry club. The clever fellow. An unbroken parade of female lovers of lyricism wandered from the door to Aatos's salon, as he called the former magazine nook in the common room.

'I understand perfectly well if you're more fond of German prose, but I'm going to have a look,' Irma said hastily, following the others. Siiri and Anna-Liisa stood in the lobby, stunned.

'I can't keep up with what's going on here any more; I feel so incredibly powerless,' Anna-Liisa said in exhaustion. She was so drained by all that had happened that Siiri had to lead her to her flat and her bed, where she fell asleep the moment she collapsed on it. Siiri stayed there for a moment watching her dozing friend, the pale, emaciated old woman who was no longer herself. Not that any of them were any more. She was equally startled every time she saw herself in the mirror; she didn't think of herself as being so shrunken and shrivelled.

Just as she was on her way out, Siiri noticed some papers on the nightstand. It was a will, its cover sheet branded with the eye-catching logo of the Awaken Now! Association, and a quick scan was enough for Siiri to gather that the document transferred Anna-Liisa's entire estate as well as that of her deceased husband, including any furniture and possessions, to the association at the moment of signing. Anna-Liisa was mercifully granted the right to stay in her flat at Sunset Grove for the rest of her life.

Siiri took the will and left her friend to sleep off her woes.

Chapter 24

A horrific din echoed from the dining room. The canteen was typically deserted, and increasingly frequently that went for mealtimes as well, as many of the residents had pronounced the three-dimensionally printed nourishment so foul they preferred to skip it altogether. But now the door was closed, apparently with some sort of vociferous mob inside. Siiri and Irma couldn't figure out what was going on.

'That's that velvet-eyed man's voice,' Irma said.

'Pertti,' Siiri said. 'That was his name, wasn't it?'

They stood at the door to the dining room and tried to eavesdrop. It wasn't one of the usual praise services, or even a collective exorcism of demons, which were also held from time to time. They had recently witnessed Margit banishing the Devil from the depths of her soul, and it had been shocking indeed. Pertti and one of the other volunteers had ordered Margit to pray harder and harder, to believe more fervently and testify more passionately. Margit had tossed her head, cried, and shouted Jesus Christ is My Lord, her prayers intensifying into a hysterical litany reminiscent of a torture victim's agonized screams. The men said they were helping Margit, but they had taken her half-grey head in both hands and shaken it until it nearly popped off. Logic should have dictated Margit dreading such treatment, but afterwards she said she felt wonderful and light, having been freed from evil influences. They hadn't dared probe any more deeply into the matter; so horrific had the procedure seemed to their eyes. But now something else was afoot in the dining room.

'It's normal for some Christians to struggle with this problem.' It was Pertti's voice. 'They feel an erotic attraction towards their own sex.'

Pertti was gentle, but now a reedier, more nasal male voice zealously uttered:

'Homosexuality is a plot of the Devil, Satan's way of luring the unsuspecting into the fires of hell! God will not abandon you, if you but turn your shameful face to him!'

Irma tried to restrain a spontaneous squeal and only partially succeeded. She looked at Siiri in horror and pressed her ear even closer to the door. A shrill female voice joined the chorus.

'Set thee up waymarks, make thee high heaps: set thine heart toward the highway. And the whole valley of the dead bodies, and of the ashes, shall be holy unto the Lord.'

'They're preaching directly to someone, they're saying "you" . . .' Irma said. Then: 'Shuffle and cut! It's Tauno! They're talking to Tauno, aren't they!'

'Lower your voice,' Siiri hissed, pressing her ear to the door, too.

The two grey-haired women leaned in towards the door, eyes wide with curiosity. There wasn't another soul in Sunset Grove's echoing lobby, and without the two inquisitive eavesdroppers the retirement home's communal area would have looked prosaic indeed: forgotten, dusty and utterly static, despite the prominent presence of modern technology that added nothing to the ambience, other than intermittent automated statements with no one to hear them: 'The. Elevator. Is. Free.' 'A. Code. Is. Required. To. Open. The. Door.' These random sentiments, repeated day in, day out, remained orbiting in the space-time encapsulated by the retirement home, where the ceiling was high and the walls distant but time so stagnant that by all appearances it had vanished entirely.

'Didn't your father show you enough love? Perhaps not. What is broken can be repaired. It's that simple.'

The woman with the shrill voice started praying in earnest, a low background murmur. It was impossible to hear what she was saying, but as the men drew breath, Siiri and Irma could make out a cry for help uttered directly at the victim:

'Holy Spirit, heal Tauno! Open not the wrong doors for him!'

Irma was already opening the door, but Siiri grabbed her hand. 'We can't go in. It would cause a huge fuss.'

Inside the dining room, the pace of the prayers picked up, as in the best opera finales, where everyone sang their own lines at the same time. The interweaving voices would have formed a beautifully building contrapuntal tapestry if the words being voiced hadn't been in such glaring conflict with all that is beautiful.

'Sin cannot be allowed to rule mortal flesh.'

'Holy Spirit, free him from lust!'

'Let out the roar of a lion. Give in to your masculinity!'

'Confess your degeneracy.'

Siiri and Irma couldn't catch the tiniest hint of Tauno's voice amid the cacophony. Perhaps it was just a rehearsal, and Tauno wasn't present? If that were the case, they could go and warn their friend.

'This man has not hidden his degeneracy, verily, no!'

Only now did they make out a male voice with a hint of tenor.

'Aatos Jännes!' Siiri hissed out of the corner of her mouth.

So the amateur poet cum insatiable lecher as a result of his memory medication had joined forces with the religious fanatics. It was nothing if not tragicomic. Siiri glanced at Irma, who had been uncommonly reticent about the poetry club at Aatos's salon. Irma looked bewildered, unable to believe her ears. The thundering beyond the door continued, mightier than ever. Now Aatos's voice bellowed above the others.

'The dark corners of railway stations and sleazy public lavatories is where they belong, not among decent people. Normal taxpayers aren't safe from this trash, even in retirement homes. Isn't homosexuality the greatest sin imaginable? What could be worse?'

'You're right, Siiri. It's Aatos,' Irma said sadly. 'He's the one who's sick, as we know. Even at his poetry salon he'd slip into incredibly lewd language; he has absolutely no control. Some people find it amusing, but I can't understand it. I stopped going. You knew that, didn't you? It made me as nauseous as these religious lunatics' broadsides.'

'Yes, Aatos. Homosexuality is the worst possible sin.' The speaker wasn't Pertti; they didn't recognize the other volunteers' voices. 'But Tauno need not shrink from that. Awaken Now! can help. We will make you whole.'

Then it was absolutely silent, and Siiri and Irma nearly burst with curiosity. Tauno had to be in there; they wouldn't be putting such effort into a rehearsal. But why didn't Tauno say anything? Generally he was quick to defend himself, regardless of the circumstances, and tenacious beyond belief, as they had witnessed during the plumbing retrofit: Tauno had been the lone resident to soldier through the cataclysm, sleeping on a thin mattress on the floor, the last of the Mohicans.

'Don't lose heart. God is stronger than the Satan within you.'

'You don't need to end up in the fires of hell, Tauno.'

Irma could take no more of the secret society's attempts to heal Tauno into heterosexuality. Without further deliberation or asking Siiri for permission, she yanked open the door to the dining room and stepped in. Siiri's digestive organs threw a somersault, and the rushing in her ears was intolerable. She followed Irma on unsteady feet.

Upon seeing his friends, Tauno let out an unintelligible howl. If it included words, they were impossible to make out, as his wail was a mixture of tears and outrage. He was bound to a chair in the middle of the room. Layers of orange laundry line had been wrapped around his arms and legs, confining him to his seat, and he had been gagged with a scrap of fabric. His face was crimson, the veins in his forehead bulged blue, and his cap had fallen to the floor, revealing white hair glowing against the red. He mumbled desperately, twitched and writhed in rage. Tears damped his face, and his eyes burned with a terrified fury. Siiri had to sit down on the nearest chair to keep from fainting.

Tauno was surrounded by Aatos in his brown weekday suit, four volunteers in suits and socks, and Sirkka the Saver of Souls in her eternal artificial-fabric tunic and green high heels. When the door opened, they had all fallen silent and now glared icily at Irma and Siiri. Siiri felt disgusted and impotent, but Irma smiled angelically.

'Oh, excuse me, are we interrupting?'

No one answered.

'Siiri and I were just coming in to eat, but it looks like we've completely misjudged the time. Can anyone tell me what time it is? Is it Tuesday? We're so dotty, you see, and when you spend all of your days inside four walls and the sun doesn't even rise outside, it's easy to get mixed up, and you never know whether it's day or night or time to eat, no matter how many reminders you get from the smartwall. It tries to send us to bed at nine p.m., too, repeats it as tirelessly as the radio announcers who read the same news headlines every hour on the hour. Have you ever heard anything so silly? I stick out my tongue at it every night at nine p.m. Like this!'

Irma made a face at the healers and broke into her tinkling laugh. As she spoke, she calmly walked up to the circle, radiating an aura of sweet innocence. Siiri almost started laughing, and her revulsion evaporated. How ingenious and brave her Irma was!

'Yes, well . . . today is Wednesday, isn't it? And the time is . . . Hmm, does anyone have the time?'

Pertti clawed at his wrists searching for his watch, then slipped a hand into his pocket, but when he couldn't find what he was looking for, spread his hands and looked helplessly at the other evangelists. Sirkka was the first one to rouse herself enough to come to Irma's aid.

'The time is seven minutes past ten. Ten a.m. Or ten in the morning, whichever you prefer.'

'Thank you, Sirkka! Where does it say that in the Bible? Since everything is laid out in it so precisely, there must be a verse somewhere that tells how time passes and what time it is.' Irma laughed cheerfully again and then turned towards the prisoner, as if she hadn't even noticed him yet. 'But, Tauno dear! For goodness' sake.'

Irma patted Tauno and bent down calmly to undo the knots in the plastic laundry line, and Tauno looked at her like an abandoned child, his pale blue eyes still wet with tears. Siiri rushed over to lend Irma a hand.

'What on earth are you doing tied to a chair like this? Are you playing some childish game? My darlings always loved playing bandits, and one time they rolled up the neighbour's boy in a rug so tightly he nearly lost his life; the poor thing couldn't get any oxygen or scream for help. I always told my children they weren't allowed to roll anyone up in a rug, even in jest, because you can never know if you pulled the knots too tightly and cut off the circulation. And what if the children hadn't been able to undo the knots? I wasn't always looking over their shoulders the way these professional mothers do today, perched on the edge of the sandpit day in, day out. I was just a housewife, and when you have six children and just one father providing, I had my hands full running the household. Oh dear, oh dear, what fun we had.' She shook her head and smiled at the memory. She had reached into her bag and pulled out the hunting knife Anna-Liisa had lent her. 'Cops and robbers and cowboys and Indians. Is this supposed to be a totem pole, this chair, and Pertti and his friends a tribe of Indians? Is that what you've been playing at, you naughty boys. Dratted knots, I can't even undo them with my knife. Could you lend me a hand, oh Great Indian Chief Pertti?'

Pertti gaped at the well-dressed, rotund old woman, diamonds glittering at her ears and bracelets jangling as her knobby fingers sawed away, faster and faster. The neo-charismatic leader obeyed Irma like a schoolboy, took the knife and severed the ropes. Siiri had worked the cloth away from Tauno's mouth and removed it while Pertti spooled up the plastic twine. Siiri was afraid Tauno would start hurling ill-considered insults at his healers, but he didn't. He just sat there trembling silently, his eyes glued to the floor.

'Well, well. These charming ladies are riding to the rescue, I see. I believe I have some things to take care of. Thank you, one and all. Until the last time!' Aatos Jännes took a couple of steps towards the door and waved. It seemed to him no one had understood his joke, and he stood there scratching his ear. 'They used to say "until next time" on the radio and telephone, do you remember? At this point in our lives it seems more fitting to say until the last. A little innocent wordplay. Or should I say till the very last time? Would that be more fitting?' He laughed nervously, turned on his heels, and fled the scene like a hardened criminal.

'Tauno, get up, dear,' Irma said, grabbing Tauno by the elbow. 'You're fine, my dear. We're with you and we will protect you. You don't have anything to be worried about. You're a wonderful man just the way you are, in that sense things are undeniably rather simple. Only a gargantuan blockhead could think anyone needs to change at this age. Like when they told my cousin she needed to stop eating sugar when they detected a little diabetes at the age of ninety-two. I said to her, don't talk nonsense, and then I told her I always pop one of the Amaryllie pillies into my mouth after I have a piece of cakesies or an ice cream cone, and my blood sugar has remained so superb that I won't be dying of that, at least. Oh dear, oh dear, this world is full of crazy people. Don't you fret, Tauno, about this idiotic Indian chief and his warriors.' Irma turned towards Pertti and made a face: 'Ugh!'

Siiri rushed round to Tauno's other side, and together they managed to help their trembling friend out of the chair and to his feet. The paralysed volunteer healers looked on as the frail trio wandered out of the canteen, leaving the door ajar behind them. When it had proceeded some way down the corridor, they heard a cheerful voice ring out:

'What if we sang a little? Would that help?'

And immediately afterwards, the women started belting out an old Austrian folk song.

'Oh, my dear August, my dear August, my dear August! Oh, my dear August, I fear all is lost. My trousers are lost, my shirt is lost . . .'

And then an unsteady male voice joined in.

Chapter 25

'I can't take this prison any more!' An overcoat-clad Irma was standing at Siiri's door, which she had managed to open with her own fob for once. 'When was the last time we saw the world? Back when we escaped the plumbing retrofit at Sunset Grove for that pornographic lair in Hakaniemi. I'll go mad if you don't take me for an adventure this minute, even if it's just a tram ride.' She had pulled her winter beret down over her ears and attached her anti-slip plates to her ankle boots; the spikes clacked against Siiri's plastic flooring as Irma paced back and forth in exasperation. She was clearly ready to face the outside world no matter how arctic it was.

Siiri had no trouble understanding Irma's restlessness. Things had been extraordinarily bleak of late. Tauno's attempted conversion had been hard on them; they had all been out of sorts since. Tauno had retreated to his C-wing cubbyhole too shaken to show his face, even for card games, Anna-Liisa lay ensconced in her bed reading *The Magic Mountain*, and Margit ran from praise service to prayer circle more frantically than ever. Only Ritva continued to man the card table undisturbed, yearning for a pint.

'Oh for goodness' sake, calm yourself, Irma!' Siiri said. 'I'd be happy to join you for a ride. It's been ages since I set foot in a tram.'

Siiri put on her coat and shoes, spent a moment looking for her handbag before finding it in its place next to the telephone table, verified that she had her fob and wallet in her bag, glanced in the mirror to find an ancient, withered creature there, adjusted her beret, grabbed her cane from the hallway cupboard and was ready.

'Aren't you taking your cane, Irma?'

'My Cane Carl has abandoned me again. I don't understand where he's gone off to, seeing as I haven't been anywhere. Do you suppose I left it in Anna-Liisa's apartment after our book club? I nearly fell asleep yesterday when she read Settembrini and Naphta's quarrel over the role of monks in the universe in such a monotone voice that I must have sleepwalked home. *La Sonnambula*, isn't that the Bellini opera? Shall we go and fetch my cane? Maybe Anna-Liisa will join us for a joyride. It would do her good; lounging about in bed for days on end is life-threatening. People just grow sicker and sicker in hospitals too, when they're kept lying there with nothing to do.'

Irma had heard about this on the radio; it was part of the structural change. Politicians had heaped all societal problems – the ill, the elderly, the disabled, the unemployed, drunks and immigrants – into one jumble. Assistance was offered from a single service point and no one was put up in institutions; instead, they were encouraged to get by on their own. Everyone did better that way, enormous sums of money were saved, and the government was able to cut unnecessary jobs, especially in social services. That was the end goal of all government activity: cutting costs and replacing people with machines or a single service point. Too much money was wasted on people, and Finland could no longer afford all its citizens, especially the unemployed elderly.

'Yes, we don't belong to society's productive sector,' Siiri said with a smile. 'Our time is worth nothing.'

'But we're doing our part! We're putting our lives on the line to test a money-saving monitored existence for the elderly.'

They knocked on Anna-Liisa's door, but she didn't come and open it. She was sleeping, no doubt; she slept nearly all the time now, and Irma felt that was the influence of Thomas Mann, whereas Siiri was concerned indeed and suspected it was due to the pressure from Pertti and his co-volunteers, which she knew weighed heavily on Anna-Liisa. And so they were bowled over to discover Anna-Liisa in her black dress at the card table in the lobby, in the company of Margit, Tauno and Ritva.

'Cock-a-doodle-doo and the latest! We're going out for a bit of fun! Come with us!'

But no one responded enthusiastically. A driving sleet was coming down, and a bone-chilling wind whipped across the faces of those who dared poke their noses outside. Siiri was rather disappointed when Irma nonchalantly plopped down with the others and started stripping off her beret and overcoat. She would have so loved to peer through the windows of Töölö, Punavuori and Kallio into strangers' homes. Now that it was cold and dark outside, the apartments looked so cosy inside. Such views reminded her of all the homes she had lived in in Helsinki's various neighbourhoods over her lifetime. But it was no good. Their lives had shrunk so far from their former parameters that few of them could even be bothered to wonder if there was life beyond the walls of Sunset Grove. Siiri also took off her outerwear to join her friends.

'Nothing is as important for people as other people,' she said, sitting next to Anna-Liisa.

'They certainly forgot that when designing this space capsule,' Irma huffed. 'The only living creatures one sees here every day are rats. Where have all of you been hiding this past week?'

'I just saw you yesterday at book club, Irma,' Anna-Liisa said, sighing deeply.

Then she called off the game of double solitaire she was playing with Margit. Anna-Liisa was vexed that Margit wasn't concentrating properly and had left many chances unplayed. The whole point of double solitaire was striking a balance between one's personal benefit and the common good, but Margit didn't seem to grasp this, as she served Anna-Liisa all the easy moves on a silver platter.

'Today I've done nothing but read *The Magic Mountain*. I also watched Chaplin's *Limelight*. Ritva taught me how to watch movies on my smartwall,' Anna-Liisa said.

'*Limelight*! I never would have taken you for a fan of that tramp Chaplin, he's such a ne'er-do-well,' Irma said, and helped Margit reduce Anna-Liisa's pack with a large stack of face cards.

'Despite its humorous moments, it is not, first and foremost, a comedy. You'll allow a brief refresher, I hope, since it appears you don't remember. *Limelight* is the touching story of an old circus artist who can no longer perform and eventually dies backstage. Modern technology came along and replaced variety shows. The story shares many similarities with *The Magic Mountain*.'

'How on earth is that possible?' Siiri asked. She could not see how the young Hans Castorp's obsessive need to cling to the past had anything to do with the death of an old circus performer. But it must have been dozens of years since she'd seen *Limelight*. She remembered having viewed it with her husband at the Blue Moon Cinema in Töölö, and that had gone out of business half a century ago.

'And there was the Bio Kent cinema in Munkkiniemi, remember, where the Muslim prayer room is now. And the upper Low Price Market is where Bio Riitta used to be!'

None of them could recall this as clearly as Irma, and even Irma's funny intuition couldn't tell them when Bio Riitta had last been in business. But she swore she'd seen several Chaplin films there. Irma wanted to know how she could get movies on her smartwall, too, and Ritva started to explain.

'. . . and first you choose "Media", and a new site will open on your screen, and you swipe that to access a dropdown menu. It has all sorts of options, like "Photos", "Music"—'

'Music! Can I watch Mozart on my smartwall?'

'Theoretically you can listen to Mozart,' Ritva continued, 'but it depends on what's uploaded there, and it looks like it's mostly adult contemporary. I've been listening to the Rolling Stones and Peter, Paul and Mary.'

'I see; in other words, rubbish. Luckily my old hand-cranked CD player still works even though it's not particularly intelligent. How are you doing, Tauno?'

Tauno seemed reluctant to answer. He glanced anxiously at Irma and Siiri as if begging them not to speak about what had happened in the canteen the week before. Irma understood and threw herself wholeheartedly into coming up with a new topic of conversation.

'Has Oiva been by this week? I haven't seen him since, since you were . . . since . . . How is Oiva? What about the rats? Why did Oiva make me think of rats, it must have been just some sort of *apropos*, but about . . . *Limelight* . . . Anna-Liisa, could you perhaps . . .'

Anna-Liisa rushed to Irma's aid and held forth tiredly but tenaciously about *Limelight*, which was set in the same period as *The Magic Mountain*, in the years leading up to the First World War. She saw uncanny similarities between that tragic, restless era and the present one. In addition, the proximity of death spoke to her, because in both the novel and the film the characters regarded death as salvation.

'I suppose it doesn't need to be said that nearly centenarian government expenditures such as ourselves have little comfort other than death and the fact that in this mad society hurtling towards catastrophe we're the sole group of humans who still remember that life ends in death.'

Anna-Liisa drew a breath to continue, but instead closed her mouth and stopped. To Siiri it seemed as if she were too tired to go on; the brief lecture had drained her utterly. Concluding her address with death perhaps came as a surprise to Anna-Liisa herself, but her lofty tone made probing deeper into questions of life or art impossible.

They sat in silence, and it felt nice. Time passed mercifully. When they were together like this, its passage was neither a waste nor the least bit arduous, as it was when day never slid into night or night into morning. And what were they waiting for at those instances anyway? Why did time need to run so swiftly that people were always impatiently anticipating the next moment without enjoying the present one? Siiri smiled happily as she looked at her last remaining friends; Irma was the only one she had known before moving to Sunset Grove, and then only distantly. Chance had thrown her together with these people, who had grown so important to her during the last few metres of a long life. She hadn't paid the slightest attention to Anna-Liisa in the corridors of Sunset Grove until Irma fell ill and had to be rescued from the locked unit. Back then, Anna-Liisa had been energetic and in love, and now she was a diminished, anxious widow. And what about Margit, who had rubbed her the wrong way until she joined Siiri and her friends during their plumbing-retrofit exodus and who had taken Siiri into her confidence during her husband's difficult death. Margit was her friend, of course. But Margit had also changed. She was no longer brusque, strong in body and in spirit, but lost and in need of help. Siiri saw no other explanation for Margit's clinging to a religious cult.

'You mentioned catastrophe, Anna-Liisa. Are you saying there will be a Third World War?' Ritva asked seriously, and almost excited.

'Oh, I can't say. War isn't what it was in the days when I was washing corpses at the Karelian Isthmus. Even war is waged in technological terms these days. There are these cyberwars and hybrid wars, in which manipulating information, system infiltration and psychology are central to the strategy.'

'Where did you come up with that?' Siiri asked, dumbfounded.

'I keep up with the times. The world will not survive technological dominance, that's plain as day. Moving on to another matter, did you hear three residents of the dementia unit died during that absurd electricity outage? They were lethally left without medication, monitoring or care. But no one is interested in their deaths. Except the city's financial manager, and for him it's a cause for celebration, as now there are fewer near-cadavers that need to be turned by machines.'

Irma covered her face with her hands. 'Anna-Liisa! That's awful!'

There had been rumours about the dementia unit deaths, but no official notification had been forthcoming from the smartwalls. As part of this pilot project in monitored eldercare, the dementia unit was even more securely locked than it had been in the past; access was strictly forbidden, and not even the volunteer staff members had been seen opening the ghostly automatic door to the vault. The other residents didn't know who was confined to the dementia unit, how the machines cared for them and who was possibly dead as a result of the technical malfunction. The incident was so surreal it was difficult to find the words to discuss it.

'What is the meaning of old age?' Anna-Liisa asked suddenly, as if moving on to the next item on the agenda of their little convocation. The others were silent for a moment.

'Could it be accepting that nothing matters?' Siiri eventually said.

'Yes, waiting for death,' Margit reflected.

Irma started getting bored and squirmed restlessly in her chair. 'Listen here, you apostles of death. We have to come up with something to do other than worry about the Day of Judgment. I can't stop thinking about the catastrophe Anna-Liisa just mentioned. I think we should start a war here at Sunset Grove. Why wait?'

The others gaped at Irma, whose eyes were twinkling with enthusiasm. She dug into her handbag in pursuit of her tablet and found it surprisingly swiftly. She started swiping with sweeping arcs, and it seemed to Siiri as if Irma were declaring war from her gadget then and there. Just like Ronald Reagan, who could have made the Cold War a physical reality with a single press of a button.

'What are you doing, Irma? What are you implying with this talk of war?' Anna-Liisa's voice was weak and agitated and it appeared as if she were genuinely afraid.

'I've had enough of this caregiving technology tomfoolery. How many more bodies need to turn up, friends, before you're convinced that cleaning robots and a food printer can't care for the elderly? The electrical outage was the real guinea pig test in this madhouse. It proved that the notion of replacing humans with machines is dead on arrival. But no one is doing anything about it.'

'I've been wondering the same thing, since there hasn't been anything on the news about the accidents here,' Tauno said faintly, as if he had given up. Siiri had never seen Tauno like that before.

'No one is interested in a couple of old people who got squished by robots. Or maybe they would be, but talking about it is blasphemy. Technology is the new religion, and when something is as sacred as a religion, you're not supposed to question or criticize it. Humour is forbidden, too. Beware mocking a caregiving robot!'

'That's no doubt true, Irma. But how were you planning on starting this war, and what are your aims?'

Irma didn't have a plan. She suggested that for starters they pull the plug in the Holy of Holies, located in the cellar.

'One flick of the wrist, and this entire pilot project comes crashing down.'

'Are you talking about the server? What makes you think it's in the basement?' Ritva was clearly interested, but the others paid her no attention.

'What a superb idea, Irma,' Anna-Liisa said sourly. 'And when four more residents die as a result of your cyberattack, what happens then?'

'Then . . . then we save all the residents and become heroes.'

'I like it otherwise, but the doors need electricity to work, so we won't be able to open them.'

Tauno had a point. Siiri smiled at Irma, who firmly believed the time had come to take action. Siiri agreed; this could not go on. But she didn't know where to start unsnarling this technological tangle. Pulling a plug out of a wall wouldn't cause sufficient damage, and in some strange way the thought of Sunset Grove suffering a major catastrophe appealed to her, as it did Irma. Long after the others had forgotten Irma's military strategy and started volubly arguing about the correct answer to a trivia question posed by the smartwall, Siiri closed her eyes and ears and tried to think. 'Think, think,' she said out loud without anyone noticing, and felt as stupid as Winnie the Pooh.

Chapter 26

The Ukko-Munkki, the old dive bar across from the combined elementary and middle school, was a Munkkiniemi icon like the wooden kiosk, the Kalastajatorppa hotel, the former cadet academy and the cobbler on Munkkiniemi Allée. Siiri had walked passed it since the 1950s, but now she had Irma's support, and together they stepped boldly into the pub's infamous cellar. At least the main floor was occupied by a proper restaurant. Siiri and Irma had attended a peculiar memorial service there, during which the deceased's former co-workers tossed back booze with both hands and the pastor played the saw.

They stood clinging to each other at the threshold of the Ukko-Munkki like Thingumy and Bob arriving in Moomin Valley and looked around. Most customers leaned in solitary silence against the tall tables, but a few stood in a row at the bar. Some skimmed through the tabloids spread out before them without so much as a glance at the headlines; one pounded at the fruit machine, whose colourful lights provided the only bit of cheer in the room. Even though it was still morning, the bar was surprisingly full, with the smattering of young men staring reverently into the void as if time had blissfully stopped. For a moment it seemed to Siiri as if the ambience in the public house had been lifted directly from Sunset Grove.

Ritva waved at Siiri and Irma from the brown-and-grey sofa and croaked out a 'Cock-a-doodle-doo', somehow managing to make it sound much more prurient than Irma's crowing. The bar came to life instantly. The philosophical souls sunken in self-reflection raised their heads a centimetre, one rubbed his neck and a few stirred sufficiently to order another pint when two women who looked to be about a hundred shattered the bar's daily routine.

'Hello, everyone,' Siiri said, giving the walls a broad smile.

'It doesn't look like this place has been cleaned since the 1950s,' Irma said. She sat next to Ritva after first swatting at the sofa with her glove as if driving out evil spirits. Siiri hesitated for a moment as to where she should sit, as there was a black smudge on her stool, perhaps chewing gum that had been there for years, collecting lint from the trousers of thousands of customers. She noticed a slightly more tolerable chair at the next table and politely enquired from a man sitting there if the seat might be free.

'Huh?' he answered.

Siiri cheerfully thanked him, dragged the chair over and seated herself across from Irma.

'Stop being so snooty. They just remodelled. Now you can even see out the windows,' Ritva said, laughed hoarsely, and started reminiscing about the old days at the Ukko-Munkki, when you could still smoke inside and employers weren't so uptight if you popped out for the occasional beer in the middle of the day. 'The only time the bar emptied was lunchtime, when everyone headed out to eat. Other than that, the place was constantly packed.'

Ritva called out to the bartender by name, and he generously carried over a cider for Irma and a beer for Siiri, although they should have actually collected their drinks at the bar. Irma's was served in a pretty glass with a stem, but Siiri was forced to settle for an enormous mug she had a hard time lifting, even with both hands. She didn't remember the last time she had drunk beer, presumably some summer evening after the sauna when her husband was still alive.

'Yes, *ölyt*, as my cousins and I used to say. Oh dear, oh dear, my Veikko always drank *ölyt* after the sauna, too. And he drank it at home on weeknights, too, but moderately, three bottles while he watched the news. And now I miss my Veikko again, my darling husband! We had so much fun together. Do you know that lovely song by Sibelius, "Första kyssen"? I listen to it all the time; I have a superb recording by Soile Isokoski, and "Första kyssen" describes our first kiss during the interim peace down to a T – have I told you about how passionately Veikko kissed me, how manfully?'

'Yes,' Ritva said curtly. 'You've also told us how he swore when the bookshelf came crashing down on his neck.'

'I have?' Irma asked, feigning surprise at having ever mentioned the story they heard from her lips at least once a week. 'But who can be bothered—'

'To tell a dull story, yes,' Ritva continued.

'Exactly. I'm just an old fuddy-duddy. I always tell my darlings that—'

'Irma, not now.'

Ritva wanted to get down to business, and it was true that they had decided this conclave take place specifically at the Ukko-Munkki, because the topic was top-secret and could not be discussed among the cameras and microphones of Sunset Grove. Siiri had noticed that Ritva was very skilled with buttons and electricity, and could thus provide crucial information. And everything was more fun whenever Irma was involved.

'You used the word "server". What does that mean? Is it the same as the Holy of Holies, as Irma calls it?'

'A server controls Internet connections. And it really serves, unlike public health centres or post offices, where the business models are based on self-service.'

Ritva knew the Holy of Holies existed. All the computers and robots worked at the pleasure of the Great Server. She mentioned components, and Irma started smacking her lips and thinking about the fruit compote they always spiced generously with cinnamon, before drifting off into longing for her Veikko again and remembering how he had faithfully maintained their compost pile.

'But that was an endless battle against rats. We had to get rid of the compost, because there was no way we could kill them all, and the decomposing delicacies attracted them. This was at our villa, of course; you can't have a compost pile in the city. Although on the other hand, why not? Since there are already plenty of rats, they wouldn't be a hindrance.'

Ritva coughed for a moment, drained her pint and fetched another. Then she went on at length about the world of buttons and gadgets. For the most part, she used incomprehensible terms like 'operating system', 'application software' and 'internal database', which led to Irma flipping over her coaster to play a solitary game of Words in a Word. Siiri got the impression from Ritva that the Great Server miraculously brought all these long terms together and caught them up in some sort of net that created its own little universe, their Sunset Grove.

'Sunset Grove might be buying this service or tailoring it themselves.'

'Tailoring?' Irma interrupted. 'That makes me laugh. Everything is tailored these days, and I doubt Jerry or any of his friends has ever set eyes on a real tailor. And architecture, isn't that also a word applicable in just about any context these days?'

'Architecture refers to the operating environment. And orchestration is used when discussing division of labour,' Ritva said. She had sucked down half of her second pint and sank into a reverie. Suddenly she said: 'I would have so loved to play the violin, but my mother always wore trousers. Our maintenance man had such pretty hair, too, when he let me paint my party frock and I never learned to ride a bicycle. I just went off to school.'

Irma and Siiri exchanged horrified glances. Was Ritva already this inebriated? Or suffering from dementia? Ritva was their sole lifeline to the world of robots, and nothing would come of their war-mongering if she cracked up on their hands in a pub in broad daylight.

'She gets a little confused sometimes,' the man at the neighbouring table said, the one who had lent Siiri the chair. He had collected his sparse, long hair into a rat's tail at the nape of his neck and was wearing nothing but a jeans jacket on the frigid winter day. 'Give her a minute, she'll be all right.'

'I see, thank you,' Siiri said. 'I suppose we'll just . . . wait, then.'

'You could throw darts,' the man suggested, rising unsteadily to his feet.

'Goodness, isn't that dangerous . . . in that condition?' Irma hesitated but then stood, as her game of Words in a Word was winding down with words she wasn't sure were real words, such as *pliate*, *clints* and *fapple*. They left Ritva to her muddled mutterings and followed the scrappy fellow towards the dartboard at the back of the bar. It was the English kind, not like the one Irma's darlings had hung on the door of the woodshed at the villa. She and Siiri could make neither head nor tail of the man's instructions. There were sections and pies and multipliers, but they gathered that the smaller the area they hit, the better. Their denim-clad tutor offered them a demonstration, and every one of his darts missed.

'Your turn,' he said to Irma, who enthusiastically accepted the handful of darts and asked the man to hold her handbag.

'Why, they're all sticky,' Irma said with a laugh, and the man suggested they throw from a shorter distance than him, because they were women. Irma peeled her foot from the equally sticky floor and took a step forward. Then she aimed, closed one eye, stuck out her tongue, and threw all five darts into the target with ferocious speed. The man guffawed loudly, making the rat's tail at his neck waggle.

'Goddamn, lady, nice score!'

People started to collect around them. Beckoned by the commotion, pensive philosophers wandered over to lurk around the fringes of the dartboard. Irma's points were totalled, and a short man with a big belly wrote the result on the chalkboard. Irma laughed her falsetto laugh and jubilated in her success.

'You go now, Siiri,' she said, placing the tacky darts in Siiri's hand. 'It's easy.'

Siiri concentrated. Left foot forward, legs in a sturdy straddle. She waited for her breathing to steady and raised her right hand to her face. She tried to close one eye but accidentally closed both. A violent wrench and a toss. The first dart hit the upper part of the target, to enthusiastic applause, as Siiri had struck a square worth a lot of points. She closed her eyes again, actually squeezed them shut, threw the rest of the darts and received even louder ovations from the daytime drinkers than Irma had. Everyone was delighted that two old women were lobbing darts into the board better than Ukko-Munkki's regulars did after years of practice.

'This is a lot more fun than flailing about with the fitness console,' Siiri exclaimed, and let the big-bellied fellow give her a hug.

226

'I'm buying the winner a round,' the man in the jeans jacket slurred, staggering over to the bartender. Siiri and Irma tried to stop him, as they had no intention of getting inebriated, and their first drinks still stood on the table, nearly untouched. But he was persistent. He had never seen a hundred-year-old throw darts before, and he wanted to make the most of the moment.

'Why don't you offer *ölyt* to our fans. You can't set an athletic record without the support of a good crowd,' Irma said as if she were a modern, media-savvy top athlete.

The men at the bar cheered, everyone got a drink, and after that the crowd moved back to the dartboard to beat Siiri's and Irma's scores. Gruff cursing and good-natured laughter echoed from the dartboard, but Ritva had disappeared from her table.

'She left an unfinished beer here. She'll be back,' Irma said confidently, reclaiming her spot on the sofa. And before long Ritva materialized, her normal self. She had gone to the restroom and been confused when she hadn't found her friends there.

'I thought you went to the toilet. It's pretty filthy here, maybe not what you're used to.'

'Oh dear, Ritva – if you only knew the sorts of thickets and bogs we've had to do our business in when it was cold enough to freeze our behinds,' Siiri said, and laughed cheerfully. 'But where were we? You were talking about the Holy of Holies, weren't you?'

There was no longer any trace of Ritva's confusion. She mused on the role the Awaken Now! Association played in

Sunset Grove's infrastructure and reflected it was possible a cloud service existed somewhere that some select group of the association's members could access.

'You're saying they can't all get to heaven? Do you need a code to get in?' Irma asked.

Ritva jabbered on about server interruptions and fibre optics. Siiri didn't fully understand and wanted to know what electricity had to do with this. According to Ritva, the entire world ran on electricity, which was why the electricity outage had paralysed Sunset Grove, down to the robots that carried out all the commands.

'When there are no commands, the robot doesn't do a thing. That's why we ended up with a body count. It's completely obvious, but I doubt the Finnish justice system cares.'

'This is worse than awful,' Siiri said. 'You'd think it would be easy to discover the culprits, since everything is being recorded somewhere. These breadcrumbs and sensors, they're gathering information incessantly.'

'Sure, but the question is where. There's a router somewhere, maybe in the basement, but the server could be anywhere, even the Ivory Coast.'

'So we can't just follow the cable and pull the plug?' Irma asked, and then sighed in disappointment. She drowned her sorrows in a couple of sips of cider and grimaced, pressing her upper abdomen. 'I must say, this is terribly bitter. It's making my stomach lurch.'

But Ritva was on a roll. She ranted about international security breaches, the twin towers in Manhattan and data gathering in the United States.

'Thousands of computers are gathering information on everyone, not just American citizens, because you don't have to be an American citizen to be a terrorist.'

Siiri couldn't grasp what some monolingual bureaucrat in Tulsa would do with her nightly sleep report. Irma constructed ever-wilder visions of top-secret meetings where the mashed balls printed for her consumption and the path she trod each day were presented to the US Minister of Defence through the mediation of interpreters. A team of lieutenant colonels analysed the series of images of her sticking her bum out at the camera and sticking her tongue out at the smart-wall.

'I certainly feel safe now!' Irma found this so funny that she had to dab the tears from her eyes with her lace handkerchief. Siiri started to laugh, too, and their hilarity didn't cease until Irma cried: 'And now I've wet myself!'

The men at the dartboard turned to look at the old women and burst out guffawing. Pints were raised in a toast and Ritva wondered why the men were calling to Siiri and Irma with such familiarity. They couldn't be bothered to explain how masterfully they had dived into the pool of pub-dwellers while Ritva regressed into her own thoughts. They had to proceed quickly, while Ritva was still clear-headed.

'I'm sure data collection is a serious matter, but it's not our problem,' Siiri said.

'It's not just that,' Ritva continued. 'Finnish law doesn't apply to servers located elsewhere.' She stood lazily and slouched over to her bartender friend to fetch a fresh bucket of beer, by Siiri's count her fourth. Ritva had to be rather intoxicated by now. Siiri had only managed to take a few bitter sips of her own brew. She hadn't remembered beer tasting so foul.

'But this is all guesswork, right?' Siiri finally said. 'We don't know how Sunset Grove has decided to handle this cloud box, do we?'

'There has to be a cable somewhere. We'll follow it!' Irma said, raising her fists like a classic political agitator.

'There must be a backup system, unless those religious fanatics are really stupid,' Ritva noted, draining half of her pint in one greedy gulp. She was already slurring badly.

'But all cables lead to the basement,' Irma said. 'Or Rome.'

'How can you be so sure?' Siiri asked.

'I have this funny intuition.'

'The board of directors is wrong!' Ritva's gaze started to wander. 'So goddamn wrong it's not even funny. No one listened to me again. They didn't care. The teachers didn't even know my name, even though my grandma had the best carrot patch. Rows as straight as arrows and all the kids' teeth were weeded on time, goddammit.'

Irma and Siiri wanted to take Ritva home with them, but they had trouble helping her up, and she was incapable of standing on her own. Irma called over to the dartboard crew for assistance, and the fellow with the rat-tail and his big-bellied friend grabbed Ritva under the arms with a familiarity that suggested this wasn't the first time.

'Would you mind walking Ritva home with us? We can't do it,' Siiri asked.

'Sure, no problem. Never leave a friend behind,' the big-bellied man said.

The bizarre little band proceeded carefully down the grey February ice crusting the pavement. First came the two beer-guzzlers lugging Ritva, who was in such bad shape her feet refused to work and dragged limply behind her in the sand the city's maintenance crews spread to prevent slipping. They were followed by Siiri and Irma trudging arm in arm, each leaning on her cane in the other hand. Irma was hiccupping horribly, and they nearly toppled over every time she hicced. The sun had nearly set beyond the bay. The entourage advanced slowly, but as there was no rush, arrived without incident. The rat-tailed fellow and his big-bellied friend were incredibly sweet and promised to escort Ritva all the way to her flat.

Chapter 27

Loud swearing echoed from outside the door to the guarded caregiving facility known as Sunset Grove. Siiri glanced over to see who was trying to enter, but was unsuccessful in the attempt, because it was dark outside and brightly lit indoors.

'Quite an unusual action point, trying to get in here,' she said to herself and smiled, until she reached the door and saw that the big bald fellow cursing foully outside the door looked familiar. 'Is it possible? Oh, for heaven's sake . . .'

She opened the door a little anxiously with the fob she kept on her watchband like the bells berry-pickers used to ward off bears. It actually would be rather practical if each fob came with a little bell that indicated where its wearer was roaming at any given moment. She had to fight with her fob for a moment before the automatic door smoothly opened in the incomer's face.

'Goddammit!'

'For goodness' sake! It really is you! Oh, Mika, you don't know how much I've missed you.'

Mika Korhonen, motorcycle enthusiast, occasional taxi

driver and Siiri's personal guardian angel, stepped in from the blizzard, bedraggled and irate. He looked grimmer and weathered, but his sky-blue eyes were still as mild as Siiri remembered. For a moment it seemed as if Mika had no idea who Siiri was, but when she held out her hand, the familiar smile spread across his face. The handshake was as manly as it had been so many years ago, and it seemed to Siiri as if her friend might have bulked up a bit. His head was still shaved, but the ever-present leather jacket with its skulls and yellow wings had been replaced by a black parka. Siiri would have loved nothing more than to throw her arms around Mika's neck, but something in his demeanour repelled any sort of nostalgia.

'It's been a long time, Mika. I was starting to think I would never see you again. Where have you been?'

'In prison,' Mika said gruffly and without further explanation. Siiri was stunned. She hadn't had the slightest clue about what Mika had been up to, and she started to fear the worst. What on earth had happened?

'Oh, a bunch of little stuff,' Mika said vaguely.

'I'm sorry to hear that. But now you're a free man and you finally came to see us, is that it?'

'What? No.'

'I know, I didn't seriously think you were here to see me. You're carrying that enormous box, too, and it looks very important. No one comes here unless ordered to by the authorities.'

Siiri tried to laugh a little, so Mika would understand the moment wasn't so serious. She felt a lovely warmth in her stomach, gazing at long last at her angelic Mika Korhonen, whom fate had thrown into the role of their saviour when the beautiful boy in the kitchen died under ambiguous circumstances. How many years had it been? It felt like an eternity. Chance was probably pulling the levers this time, too.

But Mika was remarkably glum and didn't appear the least bit delighted by their reunion.

'I'm here to kill,' he said, and paused. 'Rats. Community service.'

'Bless you! You're the one they settled on to solve our rat problem? Or did you request to be sent here yourself, seeing as how you already know the place? Although I suppose Sunset Grove has been renovated beyond recognition since your last visit. Would you like me to show you around?'

'No thanks.'

Mika shoved a paw into his jacket pocket and pulled out a crumpled piece of paper, some sort of floor plan of Sunset Grove. He slammed his heavy box down on the floor so violently that Margit, who had drifted off in her massage chair, started, but then her resonant snoring continued.

'Now you listen here, Mika Korhonen,' Siiri said, raising her voice, heart pounding. She felt the colour rise to her cheeks and her cane-holding hand tremble, but she meant to say what was on her mind. 'You're behaving as if we'd never laid eyes on each other, and you're my legal guardian, and Anna-Liisa's, too, if my memory serves me. You sat in our flats and had us sign papers after you made head nurse Virpi . . . Virpi . . .'

Awkward in the extreme, that suddenly the surname of Sunset Grove's former monstrous head nurse escaped her. The idiotic pause dulled the keenest edge of her anger and turned her into an addled old lady. She rapped the floor with her cane as if restarting her degenerated receptors to find the right keyword.

'Hiukkanen,' Mika suggested indifferently.

'Oh, thank you.' Siiri laughed off her disconcertion and continued her jeremiad. 'My brains probably wanted to forget the whole woman. But when you convinced Virpi Hiukkanen to pay back the money she swindled from us, we made you our guardian, Anna-Liisa and I. You remember that, don't you? Anna-Liisa could use your help now, because this place is teeming with grasping religious fanatics who are trying to transfer Anna-Liisa's property over to a revivalist association. We have to do something. Irma intends to start a war, and it doesn't make the least bit of sense, but I can't think of any wiser course of action. And then you appear at the door to our prison with your strongbox as if someone had sent you to save us. We need you, Mika, and I sincerely hope you'll stop scowling and be a good boy and come to my place for a cup of coffee.'

Mika grunted and scratched his bald pate. When he raised his arm and turned to look at the box on the floor, his shirt hiked up, revealing a massive tattoo on his belly, some sort of snake surrounded by impressive flames.

'Siiri,' Mika finally said, looking her in the eye so beautifully that she forgot the last of her vinegar and smiled tenderly. 'Things aren't going so great for me. Community service and an ankle bracelet, see? It reports everything. I'm here to kill rats, and that's it. So stop blubbering, OK?'

'Mika, I'm not blubbering. I want to talk with you; I've missed you and was actually quite concerned with you disappearing like that.'

'No more about that, all right? Now it's rats. Where have they been seen?'

Siiri told Mika about the rats, how the same perky one visited her apartment every morning in anticipation of being fed. She really wasn't very enthusiastic about Mika killing her sole living daily contact. She started off towards her apartment, and Mika followed reluctantly, dragging his strongbox. It contained his extermination equipment, various poisons and traps. Mika couldn't believe Siiri was feeding a rat, even though an urgent report had been made to the municipal Department of the Environment because the rats had been causing such a disturbance at Sunset Grove.

'You're saying you don't even want the rats to leave.'

'A lot of people have complained, including Irma. But I don't have anything against the rats myself.'

'This place is nuts.'

Siiri explained to Mika that he didn't need to fret about his anklet. Everyone was being watched these days, it was the latest, and it was impossible to take two steps without it being recorded in the United States. She showed Mika her fob and tried to remember all the information hidden in it, but couldn't get the list to sound as impressive as Sirkka the Saver of Souls had on that one occasion at the ATM.

'At least I can use it to withdraw money, drive a car and travel abroad.'

'Yup,' Mika said, stepping into Siiri's apartment in his big, grimy boots. He went straight into the kitchen and opened the door to the cabinet beneath the sink. He didn't find a rat there, or even any rat droppings, just a yellow saucer holding the morsel Siiri had set out that morning.

'It looks like he doesn't care for blue cheese,' Siiri said, a little disappointed.

Mika unpleasantly pushed Siiri out of the way and pumped a foul-smelling, bluish mist under the sink with a device that resembled a fire extinguisher. The fog quickly spread everywhere.

'Oh dear! What are you doing? You'll poison us both, and there's not a rat in sight.'

'Mild stuff. Keeps rodents and bugs away.'

Mika rose to his full handsome height and clomped back into the living room looking for the next corner to aim his poison at. Siiri followed him in concern, and felt her circulation stirring again.

'Mika, I won't have this. Please sit down.' Her commands were so firm that the big boy collapsed obediently in her armchair. She took a seat too, and started telling him about life at Sunset Grove these days. Mika didn't appear to be listening, but he sat there silently and stared at the wall, which hadn't forgotten its manners and greeted the guest with a personal message: 'The Devil was a murderer from the beginning, and abode not in the truth, because there is no truth in him. When he speaketh a lie, he speaketh of his own: for he is a liar, and the father of it. John 8:44.'

Siiri started from the skeletal robots and smartwalls, went through the food-like substances, AGVs, fitness consoles and seal pups, then moved on to listing the deaths caused by healthcare technology before describing the army of volunteer staff, especially Pertti and Sirkka the Saver of Souls, Tauno's attempted healing and Margit's convulsions, and ended with Anna-Liisa's will, which she was holding in her hand, because she hadn't decided what to do with it yet. Anna-Liisa had signed it, but Siiri knew her friend didn't want to turn over all her property to the religious graspers, especially before she died.

'And since you're Anna-Liisa's guardian, I thought you should have a look at this document and confirm its invalidity.'

She handed the will to Mika, who glanced at it indifferently. According to Mika, a guardian's rights only came into force when the individual in question was incapable of making her own decisions.

'How's Anna-Liisa doing?'

'She's . . . fading . . .' Siiri's voice started to tremble frustratingly as she told Mika she was afraid the estate-disbursement process had been too much for Anna-Liisa after everything she'd been through in recent years: Onni's death and his dirty business affairs and squabbling heirs. Anna-Liisa languished in bed, reading gloomy German literature and talking about death in a completely different way than before. Irma didn't even dare say *döden, döden, döden* any more.

'Got it. So she's conscious.'

'Anna-Liisa? Of course. Right in the head, as Irma would say.'

'Then you guys can handle it. You don't need a guardian.'

Mika stood and prepared to leave, packed up his poison mister and locked his toolbox. Siiri was panicking and she didn't know what to say to convince Mika to help them one last time. He had to; they didn't have anyone else. But he seemed to harbour resentment over his earlier escapades with Anna-Liisa and Siiri. Perhaps they had caused him trouble.

'Mika, wait!'

The big lunk stopped at the door and looked Siiri beautifully in the eye. Siiri thought she caught a small smile on the hardened face. Maybe they were still friends after all?

'Are you upset with me? Are we the reason you went to prison?'

'No. Old stuff. Almost finished doing my time. See you.'

Mika went on his way. The door banged behind him, and Siiri was left alone in the hallway amid the echo and a faintly sweet, strange aroma: the smell of rat poison. Didn't Mika really want to help them? Or had he unintentionally given Siiri an idea for solving their conundrum?

Chapter 28

'Dead, every last one,' the burly man in red overalls and neon vest said into his phone outside Sunset Grove. Siiri was just coming from buying her daily serving of liver casserole from the upper Low Price Market and couldn't believe her ears. She looked around in a panic. There was no ambulance, only a blue van. Perhaps the ambulance had already left; after all, they weren't meant for transporting the dead, only the living. But the blue van didn't look like a hearse; it looked more like an unmarked police vehicle.

'No, no signs of life.'

Siiri felt her heart stop, then drum at a terrific tempo, *prestissimo agitato* at the least. Why wasn't there a soul in sight at Sunset Grove, aside from this fellow in coveralls? A brigade of day-care children was marching down Perustie, wearing the same sort of neon vests as the burly bellower, who was perhaps a fireman. The children were en route from the old bank to play in the park. The display-window day-care was a daily source of joy for Siiri; she always paused for a moment to watch the children play, eat or crawl onto their mattresses for their naps. It must have been two o'clock, since the four-year-olds were embarking on their outdoor adventure. Siiri leaned against Sunset Grove's cold walls, drained, and listened to the rushing in her ears intensify to a dreadful thundering. The electricity wasn't out, as the lobby smartwall was glowing so brightly she could see it all the way outside.

'We haven't all died, have we?' Siiri said to the man and realized she was panting distressingly. 'After all, I'm alive . . . at least I think so.'

'What's that?' The man looked at Siiri and put his phone in his pocket. 'Do you have a key? I need to get inside.'

How did he plan on carrying out the bodies on his own? And without a stretcher? Siiri felt dizzy and was afraid she was getting confused. Where was Irmu? Hadn't her daughter-in-law come by to pick her up for book club somewhere in the boondocks? That meant Irma might still be alive. What about Anna-Liisa, who spent her days lounging in bed with Thomas Mann?

'Was it the gas? A leak of some sort? Or is it another computer malfunction?' she asked.

The man looked at her, perplexed, and jangled the jumble of key-fobs in his large fist. It seemed to Siiri as if he were starting to get upset. She desperately rummaged around in her bag for her own fob, then remembered she kept it on her watchband and drew it out from the sleeve of her overcoat. But her hands were trembling so badly the device wouldn't obey. The door remained shut.

'Goddammit,' the man said, pulling out his phone, as if threatening to call in more hearses unless something sensible happened soon. 'Is that dead, too? These fobs are a real pain in the ass.'

'You're the one who said it, but mine usually works impeccably. Let me try again.' Siiri flashed her fob at the reader rather viciously, and wouldn't you know, the door began to open in their faces. 'Hocus pocus! See, it works!'

'So that fob wasn't dead. But these are,' the man said, shoving the stash into his vest pocket.

'You were talking about the fobs when you were saying they were all dead, is that it? And here I was thinking you meant . . .'

The man burst out laughing. 'The residents? I love it! Hilarious!'

Siiri also laughed gently in relief, because even though they all hoped for a speedy release from their computerized existence, and to be carried by a merciful bout of pneumonia to technology-free zones, the thought of the simultaneous death of all residents of Sunset Grove was unpleasant. Now she wondered how she had ever imagined something so unnatural. A life of monitored care had estranged her from all that was natural; that must be it. When old people died from the embrace of automated seal pups, the clutches of robotic companions and virtual exercise, wasn't it just as likely that a sudden lethal epidemic could sweep through all of Sunset Grove? She found it funnier and funnier, and also a little embarrassing, and the maintenance man at her side concentrated on studying a floor plan of the building from his tablet.

After wiping away her tears with a handkerchief, Siiri

took the man's arm and asked him what he was doing at their retirement home, if it wasn't to cart off bodies.

'Outsiders aren't allowed in here. You must have some extremely valid reason for your visit, I presume. I'm assuming you're not a fob resuscitator?'

The man laughed again. 'No. I'm here to switch the cables. The server is being updated.'

'The server? The . . . sacred server, is that it? Is there something wrong with it? There wasn't a single Bible passage this morning, and that's usually a sign of a technical malfunction.'

'A normal update, but we're going to switch over to the backup system for the duration.'

'How interesting!' Siiri said, more eagerly than was necessary.

'I'm not so sure about that. Is that the C wing?'

The man started walking across the communal area towards the C-wing corridor. Siiri was forced to take a few running steps to keep up with him, and her heart shuddered slightly again.

'Excuse me! Wait a moment! What are you going to do to the server?'

'Nothing; I just take care of these cables. Old one out and a new one in; no big deal,' the man shouted over his shoulder as he vanished through the heavy door leading to the basement. Siiri listened to his heavy boots recede down the stairs. She felt a tingling curiosity as she thought about all the thrilling things one might find in the basement. It looked as if Irma was right after all: the Holy of Holies was in the catacombs.

'What are we standing around here for? Are we lost?'

Siiri recognized the voice and guessed the colour of the shoes before she turned around. Yet again, Sirkka the Saver of Souls had materialized out of thin air and was looking at Siiri as if she had escaped from a precision-programmed bed in the dementia unit, where the carcasses had received so much caregiving they couldn't move.

'CAN YOU TELL ME WHAT DAY IT IS? DO YOU REMEMBER YOUR NAME?'

'Thanks for asking. Today is Friday, 19 February, and those celebrating their name days today include Eija, or according to the Swedish calendar Fritjof and the Orthodox calendar Arhi and Arhippa, even though I've never heard of anyone named that. My name is Siiri Kettunen, and your name is Sirkka Nieminen; we've met on more than one occasion. You have a peculiar tendency to show up in surprising places. Are you starting up a prayer circle or are you planning on healing one of us demon-possessed old people?'

The carefully rehearsed empathy drained from Sirkka's face, to be replaced by a magnificent blankness. Her mouth twitched, and her uncertain, quite fearful eyes didn't know where to focus. Siiri gave the missionary a moment to think of a fitting Bible phrase, but there was no response.

'Is it money you want? Alms and indulgences?' Siiri asked, attempting a friendly smile. She took a few resolute steps to remove herself from the situation, as the conversation didn't appear to be going anywhere, but Sirkka blocked her way.

For a moment they stood in unpleasantly close proximity to each other. Siiri caught a faint but pungent whiff of sweat and looked at Sirkka's turquoise artificial fabric tunic. Rayon or what have you, no doubt it didn't breathe.

'Who went down to the basement? I heard the door slam. Did they tell you to stand here and act as lookout?' Sirkka asked.

Siiri found it curious that the basement could agitate the volunteer staff member so badly that she lost all semblance of courtesy. Suddenly the devil got in to Siiri, no doubt Lucifer himself, and she said casually:

'Irma Lännenleimu went down there. You're right, I'm acting as lookout to make sure no one noticed, but you noticed anyway.' Sirkka's fearful eyes went as wide as her large, plastic-framed spectacles and she gaped at Siiri before yanking the basement door open and disappearing behind the steel door herself. The green high heels produced a distinctly different sound in the stairwell from the maintenance man's clodhoppers. Before long a shrill squeal echoed, and then all was silent. Siiri waited in suspense. For the first time in her life she regretted not having a mobile phone to call Irma and her other friends to let them know there was some fun in store. When she heard nothing from the basement for a moment, she rushed to the end of the corridor and peered into the communal area, but there was no one there. Pity. She was so excited that her stomach felt like an anthill, just like decades ago, when something unusually fun was in the works. It had been so long she'd forgotten how refreshing a little practical joke could be.

At long last the basement door opened. The maintenance man stepped out, followed by a tear-faced Sirkka Nieminen. The gruff, growling fellow was trying to soothe the increasingly hysterical woman, who was sobbing incomprehensibly. They approached Siiri, and it was only then that her delighted suspense turned to horror. She had lied to Sirkka like a naughty schoolboy. Maybe it hadn't been so funny after all, fooling the poor woman into going down into a dark basement that was probably teeming with rats.

'You, wait a minute, you there!' Sirkka shouted as she approached Siiri, who had frozen on the spot and clenched her handbag in bewilderment as if it were a security blanket. 'What are you up to? Why did you egg me on like that? What are you trying to do here?'

'Actually, no one should be going down into the basement except for maintenance company employees,' the man in coveralls said.

'I thought there were old people down there who were snooping . . . prying . . . endangering . . . that client, I mean that resident, told me that she was keeping a lookout . . . that there was some spying operation . . . the basement's where . . . what exactly were you doing down there?'

'Maintenance work,' the man said, and went on his way. As he passed Siiri he winked and gave her the thumbs up. It was a common gesture these days, depicting some sort of accepting encouragement, was how Siiri interpreted it. The man paused at the bin, reached into his vest pocket and discarded the dead fobs.

Sirkka didn't follow him; she remained quaking and confused with Siiri.

'I've had enough of old people. I can't do this any more. I've asked Pertti so many times to assign me to the expenses department, but he won't let me. The pay here is so bad, too.'

'We thought you were volunteers. Are you really working here? What's your job?' Siiri asked in surprise.

'Job. My job is to talk about the Holy Spirit, that's my calling, that's all I have. But I sinned and I must pay the price. I have to start from the bottom, from the old people. It's called volunteering; it sounds better that way, like we're practising charitable works. I don't have any training in working with old people, that's why I shouldn't even be doing this. You can't imagine how hard this is for me.'

'No, there's no way I can imagine that. But everyone is always talking about how inhumanely hard it is for healthy people to work with the elderly. That's why there aren't any staff here, just machines.'

Sirkka burst into tears. She collapsed against the wall and slid slowly to the ground, letting out a broken, whimpering wail. Siiri looked around but didn't see a chair. She couldn't sink to the floor to sit like the Saver of Souls; if she did, at least two Ahabas would be required to hoist her up. She bent down next to the quivering Sirkka and stroked her quaking artificial-fabric shoulder.

'Now, now, that's enough of that. You're a sensitive woman. What's making your life so difficult? Is it that religion of yours?'

'No . . . maybe I'm not strong enough in my faith . . . salvation and mercy, but I can't lose weight, my fat percentage is too high and . . . weakness, a sign of weakness, Pertti said . . . I'm, I have to work for the movement, as a volunteer, even though my calling . . . all that debt and my former life, that burden, but I never collect enough donations . . . My calling, the road to salvation. That's it. But I'm, I feel so . . . insufficient, the demands are enormous, the training doesn't strengthen me . . . I don't find . . . group sex liberating, even though . . . the exercises, sometimes they feel . . . external, my corporal self and inner soul performing acts like that . . . I don't know. My imperfection, I have to get stronger, but my path . . . strewn with thorns and . . . And yet in weak moments I feel as if I can't do this, that . . . the journey to eternal salvation is . . . too hard. Why am I talking to you about this? Some old person I don't even know. My Lord Jesus Christ, forgive me my weakness! You suddenly felt so . . . but I shouldn't be talking this way to a client. Will you promise me you won't tell anyone? God will punish me; you don't have to.'

Sirkka's black hair, usually so glossy, was a fright, and her eye make-up was streaming down her cheeks. Her voice was thick with tears and the hands that were gripping Siiri were shaking more violently than those of a single Sunset Grove resident. Siiri looked the woman in the eye, wiped the black smudges from her cheeks and helped her to her feet. She rummaged around in her bag until she found what she was looking for and handed the poor woman a lifeline: a comb.

'You shouldn't agree to anything that doesn't feel good.

Especially sex. You're a modern woman, how can you subject yourself to that?'

Sirkka's breathing gradually started to level off. She combed her hair compulsively and started cleaning her spectacles on the hem of her tunic. Now she spoke very quickly, without looking at Siiri and sounding a bit like a smartwall that was breaking up. 'Woman is the vessel of man. A jug of clay. Every open vessel whose mouth has not been sealed is unclean. Woman is man's property, and man will do with it as he sees fit. The desires of the flesh are not those of the Spirit, those of the Spirit not those of the flesh. Woman is the flesh of the man. Woman is a snare, her heart is a trap, her embrace shackles. I'm an unhappy woman and I bore my soul to God. Let your women be pleasing to man, let your women keep silence in the churches.'

'That doesn't make the least bit of sense. You live in Finland where men and women are equal, and you can make your own decisions,' Siiri insisted.

Their roles had undergone a peculiar reversal: Siiri was caring for the volunteer staff member and converting her to her ideology. This was atypical for Siiri; she thought it was important to be respectful and refrain from forcing her own ideas on those who subscribed to different worldviews. But this woman was in great distress, perhaps so great she didn't realize it herself. The more Sirkka perked up in Siiri's care, the more vigorously she clung again to doctrines handed down from above.

'You don't understand. I don't want to make my own decisions; that's why it's safe for me to serve the movement.

I obey. I believe, and if I work hard and test myself, my faith will grow stronger and I'll be rewarded. That's all I need.'

She applied a coat of lipstick so dark it was more brown than red and tugged the neckline of her tunic into place. Then she sighed deeply, shot a look of busy agitation Siiri's way and left, green high heels clacking against the plastic flooring. But before she stepped from the corridor into the common room, she turned round and said in an icy tone:

'Why did you tell me Irma Lännenleimu was in the basement? And that you were keeping a lookout to make sure no one noticed?'

Siiri brushed away the question as casually as Irma, even though she had no gold bracelets jangling at her wrists. 'Is that what I said? Oh dear, silly me. Don't take anything I say seriously; after all, I'm ninety-seven years old and a bit dotty.'

Chapter 29

'You have to take the will back to Anna-Liisa,' Irma chided Siiri, after licking the lingonberry jam from her plate.

Siiri had been holding on to the will she'd found on Anna-Liisa's nightstand for weeks without figuring out what to do with it, what with Mika refusing to take it. The steeper Anna-Liisa's decline grew in the company of German literature and Charlie Chaplin, the worse the idea of bringing up the will seemed. But of course Irma was right. Siiri would have to grab the bull by the horns and deliver the document back to her friend. Siiri could tell her firmly but kindly that she'd be wise to retract her wish to turn over her property to the Awaken Now! Association. Siiri and Irma knew it wasn't what Anna-Liisa really wanted, but that she simply didn't have the energy to resist the pressure on her own, and now they had to present a solid, united front on behalf of their friend, as they always had in the past. Sirkka the Saver of Souls' breakdown and the scandalous revelations she had leaked simply reinforced what Siiri and Irma had suspected from the start: the motivations of the religious volunteers weren't altruistic, but suspect. The further away they stayed, the better.

'Although I'd love to go down to the basement and nose about a bit,' Irma said before they set off for Anna-Liisa's to return the will.

It was a normal morning at Sunset Grove: not a soul in sight. At the elevators, a lone cleaning creature spun in a circle and beat its head against the wall. It reminded them of the wild animals at the zoo that were confined to enclosures too small for them. Siiri and Irma meandered down the empty corridors and remarked on the machines' narration as they passed.

'Door. Opening.'

'Why thank you; how very sweet of you.'

'The. Elevator. Is. Empty.'

'Ooh, how fascinating! Thank you for the information.'

'He delivereth the poor in his affliction, and openeth their ears in oppression. Job 36:15.'

'Hallelujah and Amen! Maybe Margit can finally get rid of her hearing aid.'

Siiri missed the rats; it had been days since she'd seen a single one. Had Mika been so effective in chasing them from Sunset Grove? A couple of days after his visit, Siiri's rat had come by to nibble at its piece of cheese, but since then its daily ration had remained untouched, which made Siiri sad.

'I'd rather talk with a refrigerator than feed filthy vermin,' Irma said.

An abandoned or overworked caregiving robot, one of Ahaba's relations, was lying in the middle of Anna-Liisa's corridor. It had become clear of late that toiling with old people was even too onerous for many of the machines.

Overstressed, inattentive, immobile and completely non-functional equipment was turning up with increasing frequency in random corners of Sunset Grove. Ahaba's cousin didn't show the least reaction, even though Siiri patted it.

'Keep your head up, you'll be fine. No one's expecting miracles here. A bit of company and the occasional touch, but I don't suppose you've been programmed for that.'

'Yes, it's not that contraption's fault. The poor wretch isn't to blame for its circumstances, just like us.'

They left the stunted mechanized runt to its dozing and knocked on Anna-Liisa's door. There was no answer, despite frequent attempts. The knocks echoed with a dreadful hollowness in the silent building, as if someone were endlessly repeating the first two counts of Beethoven's Fifth Symphony, but Siiri and Irma didn't give up. There were no doorbells on the doors any more, so old-fashioned knocking was the only way to try to get in.

'Cock-a-doodle-doo! It's us, Anna-Liisa! Good morning!' Irma screeched in her high singing-lesson voice, rousing the companion robot. 'The sun's already shining!'

Then Irma retold the story of how she'd been at the villa and one of her darlings had come to wake her up at five in the morning to go fishing, crying in his bright boy soprano in the middle of the night that the sun's already shining. Like many of Irma's stories, Siiri had heard it thousands of times, and she smiled in satisfaction, as Irma was always so enthusiastic and happy as she recalled times past.

But Anna-Liisa didn't open the door for them. Then Siiri remembered that everything was connected to everything else and her fob would also open Anna-Liisa's door. She pulled her watchband out of her sleeve and flashed the fob at the blob on the wall. Open Sesame, the door started opening in their faces. 'Eureka, it worked!'

The air inside was stale, and the apartment was very dim. Anna-Liisa had drawn the curtains across the window and clearly hadn't remembered to air the place for a few days. A curious agitation came over Siiri in the hallway, as if something were awry.

'Yoo-hoo, Anna-Liisa! Are you still asleep? It's broad daylight!'

Irma marched in to pull back the curtains. The March sun shone in through the grit-spattered windows, revealing the dust motes that had descended over Anna-Liisa's scant furnishings. Siiri went into the bedroom and found Anna-Liisa in her marriage bed with her reading glasses on. Thomas Mann's *The Magic Mountain* lay open on the bedspread, and Anna-Liisa's hand was resting on a page of the book. She had fallen asleep while reading and hadn't even woken to their cries. The random pile of yellow Post-Its was still on the nightstand, along with a small black notebook and four pencil stubs that had been sharpened down to the quick.

Siiri reached down to remove Anna-Liisa's reading glasses, but before her fingers touched them she felt Irma's hand on her shoulder and started. She hadn't heard her friend enter the room.

'Siiri, she's dead.'

Irma whispered so softly her voice was barely audible. Siiri looked at Anna-Liisa, who didn't look dead. She had genuinely believed her friend was asleep and had been trying not to wake her. Now she took a closer look at Anna-Liisa lying in the gloom, and her heart started racing arrhythmically. She carefully took hold of Anna-Liisa's hand. It was cold and stiff. Her eyes were closed, and she had a restful look on her face, although her mouth hung open slightly. She looked incredibly beautiful, miraculously smooth-faced and younger than normal. Anna-Liisa Petäjä had truly died.

Siiri could hear Anna-Liisa's voice in her ears, resonant and powerful, and could picture her smile, slightly amused but accepting when Siiri and Irma had acted up in the middle of one of Anna-Liisa's book clubs or lectures. And her laugh! It tinkled in Siiri's ears as it had back when the new red spring hat, a token of Onni's love, had appeared on Anna-Liisa's head. So this was how Anna-Liisa had died and left them? Anna-Liisa, who had brought so much sense, order and grammar to their lives?

'She bowed out in style,' Siiri said, stroking Anna-Liisa's cold forehead. She bent down to give her friend a kiss, her final farewell, even though Anna-Liisa was who knows where by now. Then she gently removed the reading glasses from Anna-Liisa's nose and stroked the coarse, silver-white hair. She had read somewhere that hair kept growing after death, and thought it might still somehow contain a hint of the living Anna-Liisa.

'Oh heavenly days! What a calamity! How did this happen?'

Suddenly Irma was vociferously upset, bustled back and forth at the foot of the bed and clapped her hands together without looking at Anna-Liisa. Siiri left the bedside and went over to Irma, wrapped her arms around her friend and soothed her, rocking her like a little child. It put her at ease, too, feeling another's warmth.

'Anna-Liisa was lucky. She died in her sleep. Look how her eyes are so beautifully closed. She was reading *The Magic Mountain*, shut her eyes, and died. Could there be a finer end to a life?'

Irma sighed and looked doubtfully at Anna-Liisa. She had to admit that it was a lovely sight. Anna-Liisa's grey hair was clean and combed, and her white nightshirt looked like it had just been pressed. Everything was like a scene from an American movie; even the light from the living room fell magically on Anna-Liisa's face. The serenity there was con-clusive, and for that reason merciful. Downright enviable, at least in the minds of her still-living contemporaries. The crowning touch was the book Anna-Liisa had studied so diligently in her final weeks, as she prepared to welcome death.

'It is wonderful that she was able to die with her passion at her side,' Irma said, bending down to pick up *The Magic Mountain*. She glanced at the page open there. It was from the end of the long chapter 'Snow', when Hans Castorp gets lost in a blizzard and wanders at the fringes of his conscious-ness. When he recovers, he feels unusually clear-sighted and ponders death, without which there would be no life.

'Remarkable, Anna-Liisa knowing to die over such reflec-tions,' Irma said in astonishment.

Anna-Liisa knew the novel from front to back and might

well have opened it at the desired page when she sensed death approach. Was it possible to intuit one's death? Siiri believed it was. So many stories supported the notion. People expressing important things before expiring, completing tasks and then being prepared to close their eyes. Those long-term cancer patients who refused to die, confounding their physicians' prognoses until they were able to see their loved ones and only then loosening their grip on life. That couldn't be chance.

'You must be kidding. Look!' Irma suddenly cried. Siiri had been so lost in thought that she hadn't noticed Irma had risen. Now she was standing at the smartwall and pointing at it.

'Fatal error! No measurable sleep results! Verify that 1) the sensor is in place 2) the device is on 3) the patient is alive.'

'I wonder how long that announcement has been there?' Irma huffed. 'If we hadn't happened to come in here, Anna-Liisa would have rotted away before the automatic alarm system alerted some volunteer lazybones to check the sensors and verify the death. This voycurism-based eldercare is even more preposterous than enhanced in-home care! The only thing more absurd would be a cross-eyed Cyclops.'

'Should we call a doctor? A doctor always has to confirm the death; otherwise there will be problems.'

Irma started reminiscing about her various cousins' deaths, how one had been found in a pool of her own vomit, and how even though a blockhead would have realized that her cousin Heddi was no more and guessed the cause had been a heart attack, Heddi had been frozen for weeks until someone had time to perform an autopsy. To everyone's great surprise, the cause of death was determined to be a heart attack.

'Madness, in other words. And my cousin Erik starved to death, on purpose of course, after having been left a widower for a third time at the age of ninety-eight and ending up in a municipal retirement home, but investigating his death also demanded enormous resources and costly hours of professional input from a variety of fields. In the end, his grandchildren received a piece of paper in the mail noting cachexia as the cause of death and then presenting bizarre suspicions regarding supposed neglect, even though cousin Erik was never in anyone's care. There can be no neglect, can there, if there's no one to do the neglecting? Oh well, I suppose some random social worker came by once a week with her computer to report on her own doings. That is a delicious word, though, cachexia. But let's not rush now; let's take our time and enjoy Anna-Liisa's company while we can before the authorities barge in to bag her up.'

They perched a little uncomfortably on Anna-Liisa's vast bed and gazed reverently at their friend. For a long time nothing happened. They simply sat there, lost in thought, and it was lovely. Siiri felt a warm touch on her shoulder, even though there was no one there. It seemed as if Anna-Liisa's scent was surrounding her with an unusual intensity; it was a smell she'd never paid any attention to but now recognized. As if Anna-Liisa were present. Odd how death could involve so many inexplicable phenomena, even at the age of ninety-seven. Siiri remembered the composer Jean Sibelius's death, the flight of cranes that had flown over his home, one of which had broken off to circle the house before rejoining the flock, and the simultaneous radio concert being broadcast from the university's great hall, where a white butterfly had fluttered indoors in late September to bear news of the death to the audience. There was something awe-inspiring about such events. Maybe it was a good thing humans couldn't explain everything.

Eventually Irma got up and started studying the notes on the nightstand. They contained muddled phrases, random sentiments from various sources and Anna-Liisa's thoughts.

'Sobriety and gravity are the pillar of existence (Sepeteus, *The Heath Cobblers*). Youth hopes for everything, old age for nothing (Sakari Topelius). That's all any of us are: amateurs. We don't live long enough to be anything else (*Limelight*). To this class old age especially belongs, which all men wish to attain and yet reproach when attained (Cicero). Wagtails in February, not a good sign. The reporter from YLE Radio 1 said: "if she was".'

Irma arranged the notes into a tidy stack and shook her head. They portended death and the end of the world. And when the announcer from public radio's cultural programming abused the subjunctive form and wagtails arrived in southern Finland three months early, the final shreds of Anna-Liisa's will to live had blown away.

Irma found one more note that consisted of nothing but numbers.

'What's this? She wrote 484548 on a slip of paper.'

Anna-Liisa's hand had been extremely weak, and they had a hard time making out the numbers. They racked their brains trying to decipher the reference.

'What if it's two numbers?' Irma said.

'And they're hymns?' Siiri suggested.

'Shuffle and cut!' Irma exclaimed. '"Spirit of Truth" and "Walk with Me, Lord". Hymns 484 and 548.'

'I'm glad one of us is still playing with a full pack. Do you suppose Anna-Liisa was planning her funeral?'

'Good heavens! We'll have to find the strength to arrange that, too. Although it might actually be quite nice, and we can plan our own funerals while we're at it. Let's make a template, a funeral template: enter the church here, the Bach chorale there and a tasty sandwich cake there. It will be fun and therapeutic! That's what they say these days, therapeutic. People turn to their doctors for happy pills to be able to stand their grief, and I'm sure they're offered funeral therapy too, as needed. That way they can avoid facing their sorrow. Isn't that odd? This bit of paper is a good start for a funeral; I like these hymns. I could use them myself. Hilja Haahti's and Sakari Topelius's gorgeous lyrics. Did you know I'm related to Hilja Haahti? She was my great-aunt. Good choice, Anna-Liisa,' Irma said, patting her friend's colourless cheek.

They started pondering when Anna-Liisa must have died. Irma had collected her glasses from Anna-Liisa's apartment around six o'clock the previous evening, and at the time Anna-Liisa had been talkative and in good spirits, despite being in bed. Irma couldn't remember what they had talked about.

'I'm sure it wasn't hymns, though,' she mused.

All signs indicated that Anna-Liisa must have drifted off into her ultimate slumber in the middle of the night. She was cold, her limbs were stiff and they couldn't get her chin to stay in place when they tried to close her mouth.

'Rigor mortis starts a couple of hours after death and lasts for a few days,' Siiri said, accurately.

'And she used to like to read when she couldn't sleep. She might have woken up after midnight to read. Was that reading lamp on or did you turn it off?'

'I didn't touch it. Maybe Anna-Liisa turned it off herself. She was always so . . . sensible. I could imagine her turning it off so she could die without wasting electricity.'

They decided to announce Anna-Liisa's time of death as 5:48, because it was the number of the deceased's favourite hymn. It sounded as precise as the times of death noted on the official documents, although death never took place in one minute.

Then they carried out a little ritual in Anna-Liisa's honour. Siiri started reading *The Magic Mountain* out loud more or less from where Irma had left off.

'Death is a great power . . . Reason stands foolish before him, for reason is only virtue, but death is freedom and kicking over the traces, chaos and lust. Lust, my dream says, not love. Death and love – there is no rhyming them . . . Love stands opposed to death – it alone, and not reason, is stronger than death. Only love, not reason, yields kind thoughts.'

Siiri read in a steady voice, rather softly, as if trying not to disturb her friend who had turned her face towards death. Each word was charged with extraordinary significance, as those lines pertained to the imminent death the lover of literature had welcomed with the beloved novel she had read so many times.

Siiri closed the book. She and Irma sang the hymns Anna-Liisa had noted, all the verses from memory, and in the end belted out the jolly Schlager 'Siribiribim', because when it came down to it this was a day of joy and jubilation. Anna-Liisa had happily forsaken all her earthly cares in one massive sigh. Everyone hoped to die just as she had at that midnight moment: in one's own bed, without pain, of old age.

Chapter 30

'What do you think, do you suppose Anna-Liisa has some red wine in her cupboard?'

Irma was already flinging the cabinet doors open. To their happy surprise, they found a bottle in Anna-Liisa's pantry next to the cream-of-wheat. It had a fancy label and a twist cap, which Irma managed to open with only a few swear words. Just as they were toasting their friend's memory at her deathbed, giggling about all the fun they had experienced together, a familiar curly-headed fellow stepped into the hallway accompanied by his paladins. All three removed their shoes at the door and crept into the dim bedroom without saying a word. Pertti had a hole in the heel of his left sock. Siiri decided it was a fitting moment to offer the fellow some darning assistance; she even had a clever little darning mushroom tucked away somewhere.

'God's blessings on this home,' the preacher said mildly. 'What are we celebrating here?'

'As a matter of fact, we're having a wake,' Siiri said briskly.

'Yes! We're celebrating our dear friend's unusually

successful death!' Irma added, making a show of taking a big gulp from her wine glass. 'But lo, when the circle finally closes, we drink and forget everything. *The Heath Cobblers*, I don't remember chapter and verse.'

Pertti eyed the women sceptically and eventually leaned in towards Anna-Liisa, rigid and from too great a distance to bid the deceased a natural goodbye. It seemed to Irma and Siiri as if this messenger of God had never seen a dead body before. His face was twisted in an expression of faint horror, and he instinctively raised his hand to his mouth and nose.

'Anna-Liisa died last night . . .' Siiri began.

'At 5:48 a.m. Or was it 4:84? Oh yes, that's not a time, 4:84. It's her favourite hymn, which we already sang before we found a bottle of wine in the pantry.'

'I see,' Pertti said, glancing uncertainly at the young men at the door, who nervously fiddled with their satchels as they stood sentry as if they had swallowed spears. 'That makes our business all the more timely.'

Siiri looked at the ringletted shepherd in disbelief. Was Pertti referring to the will? Siiri had forgotten all about the document; it was what they had come to deliver when they found Anna-Liisa expired in her bed. Siiri felt the blood rise to her face and her bile boil. She couldn't restrain herself; she started shouting insults in the preacher's face. 'You vultures! You hyenas and carrion eaters! Is there no limit to your gall? How dare you come here before Anna-Liisa's body is even cold to fill your bottomless pockets with her property. You should be ashamed of yourselves, you scavengers!'

'Actually, her body is quite cold. Downright frigid,' Irma interjected.

'You and your wealth-management advice can be justifiably accused of causing Anna-Liisa's death. She was so dismayed by your aggressive expert assistance that in the end she couldn't even get out of bed.'

Now Irma roused herself too, and jumped on-board.

'Who knows, she might have died of cachexia while she was lying here alone. Cachexia! Do you know what that is, you snot-noses? My cousin Erik, who was the same age as Anna-Liisa, died—'

'No cousins right now, Irma.' Siiri felt like she was in the prime of her life. No force in the world would stop her now. She spoke in a steady, low voice, savouring the pauses. 'Oh, don't worry, no one is going to accuse you of anything. This death was as eagerly anticipated as all deaths are at Sunset Grove. And when it comes to that dismally infamous will . . .' Siiri theatrically paused and went off to find her handbag. The men were so stunned by all they were witnessing they couldn't get a word out. Siiri masterfully claimed the stage, strolling serenely into the living room and twirling around a few times before spotting her bag on the kitchen table. She unsnapped the old handbag and started rifling through its contents, taking her time to build suspense. In the end, she struck upon her goal and victoriously pulled out the will Anna-Liisa had signed. She held it aloft, like the bare-breasted woman waving the French flag in Eugene Delacroix's *Liberty Leading the People*.

'Here it is! The document you so lust after!'

Before anyone could say anything, Siiri tore the will in half. She tore it again and again until nothing but a pretty pile of shredded paper remained. Then she gathered the mound into her fist and shoved it into her cheerfully smiling mouth.

She concluded with 'It's this simple,' but it was hard to make out the words. She was pleased with her performance and knew Anna-Liisa would be proud of her. The only unpleasant aspect of this bravura moment was the faint nausea caused by the shredded paper.

Irma clapped, spellbound. 'Brava, Siiri! A superb performance! What do you have to say now, you imbeciles and infants?'

'The destruction of an official document . . . A criminal act . . .' Pertti cried in a panic. 'In the presence of witnesses.'

'Nonsense,' Irma said with a laugh. 'Siiri ate her own shopping list. It read: "Half a litre of skimmed milk, one package of slightly spoiled liver casserole, a box of supple red wine, bread, butter, and cheese for the rat." Isn't that right, Siiri? Did I guess correctly?'

Siiri had spat the shredded paper into her bag on the sly, because she was incapable of swallowing Anna-Liisa's will as smoothly as she had hoped. Her mouth was dry, and the paper didn't soften but formed a hard clump that refused to move towards her oesophagus. She turned towards her audience, trusted in her stage presence, pretended to munch on the paper and nodded at Irma. Then she rushed to retrieve her glass of wine from Anna-Liisa's nightstand.

'There we are. Now we're ready,' she said after draining

her glass, at the same time washing the unpleasantness away. 'Will you contact the police and the funeral home or do we have to do that, too?'

'It's not actually our responsibility—' Pertti began, but Siiri shut him up.

'Listen, if there's anything that's suitable for simpletons, it's that. We don't even have phones, so just reach into your suit pockets and pull out your smart gadgets, dial 112 and tell them that Anna-Liisa Petäjä, MA, passed in peace at the age of ninety-six in her own bed and in the presence of witnesses. You'll discover that the world won't come to an end. They'll tell you what to do. We'll wait right here for the police or some other authority to show up. But you have to leave, because we want to be alone. Even though death is a mundane occurrence at this age, Anna-Liisa was our dear friend, so we have a lot to digest here. Even more than in her will.'

Siiri rubbed her belly with one hand as if the will were giving her a stomach-ache. Then she firmly pointed at the door.

'Siribiribim and good day to you!' Irma shouted as she shoved the suited men into the corridor, shoes in hand. 'Remember to be good little boys and call emergency services right away!'

Chapter 31

The next one to die was Tauno, the same week as Anna-Liisa. Oiva told them when they happened to run into him in the lobby. That was life these days at Sunset Grove: no one knew anything, and residents were dropping right and left. This may have been due to the increased median age, but the general perception was that the gerontechnological conditions at Sunset Grove had boosted the mortality rate. And ever since the accidental casualties of the electricity outage had called unfortunate attention to themselves, the smartwalls no longer published electronic obituaries.

They lived by rumours, and days could pass before word of a friend's death reached the others. Even the flag outside Sunset Grove was no longer lowered to half-mast as a sign of mourning, presumably because it wasn't sufficiently cost-effective to bring in a living human being to take care of it. All respect for the dead had vanished.

'I suspected something, but not this . . .' Oiva spluttered when they saw him. 'We last spoke the night before last . . . Just chatted about this and that.'

Oiva didn't react to Tauno's death as serenely as they had

to Anna-Liisa's skilfully executed exit. Oiva was beside himself with grief and required Siiri and Irma's support.

'He never really recovered from what he had to go through . . . I don't even know exactly what happened . . . do you know what I'm talking about . . .'

All they could do was listen as Oiva couched his tempest of emotions in fumbling words, then a cascade of sentences. They went into the canteen, and Irma carried over a plateful of cheerfully coloured cones and cylinders for Oiva.

'Have something to eat, so you don't die from cachexia, too.'

'Tauno was ninety-three years old, but that doesn't mean he should have died . . . at least not like this.' Oiva cried heart-rendingly. He was convinced the Awaken Now! Association's attempt at healing Tauno had robbed him of his will to live. 'The thought that he'd have to go through something like that, after everything we've been through together.'

Tauno had evidently committed suicide, although whether this was actually the case remained unclear to Irma and Siiri, as Oiva spoke in meandering digressions, at times with food in his mouth, and was incapable of detailed reporting. Irma and Siiri tactfully refrained from asking the shocked man too many questions. Oiva had found Tauno in his nightshirt in bed at noon, and there had been three empty pharmaceutical vials on the nightstand. Sleeping aids and something else, but Tauno had left no note.

'He wasn't on any regular medication. He was a healthy man, always had been, never got sick or complained.

Rainy-day pills of some sort, I don't know why he would have had them . . . in such amounts.'

Gradually Oiva calmed down and started remembering the life he and Tauno had shared, spooning the nutritional mash into his mouth at the same time. He was very hungry, and Irma treated him to a second serving from the Meal-Mat. Food sprayed to the table as Oiva spoke, and the story sounded like an unbroken chain of difficulties: rejection from the family, being disinherited, trouble at work, evictions, fake wives, constant fear of being caught and who knows what other subterfuges, and they couldn't follow which of the indignities had been suffered by Oiva, which by Tauno, and which by some third party. In the end, everything came to a climax at Sunset Grove, where Tauno and Oiva were refused admittance as a couple and where religious fanatics felt it was their duty to free Tauno of his demons, with tragic consequences.

'That's what broke him . . . that terrible treatment here.'

'Probably,' Siiri said thoughtfully. 'And he's not the only one who has settled on death as a sensible solution under the circumstances.'

Silence fell. Oiva had finally eaten his fill and was wiping green mush from his walrus whiskers with his napkin. Eventually Irma decided to lighten the mood.

'Oiva, did you know they invoice you for confirming a death?' she said brightly. They had found the bill in Anna-Liisa's home when they had gone to check if the fast-moving heirs had removed the furniture yet. 'That's how the City of Helsinki remembers its long-term residents.

Fourteen euros and seventy cents. And for once the munici-
pality acted swiftly; the invoice arrived before any decisions
about the funeral had been made!'

They tried to make sense of the bureaucratic bill and wondered if the city had instigated a bidding process for the
service, as mandated by EU regulations. Perhaps health-care
technology could have shaved a bit off the cost of the procedure.

'Some magnetic tube and a handy little sensor to glance at
the body, that would be handy.'

Siiri and Irma had left the invoice on Anna-Liisa's counter.
They weren't sure if the idea was that the dead person would
personally pay the bill or if it was a cost covered by the retirement home. Anna-Liisa's apartment had looked depressingly
deserted now that its resident was gone, although her belongings were in place.

'That's the way it was in Tauno's flat, too. And they hound
you to empty the apartment so they can get the next paying
customer in as quickly as possible,' Oiva sighed. He had
conscientiously started packing things the moment Tauno
had been carted off to the morgue.

Siiri and Irma had done a little poking about in Anna-
Liisa's cupboards and sniffed her belongings longingly.
They each took one of the black mourning dresses in
memory of their friend: Siiri a stylish straight dress, Irma a
loose-wrap caftan that barely fitted her. They would wear
them to Anna-Liisa's funeral.

Irma suggested they arrange a joint memorial service for
Anna-Liisa and Tauno, but Oiva politely declined. Tauno

didn't belong to the church, and he and Oiva had planned their own modest ceremony at the seashore that involved nocturnal ash-scattering.

'I have to do it on my own,' Oiva said seriously. 'And of course I will. For Tauno.'

Chapter 32

Too much was too much. One was forced to tolerate all sorts of injustices during one's lifetime, they were used to that, but with Anna-Liisa's and Tauno's deaths a line had been crossed. Siiri and Irma could no longer sit still; they decided to investigate the premises of the Awaken Now! Association at the former Enso offices in Katajanokka. Anna-Liisa had said the cult's headquarters were located there. And the more they thought about everything Anna-Liisa had told them, the more convinced they became that it was their responsibility to intervene in the activities of the criminal cult. After all, that had been Anna-Liisa's intent; she had simply been too exhausted, despite having been first to catch scent of the volunteer organization's true mission: robbing the elderly.

'And a lot more, too. Like committing psychological violence,' Irma said, as the number 4 tram sped down a grey Mannerheimintie towards downtown Helsinki.

March was a dispiriting month. A thick crust of dirty ice covered the ground, and tall snow piles blocked the pavements. Nor were they an idyllic white, as in tourist advertisements for

Lapland, but icebergs in variously shaded strata of brown, grey and black so heavily caked by road-sanding grit that the idea of them ever melting felt like an impossibility. Over a month would pass before the tiniest buds appeared on the birches. Grimy spatters smeared the windows, and no one bothered to wash them yet, as weeks of sleet and slush still remained in store. Siiri sighed deeply, her voice trembling, and felt the familiar pressure in her upper abdomen. It was sadness. Whenever someone dear to her died, she experienced this dark pain without being able to pinpoint its precise location. Near the liver, deep in the spleen, perhaps at the head of the small intestine. In the same vicinity as the unbridled joy and happiness she felt when something lovely happened. It was akin to grief. And she wouldn't be grieving so concretely for Anna-Liisa or Tauno if they hadn't brought her incredible amounts of joy in the last years of her life.

'So we march in, find the supreme god of this cult and give him a piece of our mind, is that it?'

Siiri came out of her reverie on Aleksanterinkatu, as Irma was concluding the plan of attack she had apparently been devising for the bulk of the tram ride. She gazed at the headquarters of the venerable insurance company Pohjola, the century-old structure designed by Gesellius, Lindgren and Saarinen. Logs and other national romantic conceits had been etched into the soapstone, but for some reason the gentlemen architects had turned over the design of the main entrance to a woman. Siiri loved the facade Hilda Flodin had arranged, its bright-eyed bear cubs standing stoutly and their mother slumbering off her exhaustion, the wood patterns reminiscent of Anton Gaudí, and the smiling and crying faces a reference to theatre. Had Flodin believed that to ever get compensation from the insurance company, one had to possess good acting skills? Siiri also wondered why the right-hand doorframe read 'Kullervo', the name of the most sorrow-ridden antihero from Finnish legend, under a beautiful lighting fixture. Perhaps the point was that if Kullervo had had homeowner's insurance, he would have suffered less from the incineration of his house and his belligerent tour of vengeance? Siiri grunted sourly at her own thoughts, then started when Irma jabbed her in the arm with a dismayed grumble.

'. . . and you haven't heard a word I've said, you silly architecture fanatic. What am I ever going to do with you? Why did things have to end so sadly, with the two of us the only two left in this world? Siiri, are you sleeping? Or did you decide to go deaf at this blessed moment? Aren't we supposed to get off at the next stop? I can already see that dreadful Sugar Cube, look! Are you ready for our blitzkrieg?'

The tram curved from Mariankatu onto Kanavakatu and past the president's palace, carrying them up to Alvar Aalto's marble-faced, compellingly rhythmic edifice, where each square window was elegantly embedded in its individual niche. Siiri never tired of the beauty of this much-maligned building, but kept her mouth firmly shut, as she had no interest in arguing with Irma over whether the modern building was appropriate for the city's silhouette.

A moment later, they were standing at the doors to the former headquarters of the Enso company. The doors' bronze handles had a familiar curve to them; Aalto had designed similar ones for the House of Culture, the Pensions Institute and Finlandia Hall. Siiri wondered how often she had reached for a similar handle over her thirty-six years as a typist at the Pensions Institute. At the time, she hadn't considered herself particularly privileged to be able to enjoy beautiful architecture every day. The Sugar Cube's pillared portico commanded respect and even compelled Irma to think twice about the wisdom of their venture.

'What on earth are we doing here? It's a stroke of luck the cheapskates at Enso didn't get their wish when they wanted to replace the frostbitten marble with granite. Imagine the tombstone this place would be. But the facade is no longer Carrera marble. Some funny intuition tells me this marble was imported from Portugal. Not that it makes much difference, except in terms of cost. I don't suppose Portuguese stone will tolerate Finnish winters and freezing winds any better than Italian did. The granite foundation is stylish, I must say, but to have the whole building in granite . . . I never knew the main entrance is here at the west side. Somehow I imagined you entered through that recess across from the Uspenski Cathedral. I'm sorry, I'm babbling again.'

They were standing in the immense lobby that had served not only as the port of call for the international paper giant but as the sales office for a shipbuilding company. After glancing around, they discovered a directory of clearly later vintage, a plastic plate that clashed badly with the dignified original interior. The names and logos of tenant companies were listed on it. Only one had a comprehensible name: Awaken Now! The others were progressively peculiar mishmashes of pseudo-Latin and global English: Carendo, Caritas, Sanario Senilitas, Midas, Funtander Consumer and Finnvalue Finance.

'Second floor. Let's take the elevator,' Irma said, with a press of the round button. 'Aha, this one doesn't know how to converse like our clever dumbwaiters at Sunset Grove.'

On the second floor they stepped into a slightly smaller lobby, which also suffered no lack of august ambience. Alvar Aalto certainly knew how to elevate the mundane into the stately, Siiri thought as she paused to enjoy the view of the harbour. It would have been a beautiful sea scape if the nightmarish cruise ships and enormous Ferris wheel didn't gobble it up, leaving the eye no room to take in anything else. Two broad corridors led off from the space; they were lined with cell offices. Siiri remembered this from the 1960s, when the building was held up as a trailblazer of modern workplace culture. A cell office meant that first you stepped into a foyer that served as a common reception area for the other rooms. The building's top floor, the fifth, differed from the others in the opulent materials used in its interior decor, and the sixth floor led to a restaurant that was surrounded by a terrace. Different materials had been used on each floor as a hierarchical device that let employees know their place in the grand scheme of things. The floor might be travertine, oak parquet, concrete mosaic, soft carpet or mundane linoleum, as it was here on the second floor. There was no point dreaming of leather sofas surrounded by wooden panels and copper lighting fixtures down here. The doors were also plain painted wood; gone were the bronze and the lacquered mahogany of the lobby.

Awaken Now! had taken over several cells on the second floor of the Sugar Cube. Irma barged fearlessly into the foyer of the first and interrogated the woman sitting there as to where she would find the upper brass. The child looked like a secretary in her tight skirt suit and bobbed hair.

'We want to talk to Zeus or Wotan or whatever your leader is called. Where can we find Valhalla?'

The woman slurped disinterestedly on a two-litre beverage bottle filled with normal water and stared at her computer while tapping something out.

'You guys make an appointment? You have a slot booked in his Outlook?'

'We're here now, online,' Irma answered, unperturbed. 'The name is Lännenleimu, Irma, and this is my friend Siiri Kettunen. Shall we wait here?'

The secretary pounded away at her computer, her pretty forehead furrowing uncertainly, then sucked on her massive baby bottle and stood.

'Just a sec, I'll go and ask if he'll see you.' Apparently they had stepped right into the wolf's den – or rather the *Verwolf*'s, as Irma said. There weren't any chairs to sit on, so they leaned on their walking canes and stared out at the street. Suddenly the receptionist was standing behind them;

they could tell by the gulping sound she produced while slaking her interminable thirst.

'So, like, yeah, it's fine,' she said so curtly they thought they'd misheard. 'The director's on the third floor, just look for Sanario Senilitas. You can take the elevator.' The woman pointed her baby bottle towards the north-west; clearly this was all the assistance she intended on offering her elderly visitors.

They travelled soundlessly up a storey and arrived at a parquet floor, so one level more important than the previous. They were immediately greeted by the bright, screaming logo of Sanario Senilitas, and thanks to the guidance of the hierarchical architecture had no trouble finding the most important cell. The door to the rear chamber had been left invitingly ajar. No Cerberus stood guard, and so they stepped briskly into Pluto's maw, prepared to speak German, Swedish, Latin or English, if the situation so demanded. The large office contained a compact sofa set and a sizeable table clearly not designed by Alvar Aalto; it was a cheap cherry-veneer monstrosity imported by the new tenant. Sitting behind the desk was Jerry Siilinpää.

'Jerry! Are you the one in charge of all this?' Irma cried spontaneously and in such a shrill voice that the tuft on Jerry's head trembled and the lad stood in alarm. He was wearing the same too-tight suit he'd sported at the Sunset Grove rat session, a nametag around his neck and his rubber gorilla feet. Now he leapt out from behind his veneer desk to greet Irma and Siiri, neither of whom he recognized.

'Jerry Siilinpää, hi there. Are you from Sunset Grove, the Last Leg or Hospice of Hope?'

'We're from where we're from. Mostly Helsinki,' Irma answered defiantly. 'We wanted to see the chief of the Awaken Now! Association, but the secretary on the second floor foisted us off on you.'

'Yup. I'm the area director for Sanario Senilitas Finland. It's an international corporation open to all investors. As a matter of fact, at this very moment we have a massive IPO in the works, you two could get a valuable portfolio for a good price. It's basically a hundred per cent secure, mega-profitable, because looking ahead, elder-care is going to be a huge, huge global business.'

'I'm perfectly happy with my old *portefeuille*,' Irma said icily. Jerry looked at his audience, two angry-looking senior citizens, and continued his employer's routine presentation.

'The group owns an international chain of elder-care facilities, all fully automated monitored-care units equipped with the latest technology. A turnkey service concept based on a franchising model.'

'So . . . you're not our Experience Director & Front-Line Support after all?'

'Yes, exactly right. Experience Director & Front-Line Support is part of the job description when you operate locally down at the grassroots level.' He paused to scratch himself uninhibitedly, and when no one said anything, he reassumed control of the situation. 'So what's the deal, what do you ladies have on your mind?'

'This religious cult, it's robbing us of the last of our

money, not to mention our love for life. What do you have to do with it? You don't seem like one of them . . . You're . . . our Jerry. The project manager from the plumbing retrofit . . . And weren't you in business with the Ambassador, Onni Rinta-Paakku, our good friend who died just as we were getting to the bottom of his shady dealings at our pornographic lair in Hakaniemi?' Irma blabbered so boldly that Siiri had to take a seat. She thought it indelicate to link Jerry to past sins they had no intention of digging up again.

'Okey-dokey, so that's what's on your mind. Why don't we take a minute to brainstorm this together? Have a seat and take a breather.' Jerry's face was bright red as he sat across from Siiri on an upholstered sofa hauled in from some bargain basement, a piece of junk too soft for anything but lounging. He tried to offer them slices of tropical fruit from a bowl on the table, but they declined. They had come to complain, not to be appeased. 'Just so you know, Ambassador Rinta-Paakku and I sold our shares in Sunset Grove to Sanario Senilitas during the renovation. Onni's death created a bit of a mess, but no worries, we brought the deal home without any major headaches.'

'Onni owned Sunset Grove? I don't understand anything about anything any more,' Siiri said.

Irma seemed clear-headed and unfazed by what Jerry was explaining. She looked the lad calmly in the eye and loosed such a verbal deluge that Siiri knew it would take a long time before any of them had a chance to think. Irma spoke in broad arcs, starting from events dating back years and waving her hands. Siiri shut her eyes and listened to the jangle of the gold bracelets and let the sun shining through the window caress her face.

Gradually Irma approached the present day and made careful use of Jerry's favourite expression, 'the latest', without the lad realizing it had taken on an ironic cast in the old woman's mouth. Irma remembered many details with an admirable accuracy, the machine-induced deaths of the elderly residents, the exact date of the electricity outage and the number of victims, a few of the silliest Bible phrases, Margit's ecstatic conversion, the crushing of Tauno and Anna-Liisa's spirits and all the other spiritual and technological violence that had victimized the residents of Sunset Grove.

'So we're here to tell you we won't stand for it any longer.'

'Yup yup, right,' Jerry said, unsuccessfully trying to dislodge a pineapple fibre stuck between his front teeth with his pinky nail. The strand dangled unpleasantly across his teeth and made Siiri concentrate on all the wrong things again. 'Sounds pretty bad, if what you're saying is true.'

'If what I'm saying is true?' Irma stood up, and for a moment Siiri thought she meant to wallop Jerry with her handbag. 'It most certainly is. I'm presenting a thorough and detailed complaint about the operation you're running from your veneer desk. And since you don't understand anything, you little dumb-dumb, I'm going to tell you what's going to happen next. You're going to press a button somewhere and turn off all the contraptions, click!, and forbid volunteer preachers from ever setting foot in Sunset Grove again. They're not even volunteers! So stop forcing them. My darlings have informed me the rents and service fees at Sunset Grove have risen sky-high as a result of this new cloud service. Before long we'll all run out of money, and how will you earn your bread then? And if every last penny of ours isn't swallowed up by self-service fees, some curly-haired scoundrel comes around demanding it for charity. Do the owners of this Senilitarium here belong to this religious cult? Aren't you ashamed? Are you some sort of CONSCIENTIOUS OBJECTOR?'

At the climax of her sermon, Irma's voice rose to alarmingly strident heights, her face darkened, and she pointed an accusing finger at Jerry. Siiri found the climax ill-considered.

'Wars will never come to an end without conscientious objectors. If all young men refused to bear arms, the world would be a much better place,' she observed.

'Don't get caught up on bagatelles, Siiri. We're not fixing the entire world right now, only the way old people are treated in Finland, and we cannot allow it to slide into a tax haven run by religious fanatics.'

'Umm, yeah . . . I mean, no, I did my military service. Officers' training, actually, exactly right.' Jerry stretched out his hands and cracked his knuckles loudly. He said he was just doing his job. 'Hey, look, the world's changing. This is the latest: strategic operations based on high-tech thinking. It's all about streamlining processes in a resource-efficient AI environment. Yours truly just coordinates the operational activities at the local level in accordance with the group's mission.'

Jerry didn't appear to know what was going on at Sunset

Grove in the name of his mission. Irma told him how the religious fanatics took advantage of lonely, weak old people, promised them security and a place in heaven although all they had to offer were random snippets from a two-thousand-year-old collection of fables and a cloud service in the Ivory Coast.

'Don't you understand, you poor child, that it is irresponsible to run a nursing home for severely demented patients with a couple of cameras and a fob?'

'I'm not loving your take on things, I have to say. According to studies sponsored by the company, the care-giving technology works flawlessly, is reliable and risk-free and brings epic savings. There's no proof that the deaths of those hundred-year-olds were caused by technology. I mean, hey, come on, can't a hundred-year-old die in peace?' Jerry picked up the plot from something Irma had said and asked for a little common sense on the other side of the court, too, as if they were playing a match of two-on-one tennis. When it came to the whole religion thing, Jerry felt it was everyone's personal matter. He went on and on about the ethical principles of Sanario Senilitas, to which the group was mega-committed; it included environmental destruction, world peace and ruination as well as respect for the individual in a single sentence you could share with others, hey, why not. At one point he talked about his grandmother, who was semi-religious but never butted into Jerry's life. According to him, the senior scene was involved with the religious crowd on a bunch of levels, which was why he had a hard time getting what Siiri and Irma were so worried about.

'But OK, I'll start a ticket, and the quality standards team will investigate the case through the normal processes. If something turns up, it'll be documented and reported. Sound good? And BTW, the Sunset Grove dementia unit was ramped down last month because it wasn't profitable. We have to keep trimming the excess, that's the latest. Concentrate on what we do best, focus on our core competence.'

'Excuse me? You're saying the B wing is empty? The dementia unit doesn't exist any more?'

Irma couldn't keep up either. It was somehow illustrative that none of the residents had noticed the shutting of the locked unit. It was completely isolated from the rest of the facility, and the dark, silent desolation there hadn't set off any alarm bells in the other residents' minds.

'Where are . . . where did you move the dementia patients?' Siiri asked. But Jerry just shrugged and explained that the city carried primary responsibility when contracts for tendered service were discontinued, and that health and social services re-evaluated the placement needs of the demented residents in the context of the budgeting framework. He momentarily mulled terminal repositories, contribution-based funding schemes and models of responsible municipalities and assured them that in-home care was the solution to many problems. Then he glanced at the bare wrist of his right hand and slapped his thighs. They were very muscular.

'So that's where we are! Our time slot is closing here; I

.have to get to a marketing meeting in the online conference room, so if you wouldn't mind showing yourself out.'

'Showing yourselves,' Irma said in Anna-Liisa's honour.

Chapter 33

Like all Helsinki basements, the cellar was damp and stuffy. Siiri thought it curious that the attics of old buildings always smelled completely different from the basements, but you never came across either smell anywhere else. The aroma of the attics was tinged with wind, brick and dust, that of the basements with moisture, jam jars and old soil. Irma was holding a torch she had inherited from Anna-Liisa, and Siiri had the hunting knife in her bag. That was the extent of their defensive paraphernalia, and Siiri felt her heart pounding so furiously that she was afraid it would burst out of her chest.

'Can you hear my heart beating?' she asked Irma as she followed her down the long damp corridor.

'Of course not. I'm not deaf, but I'm not a stethoscope either. Are you afraid?'

'A little, yes. But listen, why don't we turn on the lights? Do we have to wander around in the dark with a torch?'

'As you like,' Irma said, sounding disappointed. 'I was thinking creeping along in the darkness would be more exciting.'

Irma stopped so suddenly that Siiri bumped into her. It

was a harmless collision, as Irma was soft and round. They laughed cheerfully as they nearly pitched over in the darkness and ended up in an embrace instead, but in the confusion, the torch Irma was holding fell to the ground and went out. All was pitch black. They groped the mouldy walls searching for a light switch, and had nearly given up hope when the lights came on.

Only then did they see that the basement was strewn with abandoned walkers and wheelchairs. In addition to the random collection of idle mobility aids dotting the corridors, equipment had been piled high in two doorless cupboards. Three-point canes, the odd crutch, and a toilet seat booster jutted from the jumble, but it was difficult to make out any other details. Dusty cobwebs accentuated the assemblages that could have been acclaimed art installations in some other context. A nearby nook was packed with apparently decommissioned skeletal robots. Some were missing a limb, others had been crammed into awkward kinks and all stared back lifelessly and eerily from their spherical eyes. They had stumbled upon a graveyard of medical equipment and technology.

Suddenly it seemed to Siiri that one of the Ahabas moved. She panicked, thinking the robots were alive and might attack trespassers, in other words them, like in some blood-curdling sci-fi movie. But such fantasies were childish, of course. She pulled herself together and put on a brave face.

'I'm glad you found the light switch,' she said gamely to Irma, who looked dumbfounded.

'I didn't find it. I thought you did!' Irma whispered, her

eyes wide in terror, moving her lips exaggeratedly so Siiri would understand even if she couldn't hear. 'Someone else is down here.'

'Or else they have automatic lights that react too slowly,' Siiri said in a normal voice, prompting Irma to hiss angrily and clamp a perfumed hand over Siiri's mouth.

'Hello? Who's there?'

They started. Had someone followed them into the basement? The man's voice carrying from the stairwell sounded vaguely familiar. Before long, a figure emerged at the end of the corridor.

'Mika! Mika Korhonen!' Siiri cried out in relief. Their guardian angel never let them down. How did he always know when to appear to succour them in their greatest need?

Mika was wearing his black parka and big dirty boots and hauling along his rat extermination box. Irma looked relieved, too, even though she wasn't as convinced as Siiri of the convict's magnificence.

'What the hell are you two doing down here?' Mika yelled as he approached, arms protruding from his body in the manner of American weightlifters and Russian wrestlers. He must have got a lot of exercise during his time in prison, brawny as he was now. When he reached them, Mika slammed his box down on the floor so roughly that a dust cloud billowed up and the bang echoed emptily along the corridor. One of the automated dwarfs in the cupboard opposite collapsed and whined faintly.

'We're looking for the Holy of Holies,' Irma said before Siiri could think of how to best explain their silly spying expedition to Mika. 'It's a server and it's located down here somewhere. We know because all the cables and wires lead here, and Siiri almost made it down here with a maintenance man who came to replace a cable during a repair.'

Mika scratched his bald pate and smiled as if he were going to burst out laughing. But he didn't say anything; he had always cultivated an air of mysterious reticence. It was part of his extraordinary charm, along with his blue eyes and big hands.

'There's no server down here,' Mika finally said. 'But there are plenty of cables, so in that sense you're on the right track. Why are you guys looking for the server?'

'We're going to unplug it and put a stop to this madness,' Irma said fearlessly. 'We can't take living among these machines any more. Our neighbours are dropping like flies, and as the last guerrillas standing we have to do something to save ourselves before we end up in debtors' prison at the orders of some Brazilian conglomerate. District supreme chief Jerry Siilinpää didn't understand a word of what we explained to him, even though we spoke plainly. But I don't think he speaks normal language any more. He jabbers in that consultant-speak as if he were being controlled by some bargain-basement Indian cloud from the other side of the world. Can you imagine, he offered us tickets and coupons as the solution to all this! Kept on shoving tickets down our throats and then rushed off like a madman in his gorilla feet. And we were so fond of him back when he was in charge of the renovation at Sunset Grove and taught us how to use composting toilets.'

'Got it,' Mika said, as if he had internalized every word of Irma's rundown. 'Those are the cables right there,' he said, pointing at a plastic tube running along the ceiling.

'Is that the heavenly service? Is that how they control the robots and transmit biblical phrases to the smartwalls? Is that how the religious fanatics' commandments travel into our homes?' Siiri was sure that Mika was pulling their legs. She peppered him with questions like a bottomlessly curious child, one finger raised, until she realized how comical she looked and stopped. 'You're making fun at our expense, Mika.'

'No, I'm not. The cables lead there.' Mika indicated the far end of the hallway. 'That's where the routers are. And the switch.'

Irma and Siiri stared, dumbstruck, in the direction Mika was indicating, where they could see nothing but blackness. So that's where the Holy of Holies was, which reminded them of a normal light fixture, in that it had a switch. Mika calmly clicked open the locks of his death-box one at a time.

'I'm here to kill rats. Have you seen any?'

'My rat was so frightened by your blue gas that he hasn't been back in weeks for his bit of cheese. But someone said they'd just seen several rats out in the yard. Might it have been Margit? Or Ritva? Who else could it have been?' Siiri sought support from Irma, but her friend's mind was blank. As far as she could remember, it had been ages since anyone had spoken about rats, let alone mysterious deaths and empty bank accounts.

'We'll all be destitute before long. Tapping around with

our canes begging for alms, as poor as church rats, if you catch my meaning, since you're so interested in sewer fauna. They're sucking our accounts dry along that electricity cable, these miserly merchants of nothing. Not the rats. I'm not as addled as I sound. I'm just so upset; this is unprecedented thievery, and there will be no end to it unless we gnaw that wire in two,' she said. Just to be sure, she stomped her foot and shook her fist at the cable.

'Irma! That's it! We need the rats' help,' Siiri cried. She gave first Irma and then Mika a sly smile, but neither caught on to her flash of genius. She had to start from the ground up. The thought had already crossed her mind back when Mika had sprayed the poison in her kitchen, but she hadn't understood then how everything fitted together. Thanks to Ritva's inebriated tutorial at the Ukko-Munkki, now she did. Irma should have, too. And since Jerry Siilinpää had inadvertently revealed that the dementia unit no longer existed, her greatest cause for concern had been dismissed.

'Do you think you could help us a little?'

'By not killing rats?' Mika growled, kicking the lid of his box shut. It was impossible to decide from the wry look on his face if he was on their side or if he was intent on carrying out the task assigned by the city's Department of the Environment.

'Maybe not all of them, at least . . . I doubt you'll get caught if you're careful, but the rats will stay alive, right? Who's counting them? Would you do us this one last favour, Mika?'

Mika Korhonen looked at the wizened old woman staring

intently at him with her grey eyes and gripping his arm in her veined hands. He remembered that gaze and that demanding grip from a few years ago, remembered his childhood friend Tero's tragic death, and how one bizarre taxi gig had thrown this irrepressibly optimistic duo into his back seat, forcing him to investigate Tero's death and the convoluted criminal activity at Sunset Grove. Compared to that, locking up a couple of rats in the basement didn't seem like such a big deal.

'So it's settled, then?' Siiri said, throwing her arms around Mika. He looked embarrassed but laughed pleasantly the way he sometimes did. Irma looked on in bewilderment, with no idea what had just been settled in the basement corridor.

Chapter 34

It came as a complete surprise to Siiri and Irma that Anna-Liisa was Orthodox. She had never mentioned it, and upon further reflection, she had always been reticent when the conversation touched on religion. The Orthodox preferred rapid burials, within three days of the death if at all possible, which wasn't within the framework of Finland's bureaucracy. Several weeks passed before Pertti & Co.'s call to emergency services had started up the mortality mill required to grind out a document pronouncing a ninety-six-year-old acceptably dead, determining the cause of death and granting the burial permit. At long last, the official death certificate had reached the offices of the Orthodox parish, whose staff had undertaken to arrange the funeral, as there was no kin.

Irma and Siiri were joined by Margit, Ritva and Aatos for the funeral, and on a cloudy April day, the five of them took the number 4 tram from Munkkiniemi to the Uspenski Cathedral. Siiri realized that she had ended up in Katajanokka this winter time again and again, always on different business, even though in the past Helsinki's maritime cul-de-sac had seemed a town of its own. It rose in isolated loftiness on the far side downtown, a peninsula transformed into an island by a canal; for decades she had viewed it as an obscure periphery home to the prison, the customs house, the old navy barracks, the shipyards and the harbour. The prison was now a hotel, which struck her as queer. Was it truly possible that cells built in the early 1900s served as hotel rooms for foreign tourists?

An unusual suspense enveloped the elderly troop. None of them, seasoned funeral professionals that they were, had ever participated in Orthodox rites. Aatos had never even set foot in Uspenski Cathedral, and Margit was afraid she'd have to see a badly decomposed body, as the funeral arrangements had been so delayed.

'That's right, they always have open caskets,' Ritva said.

'That shouldn't be anything new for you, seeing as how you were a pathologist in your previous existence,' Siiri said.

'Medical examiner. But you're right, I can't deny this reminds me of work,' Ritva barked with a raspy laugh.

The casket was open in the middle of the cathedral, but Anna-Liisa's face had been covered with a fine cloth. She was wearing her own clothes; a small icon rested on her breast and a cross at her throat. A ponytailed young priest had donned a stunning white cape with silver trim, and when Siiri approached to admire the garment, the priest explained that for the Orthodox, white was the colour of baptism and death.

'What a beautiful thought,' Siiri said spontaneously. 'We end up right back where we started.'

'Yes. Death is not an ending, but a new beginning.' They looked around and silently admired all they saw, apart from Irma letting out the occasional and inappropriately loud ooh. It was all so gorgeous. The place was swimming in tall, fat candles, and the magnificent altar had been opened. All this in Anna-Liisa's honour!

They had to stand from start to finish, which required determination and effort. They found their spots a short distance from the casket and observed the ritual that didn't appear to proceed according to a strict formula, but meandered from one prayer or song to the next.

'. . . lead to rest, Lord, the soul of your servant who now sleeps . . .'

The magical mantra melded into the warmth of the candlelight, the tinkling of the braziers, and the fragrant, pitch-scented smoke, sinking Siiri into a pleasant stupor. She relished the movement and chanting around Anna-Liisa's casket. The choir was blessed by one soprano whose song rose above the others. Its closest competitor was a lagging female voice, but thanks to the prolonged echo, the voices filtered into a rather lovely harmony.

'. . . the resurrection, life and repose of your sleeping servant Anna-Liisa Petäjä . . .'

The priest bent over Anna-Liisa, raised the icon from her breast and kissed it. One of the women made the sign of the cross and also kissed Anna-Liisa's icon. The choir purred the same tune over and over, and Siiri couldn't make out all the words on account of the melisma.

'. . . rejoice, oh worthy . . .'

Then it was their turn to bid Anna-Liisa farewell. Irma stepped forth boldly, the first to approach the casket. She stood there for a moment, touched Anna-Liisa's hand and dabbed at her eyes with her lace handkerchief.

'. . . that the Lord lead her to rest . . .'

Siiri touched the familiar hand, too. It was a moving experience, a much more concrete way of saying goodbye to an old friend than laying flowers across a closed casket in oppressive silence, as Lutherans did. Siiri walked back to her spot in a fog, to observe how the others managed their part.

Then the casket lid was closed, and a group of men she'd never seen before came and stood around it. The chanting continued, and Siiri couldn't tell if a moment or an eternity had passed. She felt like she was floating ethereally and closed her eyes to relish the enchantment enveloping her. She, a ninety-seven-year-old atheist! What a stunt you pulled, Anna-Liisa, and without the slightest warning!

'Holy God, holy mighty, holy immortal, have mercy on us!'

It felt as if sunlight were filling the cathedral, although that was highly unlikely. Siiri opened her eyes and swayed a little. The porter led the attendees out, starting with the choir and the priest, then the casket. Last of all, the unsteadily advancing mourners proceeded into the drizzling sleet of an April Saturday.

'. . . Amen now, always and for eternity, holy immortal, have mercy on us . . .'

The elderly attendees, on the verge of wilting from standing so long, moved their stiff limbs and glanced around. The casket was lowered into the black vehicle sent by the funeral home. The door slammed shut, keenly cutting the silence that had fallen when the choir stopped singing. When the hearse slid into the Helsinki afternoon traffic, Siiri realized she would never again hear Anna-Liisa lecture on the disappearance of the possessive suffix from spoken Finnish.

They shook hands with the priest and thanked him for the beautiful funeral, as they had just witnessed one of the best blessings in their lives, and they had seen plenty. Then the quintet from Sunset Grove proceeded silently and slowly through Tove Jansson Park to the tram stop, lost in thought. Siiri paused to admire Viktor Malmberg's statue *The Water Bearer*, which depicted a woman lifting a water jar in a distinctly awkward position. She remembered how Luotsikatu and the tram line used to run through the park, but for the life of her couldn't recall when the street had been moulded into one of the park's paths. She looked up at the first pair of buildings and let her eyes rest on two very different examples of Jugendstil architecture. Gesellius, Saarinen and Lindgren had designed the red, fortress-like Tallberg Building, whereas Selim A. Lindqvist was responsible for the streamlined asymmetrical edifice named Aeolus – which wasn't, strictly speaking, Finnish; it should have been spelled *Aiolos*. Not that the Lord of the Winds wasn't the perfect gatekeeper to windswept Katajanokka.

At the tram stop, a nasty northerner straight from Siberia whipped Siiri's face so harshly that she turned her back on it and faced Alvar Aalto's Sugar Cube, although she had determined to avoid doing so on the day of Anna-Liisa's adieu.

The marble-clad cause of Anna-Liisa's death stood there brazenly, staring down on the old cathedral and the cluster of friends who had just bid their farewells to the old woman.

Siiri tried to take her mind off things by admiring the former mint, a pink edifice that was the handiwork of many architects and eras and adorably hidden between two modern buildings. Finnish markkas and pennies had been coined there for over a hundred years, until production moved to the suburbs and the old building became redundant. At first came the euros, then the cards and the chips that transferred ethereal currency from account to account with a simple flash, in their case along a white cable from Sunset Grove to the Sugar Cube and from there to tax havens in the middle of the sea. The Foreign Ministry designed by Olli Pekka Jokela framed the mint to one side, and it was only now that Siiri realized how elegantly the 1990s structure respected its environment. Development aid, to her understanding, was what took place inside the building, so invisible currents carried money abroad from there in a rather uncontrolled fashion as well.

'It was lovely not having to listen to the usual desperate reminiscences about a person the priest has never met,' Irma said as the number 4 tram sped down Aleksanterinkatu. The others were silent. 'Oh well, we never got a chance to sing those two beautiful hymns. Actually that's for the best, that way they'll be a little fresher at my funeral. Siiri, have you figured out why Anna-Liisa left us the numbers of her favourite hymns when she knew she'd end up in the Uspenski Cathedral? My understanding is the Orthodox don't look too kindly on it if someone starts belting out Protestant paeans.'

Siiri had flipped through *The Magic Mountain* to see if that would help them decipher the message contained in the numbers. But on page 484, Hans Castorp was half-audibly babbling such strange, consonant-free gibberish that he was alarmed by his own condition, and on page 548 a new visitor to the sanatorium was introduced, the Dutchman Mr Peeperkorn, an unpleasant fellow with pale watery eyes and patchy facial hair. Anna-Liisa's sole margin note there, which was reinforced by two exclamation marks, referred to an incorrectly inflected predicate she had spotted.

'Perhaps it was her phone number from the landline days? 48 45 48 would imply Munkkiniemi, wouldn't it? The Töölö numbers started with 49 and Meilahti with 47,' Irma chattered, for all intents and purposes to herself. 'It was so handy back when you could tell the neighbourhood from the beginning of the phone number. These days they're so long it's impossible to deduce anything from them. I can't even remember mine! But when we lived in Töölö, our number was 49 71 72. I'm sure I'll still remember it at the gates of heaven if I'm asked.' Siiri sat in the tram behind Irma and Ritva, with Margit at her side. Aatos had stayed further back in solitude. He had clearly stopped taking his Alzheimer's medication, and as a result had grown as listless and absent-minded as a castrated steer, to the point that on occasion Siiri found herself secretly longing for the frisson the former Don Giovanni brought to Sunset Grove with his amorous couplets.

Margit had asked Siiri to sit next to her; she had something on her mind that was difficult to put into words. It wasn't until they reached the old convention centre that she opened her mouth.

'I've started having second thoughts about my involvement with that cult,' she said, and looked at Siiri, eyes full of tears.

'Really? But you haven't done anything irreversibly foolish, have you?'

'In a sense I have. I donated Eino's bonds and stocks to them. They even made me pay the gift tax, can you imagine? And now my pension is too small to afford the fees at Sunset Grove.'

Siiri felt a flush of anger rise to her cheeks. So this was how these men of the cloth had exploited their faithful new servant. She felt like screaming in rage, but she settled for clutching her handbag with both hands, as if she believed Pertti's paladins would snatch it at that very moment and carry it off to their vault.

'Do you have any savings left?' Margit asked, and looked at Siiri in concern, as if afraid her friend had lost her grip on reality.

'Not really. I've been frugal with my pension, but I must admit this winter was difficult,' Siiri answered, discovering that her nerves had eased slightly. 'Although it's not as if I need much, aside from a bit of liver casserole now and again. Clean water comes from the tap, beautiful music comes from the radio, and I have a wardrobe full of clothes.'

'And I felt so safe at the prayer circles and praise services!

But now it seems there was something phony about it. It dawned on me back there at the Uspenksi Cathedral. The ambience there was completely different from what it is at Awaken Now! events. Hope, tenderness, mercy . . . that's what I've been yearning for.'

'Now don't start changing religions in your old age. It's too much trouble.'

Margit launched into a convoluted, agitated explanation of the Awaken Now! Association, which she still refused to criticize for trying to spread the message of Christ. But Margit had found herself alone indeed in her new congregation once her major donation had been received, as if that had been their sole interest in her. She had tried to unburden her heart to Sirkka the Saver of Souls, but instead of helping Margit, Margit had ended up supporting the poor woman.

'Ritva told me about your plans,' Margit said, no longer looking miserable. She deepened her voice and bellowed so loudly in Siiri's ears that it made them ache: 'You have my full support! We have to put a stop to this! Once and for all!'

Chapter 35

Siiri was nearly frightened out of her wits when Mika suddenly pounded on her door. Nowadays no one just walked in the way they used to, at any time. Irma was the only one who visited her, and she was easy to identify from the cock-a-doodle-doo she belted out before she even found her fob. But this time, Siiri heard a demanding, powerful beating at her entrance.

'The rats are piling up; we have to do something,' Mika said, once Siiri had opened the door and Mika had pushed past her in his muddy clodhoppers.

'Could you be a dear and take off your boots? I just mopped this morning.'

Mika looked at Siiri with his sky-blue eyes. 'Huh?'

Suddenly Mika was sockless. The lad was going around barefoot in boots, in April, even though Helsinki was suffering from a late cold snap that struck so unexpectedly that the wagtails that had arrived in February nearly froze on the lawns. Mika wore a black band around his right ankle, the same kind some old people wore around their wrist.

'So that's what tells the prison where you are?'

'Yup. I can't go anywhere without the police knowing about it.'

'Me neither. Or in my case it's not the police following me, it's some religious cult. I have instant coffee and two-day-old pound cake in the cupboard. Would you like some?'

Mika grimaced and shook his head. It was a pity, as Siiri would have gladly had a drop of coffee herself, but didn't dare serve herself in the presence of a guest who had declined so firmly.

'Maybe you'd care for a glass of red wine? This box has been standing on my counter for over a month. But then again, doesn't wine keep for decades and just get the better for it?'

'Sorry, I don't drink.'

'Oh yes, I'm sorry. You're a prisoner. How will they know if I offer you a glass of wine or not?'

'They have breathalysers. But I'm not interested. I don't drink at all.'

'Never again? That's sad.'

Mika collapsed into Siiri's armchair and started talking about rats. He had visited Sunset Grove regularly, supposedly killing rats and making sure none were seen skulking about the resident floors. But every time he'd seen a rodent, he'd lured it into a trap and ferried it to the basement. Now there were so many rats Mika felt they had to take action; otherwise they'd run into trouble.

'So what is it we're doing?'

The big bald man looked at Siiri with such confidence he

must have really believed the ninety-seven-year-old had a sensible plan for the drove of rodents. Siiri didn't know what to say. Suddenly she remembered Albert Camus' *The Plague*. Mika had never read it, so she had to explain that the story, set in the small town of Oran, was a metaphor for German-occupied France during the Second World War.

'OK,' Mika said, looking impatient.

The plague spreading through the town was an allegory for any madness that drove the masses into ecstatic deliriums. Communism, Naziism, technological frenzy, extremist religion. The town was quarantined, the bacterial plague spread to people, and in the end people were dying at such a rate that funerals were no longer held; the bodies were tossed into mass graves and eventually burned due to lack of time and space.

'The less privileged, like prisoners and old people, died first, and the others fended for themselves alone. Only in the face of widespread catastrophe do people really start helping each other.'

'Meaning?'

'In other words, it takes extreme situations for people to understand that the common good is also the individual good.'

'OK. Were you planning on releasing the rats onto the streets to spread the plague?'

Siiri laughed. 'Of course not. The rats just made me think of it. You should read it sometime. Of course *The Plague* also describes Sunset Grove, but I would need Anna-Liisa to explain how everything is interrelated. And Anna-Liisa's not here any more. She was saved. Crawled into bed and read to death.'

Mika started squirming uncomfortably. It was unfair to expect the young motorcycle enthusiast to identify with the ambience of the Second World War or a sequestered retirement home, let alone to grasp the inevitable emptiness that ensued when a loved one died. Even at the age of ninety-seven.

'Maybe we can talk some more about Camus after you've read *The Plague*. Or *The Stranger*: in it, a young man kills another man by accident and is expelled from society, to prison.'

Mika scratched his bald head and grunted.

'So this is turning into a book club. What are we going to do with those rats?'

But Siiri didn't have a detailed plan yet. In some way, Mika's rats had to be persuaded to gnaw the cable in two; Ritva had said that would make the system crash. But the cables ran along the ceiling in a plastic tube, and Mika had spoken about switches. They had to lure the rats into the Holy of Holies.

'I think we can manage that.'

'Yes! That's what I was thinking, although I'm not sure how to do it.' Mika helped Siiri formulate a plan. He took a piece of paper and drew a tall box in the cupboard at the end of the corridor and various cables running in and out of the building from this Holy of Holies. They divided up responsibilities and ensured Mika wasn't at any risk of getting caught. He couldn't come to Sunset Grove at night, as his anklet would give him away. But Mika believed that no one else ever went in the basement, which meant he could do his part during official visiting hours.

'What do you think, what do rats like to eat?' Siiri asked Mika in concern.

'No clue. Look it up online.'

'Where else, of course,' Siiri said and silently blessed Irma, as her green flaptop would finally be of use to them. She started talking to Mika about computers and how they rarely obeyed old people, who didn't care about swiping screens or competing in trivia quizzes led by little trolls or playing bingo with a screen. Machines didn't make their lives the least bit easier, just the opposite. The older one got, the more difficult it was to live without other people.

'You see, in the end, another person's touch is the most important thing in life,' she said, taking Mika's hand. 'And its importance simply increases with age. When you're young or middle-aged, you can still be so self-sufficient you supposedly don't need anyone else around, but when there's no one there any more, you remember what's important.' She patted Mika's hairy paw, and he didn't resist. 'There's not a machine in the world that can replace this. When I die, come and stroke my hand like this.' Then she let go and returned to machines. She wanted Mika to grasp why it was so difficult living surrounded by technology. It wasn't just that they didn't know how to use the devices or weren't used to them. Machines were simple; a two-year-old could master them. It wasn't a question of intelligence, but of will. 'We're not interested in managing everyday life with a robot.'

Mika seemed reflective and cast a serious look at Siiri's bookshelf.

'I didn't kill anyone, even by accident,' he finally said, looking Siiri right in the eye. The poor young fellow looked sad.

'I never thought you did,' Siiri said. 'But I've been getting the impression that you've lost your way a little. You shouldn't be doing community service in my room; you should be doing something fun and modern out there in the world with everyone else.'

Mika was quiet for a moment. Then he explained that a couple of years in prison had given him some space from the wrong crowd, as he put it. And he didn't have much anklet time left either. He said he was an optimist and had learned a lot from Siiri.

'From me? What on earth can you have learned from an ancient old relic like me, a social outcast forgotten among machines?'

'Optimism,' Mika said. 'And all sorts of things. That just like in that book *The Plague*, only people can help other people. Do you have it?'

Siiri popped up and went over to the bookshelf. She had organized her books by language, and because there wasn't much French literature and it was sandwiched between the Germans and the Italians, it didn't take her long to find Camus.

'Here. It's a gift.'

Mika looked pleased and asked Siiri to sign it. It took Siiri a minute to locate her reading glasses, and then a ballpoint pen that worked. She opened the book to its title page and realized it had been a birthday present from her husband in 1950. Oh, how many lovely emotions surged through her from the dusty pages of that volume! So it had been over sixty years since she had first read *The Plague*. She might be misremembering everything and was afraid the book would be a disappointment to Mika. The world was nothing like what it had been after the war. She wrote in a frail hand beneath her husband's firm one: 'To my good friend Mika, not long before we freed the rats. Siiri Kettunen, optimist.'

Chapter 36

Yet again, Irma's green flaptop proved of absolutely no use. No matter how they swiped and swatted, they couldn't find any simple information on the dietary preferences of rats. They were informed that rats were omnivorous, which they remembered from their own lives and the compost piles that had attracted hordes of the creatures. But the thought of strewing their kitchen compost around the basement corridor didn't feel quite right.

'On the other hand, it might look like an accident then,' Irma said.

The ingeniousness of their plan was that no one but the rats could be called to account for the damage. But they were running out of time. Mika would be incredibly upset if they didn't stick to the timetable and he was forced to keep the rodents corralled in the basement much longer. Irma read online that female rats were nearly always on heat and gave birth to a new brood every four weeks. They tried to calculate the speed at which Mika's rats were reproducing in the basement cupboard. It was a complicated equation, and they arrived at a different result every time, always such a horrendously high figure that they decided to forget the whole Internet and marched down Munkkiniemi Allée to the pet store that now occupied the former hair accessories shop.

There was a strange smell in the shop. It carried a whiff of the flavour of the cat snacks, but also the aromas of plastic toys and cat sand. The salesgirl was a very young woman, still a schoolgirl. She had completely shaved the right side of her head and dyed the scraggly curtain falling to the left violet. Her face was full of spikes and her arms plastered with tattooed symbols of death. Her lace shirt was cropped just short of her breasts, heavy charms circled her navel, and she was wearing a choke collar around her neck. The girl looked at them, batting her eyes when they said that they'd come to buy delicacies for rats.

'There are about twenty rats, give or take,' Siiri said.

'Twenty pet rats?'

Siiri nodded. 'Exactly. Unless they've reproduced again.'

'They're always on heat,' Irma interjected.

The salesperson looked horrified and wanted to know what they'd been feeding them, until Irma had a shuffle and cut moment and lied that the rats were recent acquisitions.

'We were offered this opportunity, so we came here to learn what we should be feeding them.'

The girl instantly applied herself. In her view, twenty rats was too great a burden for anyone, and Siiri and Irma should only take a few to begin with; one would be too lonely, because rats were herd animals. In the end she suggested two females. Females were lively and affectionate, unlike males, which just lay there. 'So they're not as much fun.'

'Interesting. Rats are like humans in so many ways,' Siiri said with a smile. 'What sort of rat food do you have?'

They followed the salesgirl to a rack that had been dedicated solely to rat-care. It contained bathing supplies, sunglasses, toothbrushes, toys and other time-killers, sleeping nooks, combing supplies and hammocks. As well as, of course, various treats that looked like snacks. Irma picked up a round blue object and sniffed it curiously. It was a bathtub. Then she looked at the swings and fingered the tiny scrap of fabric.

'I never had a hammock,' she said wistfully.

'Of course, you're a female,' Siiri remarked, and the half-bald pet salesperson tittered.

'What on earth is this?' Irma asked, pointing at an object resembling a pencil case in Burberry-print fabric.

The object was a lounger. The girl's enthusiasm grew as she showed them trapezes, slightly larger bundles and three different inventions to facilitate the lounging of rats in a range of colours, flipped them over under a lamp to demonstrate their ingenious designs, and looked at them, eyes gleaming.

'Adorbs, huh? Have you guys owned rodents before?'

'No. Not even a cat or a dog,' Irma said curtly.

'But we love animals; it's never too late to learn something new,' Siiri continued, as the salesperson mustn't get the impression they didn't care for pets.

The girl nodded solemnly and politely reminded them that a snake or a stick insect might be easier to care for than a horde of rats. She tiptoed forward a few steps and showed them a glass box with a fat green snake slithering in it. When Irma realized it wasn't a garden hose, she shrieked so loudly that the salesperson jumped and returned to the dietary alternatives for rats. And there were plenty. The rack was bursting with any manner of nuggets rather like the cat snacks they'd fed to Sirkka the Saver of Souls.

'Can we taste them?' Irma asked, and the girl tittered again.

'Gross! I've never heard of anyone eating these. Except rats.'

Protein was vital for rats, which was why she added dog food to the pellets she fed her own rats, named Principal and Vice Principal. Apparently rats put on weight and got bored easily, so one had to monitor exercise and food intake closely. Sunflower seeds and nuts should be avoided. Rats loved puzzles, even challenging ones, and agility competitions were very popular. Just the previous week, Principal and Vice Principal had performed very well, probably partially because they were fed nothing but low-fat organic seed mixes. Irma started to get bored by the girl's nutritional diatribe, and she moved on to examine what else the shop had to offer. She oohed and aahed over the dog neckties and fur dryers and then started lifting random unidentifiable lumps out of a bucket.

'Steers' knees and goose feet!' she read from the price tags, then began laughing uncontrollably. 'Did you hear that, Siiri?' The next bucket contained big black slabs she claimed were dried cow stomachs. 'This is madness! Oh dear, oh dear, now I've wet myself!'

Siiri stayed with the salesperson and tried to steer her attention back to their query proper.

'If we just want to pamper our little lovelies a little, what would we give them? What sort of treat would inspire a sinful gluttony in them?'

The girl looked at Siiri doubtfully and toyed with the spikes in her left cheek with one hand, the charms dangling from her navel with the other one. She tried to keep one eye on Irma's voice, and when she turned her head sharply, the choke collar made a funny clinking sound. No doubt she had good cause to be concerned about her restlessly probing customer.

'Oh, for goodness' sake! So you're supposed to slip this fake fur over a purebred cat when it's freezing outside? And here I was thinking it was a muff!'

Siiri ordered Irma back to the rat department so the salesperson could concentrate again. She warned her customers about teaching rats bad habits. It was important to avoid fat, salt and sugar. In addition, they needed to be aware that allergies, high blood pressure and elevated cholesterol levels were common among rodents. She couldn't in good conscience recommend they feed rodents treats.

'Oh my. And here I was thinking rats and cockroaches can survive anything. But a modern lifestyle is life-threatening to them, too,' Irma said. She was losing her temper with this child who wouldn't let them baby their rats.

But the salesperson was no slouch; she had an eye for divining a demanding client's temperament and could bend to their wishes when push came to shove. Mumbling slightly, she finally revealed that rats liked baby food.

'The kind that comes in those little jars. And then the best thing ever are mealworms.'

'Mealworms? I've tasted them, too. Wonderful! Where's your worm department?' Irma looked around impatiently and bumped into a stack of pizza boxes. 'Look, Siiri, we could have pizza tonight, too!'

'Those are dog pizzas,' the girl said, and then told them that mealworm larvae were sold in little bags and you could buy them flavoured or plain. She would just give the rat a few at a time, as a reward for performing some task, but Irma didn't listen and grabbed all of the bags from the rack.

'We'll take these. And we'll get baby food from the upper Low Price Market.'

The girl was still concerned about their capacity to take care of rats. The charms in her forehead spikes tinkling, she spoke about bedding and climbing equipment and warned them about sensitivity to dust and dryness. The rats' sensitivity. They should get a humidifier, too. Alder chips, linen and hemp were the best, because they didn't give off dust that irritated the rats.

'Fiddlesticks! Rats like dirt and filth, and we don't have humidifiers or climbing gyms ourselves at Sunset Grove. The worms will do.'

The girl flashed the bags of mealworms at the machine in dejection, and it sucked the sum out of Siiri's fob. Irma dumped the worms in her bag, and they both thanked the salesperson for her expert advice. She smiled cheerfully again and reminded them that if they had difficulties clipping the rats' claws, a hygiene therapist visited the pet store on Wednesdays.

'I'll bring my own toes, she can clip them too,' Irma called.

'Nice serve!' the girl tittered.

Chapter 37

Today was the day when the pilot project in monitored care-giving would come crashing down for good. Siiri and Irma had charged Ritva, Margit, Aatos and the Finnish-Somali woman with the task of spreading the word among the residents. They were to go round to their assigned zones explaining what was about to happen so no one died of fright.

At precisely the agreed moment, Siiri and Irma entered the basement. As the bolder of the two, Irma led the way again, and Siiri followed carrying the bottles of baby food and bags of mealworms. They no longer enhanced the suspense with a torch and a knife; they simply switched on the lights at the top of the stairs. Without saying a word, they walked down the stairs, opened another door, and turned on the lights in the long corridor that led to the Holy of Holies. They passed the abandoned robots, walkers and electric wheelchairs and arrived at a blue steel door that read: 'Building Control Centre'.

'That's a nice Words in a Word word,' Irma noted, pushing the door open. But it didn't budge.

'The handle! Press the handle down!' Siiri whispered nervously, even though no one was listening except for the rats, whose scrabbling carried at an agitating volume from the other side of the door. The creatures must have been hungry and impatient, since Mika had kept them in the locked cupboard for so long.

Neither pushing nor pulling served to open the door, regardless of whether the handle was up or down. An irritated Irma gave it such a swift kick she hurt her toe, but the door stayed closed.

'Dratted drat! Is this how it's foiled, our audacious plan?'

Siiri looked around nervously, pulled her fob from her bag but couldn't figure out where to flash it. There was a keypad next to the door that didn't react even though Siiri presented her fob to it imperiously. But wait a minute! The keypad was the kind they used to have on landline phones and at the entrances to apartment buildings. It needed a code, some secret combination of numbers. Of all the codes in the world, which one could be right?

'We'll never make it into the Holy of Holies,' she sighed in dejection.

But Irma refused to be daunted and dug into her handbag. She pulled out her wallet and from one of its compartments the slip of paper containing her important numbers. Unfortunately the PIN code to Irma's expired debit card didn't unlock the door. A message appeared on the screen above the keypad: 'Code incorrect. Try again.'

'Now it's your turn to try your luck,' Irma said, as if they were playing bingo.

Siiri remembered the door-buzzer codes of the past. They were often derived from the year the building was built. If Sunset Grove had been built in the 1970s, say, 1974, it might be that, or 7419. She tried the latter.

'Code incorrect. Third incorrect attempt will set off the alarm system.'

'Only one more chance? How on earth will we survive this?' Irma was really getting nervous. She paced the corridor, babbling nonsense. 'Hells bells and heavenly days. Jesus Mary and Jehoshaphat, what I would give for one reassuring Bible phrase to pop into my head . . . Shuffle and cut!' Irma suddenly cried. 'Of course those blockheads have taken the code from some Bible verse! I know a phrase or two by heart, but now we need numbers. If only Anna-Liisa were here, she knew how to spout everything between heaven and earth—'

'Anna-Liisa! That's it! You said it!' Siiri cried so loudly the rats stopped scratching inside their locked chamber. Irma looked at her in bewilderment, but Siiri was absolutely certain she had struck on the solution. Anna-Liisa had investigated everything involving the religious fanatics' activities, and surely she had managed this for them.

'What on earth are you babbling about, Siiri?'

'The hymns. Anna-Liisa's hymns, Irma. They're the key to the Holy of Holies.'

Irma instantly cottoned on and started rummaging through her bag, even though both of them remembered that the hymns were 'Spirit of Truth' and 'Walk with Me, Lord'.

'Here, look, I still have Anna-Liisa's note. It reads first

484 and then 548. And make sure you enter it correctly. We only have one try left.'

Siiri could feel her heart beating at a lethal rate and focused furiously so her hand wouldn't shake too much and her breathing would flow smoothly. She carefully pressed the six digits from Anna-Liisa's slip of paper into the keypad. An approving click rang out after each one, accompanied by a flash of the green light on the edge of the box, and when she pressed the final 8, the lock clunked open and text appeared on the screen: 'Code OK'.

'Open Sesame!' Irma squealed, yanking the door open. 'Siiri, you're a genius!'

'Not me; Anna-Liisa,' Siiri said and felt a warm sense of well-being in her upper abdomen, for Anna-Liisa's masterful guidance from beyond the grave. Without their friend's help, they would have remained crying in the corridors and perhaps themselves ended up as food for the ravenous rodents.

To their disappointment, the Holy of Holies was rather banal inside. All the room contained was a tower of skinny ugly boxes stacked on top of each other. Each one had breakers and holes and tiny yellow and green lights. The tube running along the ceiling ended at the Holy of Holies, and cables from it led to the boxes. But only one cable led from the stack of boxes in the other direction, to the outside world. That was their cable.

'Aha! There it is, the handsome devil,' Siiri muttered.

'What are we waiting for!' Irma said, attempting to squat. 'That's where we put our snacks for the pet rats, then.' The squat proved unsuccessful, and she rose, panting and red-faced. 'You try.'

Siiri had an easier time bending down, so she got to do the spreading while Irma did the handing over. The jars of baby food made a fun pop as Irma opened them one at a time, accompanied by cursing, and passed them to Siiri.

'Dratted dratted drat! Pop, there. And the next one!'

'I think two jars is plenty. Don't open any more. We only need enough to lure the rats to the cable.'

They hadn't brought a spoon or knife. Siiri slopped the yellow-orange muck around by flicking the jar. The loose liquid splattered with a convenient randomness on the cable and in the vicinity. In the end, Siiri emptied the jar with her finger and spread one more layer of sauce on the surface of the cable lying on the ground.

'This is really rather good,' she said, licking her finger clean. 'Would you like to taste?'

'Maybe later. Next you get to taste mealworms,' Irma said cheerfully and handed the unopened bag to Siiri.

'Why didn't you open the bag? Do I have to do everything?'

'I can't. Worms repulse me. I could never help my darlings, either, when they wanted to go fishing.'

'But you gobbled these down as happy as a clam at the supermarket sample stand!'

'Those were breaded and fried.'

Siiri tore the bag of mealworms open and sprinkled the stubby brown worms on the cable. They were plump and firm, a little shiny, and at a closer glance had three pairs of legs and some sort of thin carapace. Siiri emptied all the bags on the ground and placed the worms on top of and beside the cable, so it was basically covered in a mountain of rodent delicacies.

'That's quite a sight,' Irma said, raising her hand to her mouth in horror.

'Let's go. Mika will be here in fifteen minutes, and when he comes, we'll be sitting in the communal area playing solitaire.'

They still had to solve the problem of the door. It had to stay open, because it was unlikely that Mika had the correct code. Irma had the bright idea of retrieving one of the abandoned wheelchairs from the corridor. They placed it in front of the open door to prevent it from slamming shut.

Chapter 38

A restless mood filled the lobby at Sunset Grove, which manifested in a greater-than-average apathy. No one was doing anything. Aatos paced back and forth in the A-wing corridor, the Somali woman hung around the entrance to the B wing, Margit at that of C wing and Ritva kept an eye on the elevators. One elderly resident was dozing in an electric wheelchair near the main door.

Their scheme worked like a charm. A little before noon, nearly everyone moved into the dining room to eat. Just then, Irma and Siiri marched out of the basement, and when they saw the others wandering off to their last supper, they joined the procession. It felt like Christmas in the dining room; the residents were like children who couldn't think about anything but the presents under the tree. Food was moved around plates, uneaten, and no sensible conversations arose. Aatos wondered where the waiters and maître d' were. Ritva was so nervous she spilled food on her top. In the meantime, Mika came and went as if nothing were going on, right on time, and the residents paid no particular attention to him.

After eating three-dimensionally printed nutrition for the last time in their lives, Siiri and Irma started playing double solitaire at the baize-covered table in the communal area. Margit sat down with them and appeared to be praying. She folded her hands in her lap, closed her eyes, and swayed silently on the spot. None of the other members of the strike team were in evidence.

The smartwall communicated actively: 'Did you remember to take your midday medicine? To call the AGV, press #4.'

'And the strong shall be as tow, and the maker of it as a spark, and they shall both burn together, and none shall quench them. Isiaiah 1:31.'

'Remember, prayer circle in the dining room today at 6 p.m. If you can't make it in person, you can participate via Twitter @awakennow #prayercircle #dailyscripture #elderly!'

'Have a fantastic day! From the folks at Awaken Now!'

The elevator called out its status updates, the scouring device scrubbed the vestibule, lights flashing furiously, and two caregiving robots entertained each other, as no one else was interested in their efforts. For a long time, nothing happened. Time truly had seemed to come to a permanent stop. Machine and resident alike repeated the same movements over and over, waiting for the next command.

Irma won the first round of double solitaire. She and Siiri gathered up the cards and divided them into two packs, each of them shuffling one before placing the cards back on the table and starting a new game. Siiri got to make the first move. Margit lowered herself into the massage chair – one last time, as she put it. Four women in wheelchairs were parked next to the sofa, and it was impossible to determine whether or not they were awake. Aatos had drifted away to his apartment, and Ritva emerged from the elevator. There was no sign of the Somali woman. A cantankerous old soul with a horrifically tangled thatch of hair had asked a companion robot to dance with her.

So there they were, apparently, the remaining occupants of Sunset Grove. New residents hadn't appeared in place of those who had died or moved away, and no one knew why. This suited Siiri and Irma's plot better than well, as the intention was not to cause the residents harm, but to free them from their technological penitentiary. They believed their tiny deed would open the floodgates. People's eyes would be opened, and everyone would gradually rise in rebellion against technology. Around the world, everywhere.

Margit's massage chair was the first to give out. Its kneading super-fists stopped in Margit's lower back, digging so deeply into her kidneys that Margit let out a louder-than-normal howl. Then the smartwalls started flashing. Their screens mutated into an agitated chaos of tiny coloured squares before going completely black. The elevator fell silent, the cleaning robot froze in the middle of the floor, the refrigerators started giving their owners the silent treatment and unidentifiable splashes and splutters echoed from the dining room as the MealMat belched up eternally preserved mash with the last of its strength. The swill that just a moment ago had been served to the residents for lunch formed cheery, brightly coloured patterns on the walls and the floor. The DishGullet rattled a few times, collapsed in on itself and smashed a mountain of dishes with an ear-splitting crash. The AGV spun around on the spot, spitting out coloured pills; it almost looked like fireworks. After shooting out all its medicine, the trolley drove itself into a wall and dashed itself to bits. The game machines in the Fitness Console Centre whirled in a wild death dance, where Alpine vistas melded with the turf of football stadiums and the crushed clay of tennis courts, virtual balls whooshed through the air, rackets flew into dartboards and non-existent scullers pulled their last row. The sleep sensors fell into eternal slumber, the VirtuDoc wrote itself a letter of discharge, the self-service emergency first aid machines silently committed ritual suicide and the soothing seal pups were freed from their responsibilities. A tiny whimper echoed from the main door, and then nothing. The place was dead.

'What do we do now?' Irma whispered, when the silence had lasted an eternity.

'Will the rats come here?' Margit asked fearfully, still contorted in the grasp of the massage chair. The bewildered Somali woman was gaping at the ruins of the AGV, Ritva collapsed onto the sofa, and there was still no sign of Aatos. Their strike team wasn't exactly keeping up.

Tanglethatch struggled and cursed in the embrace of the companion robot that had expired in the middle of the dance floor.

'Help me, dammit! This damned contraption is strangling me!'

She was genuinely panicking. The row of wheelchairs,

the monitoring team that was supposed to ensure that no one
was in contact with a robot at the moment of doom, stirred
but continued dozing. Irma and Siiri rushed over to the
dancing couple to free the old woman from the cyborg's
clutches, but it was impossible. The creature was stronger
than they were, even in death, and its limbs were stiffer than
an arthritic rheumatic's. They couldn't free her, and instead
tried to soothe the aged foxtrotter, who simply grew more
hysterical as a result.

'Where's Mika?' Irma asked in a fit of pique, as if Siiri
were answerable for Mika and Mika were the only one who
could be counted on in a crisis.

'He couldn't stay; you know that. He has that strap
around his ankle, and he has to stick to his assigned sched-
ule.'

Siiri and Irma started singing, and Tanglethatch calmed
down. After quite a few songs, she fell asleep with her dancing partner at her side and looked peaceful but alive. Ritva
was snoring on the sofa, and the Somali woman had disappeared. It seemed to Irma and Siiri that the time had come
to withdraw to their apartments to see how things stood
there now that rats had liberated the world from the vice of
health care and information technologies. But then they
heard a horrific howl, consisting of the sirens of at least
three emergency vehicles wailing at micro intervals from
each other. They grew louder as they approached before the
dreadful screaming contest came to an abrupt end. Two fire
engines, a police car and an ambulance had pulled up outside
Sunset Grove.

'Who called them?' Margit wondered, still stuck in the massage chair.

Sunset Grove's automatic door wouldn't open, as it had been deprived of the scintilla of intelligence it had once possessed. The firemen smashed the door with an axe and marched in in full regalia. It was a handsome sight. The troop of young rescuers fought their way to the old residents fearlessly and professionally, without exchanging a single word, as they had been trained to work as a team in extreme emergencies. One of the men was black as night and had beautifully gleaming white teeth.

'It can't be . . . they all look so much alike . . .' Irma stammered.

'It's him! Goodness, Muhis! Oh, how I've missed you.'

'Cock-a-doodle-doo, Muhis!'

'Siiri Kettunen! And Irma . . . what was your last name again? Loimenlieri?'

'Lännenleimu,' Irma said, a little hurt, but melted quickly when the black fireman wrapped them in an enormous embrace. It was their fellow food enthusiast from the Hakaniemi days, the cheerful young Nigerian they had met buying innards for stews at the market. Muhis even smelled the same in his handsome uniform, a mix of salty and sweet.

'I almost didn't recognize you without that beehive-hat on your head,' Siiri said. 'It is so good to see you. I've been back to Hakaniemi, but I haven't ever seen you or Metukka.'

'You're a fireman now?' Irma asked, eyes full of admiration. 'Can you do six push-ups in a row?'

Muhis laughed his lovely laugh and was genuinely sorry

he didn't have time to chat. It had never occurred to him that the alarm the Haaga fire station received from a retirement home in Munkkiniemi could bring him back in contact with his old friends, and he was clearly flummoxed.

'We received several automatic alarms from here. Haven't you noticed? We have to check all of the apartments, because the alarm system indicates that none of the automated functions are working, and that means the lives of the residents are in danger. Are you two all right?'

'We're doing just fine. Why don't you go and free that dancer from her robot's loving arms,' Siiri said. At the same instant she remembered Aatos, who had in all likelihood wandered to his apartment and couldn't get out. It was also perfectly possible others were caught behind locked doors somewhere in the building. 'It's a good thing the firemen showed up. At least the automated systems are good for something, seeing as they knew to call Muhis in.'

The lobby was swarming with men in uniform, which was a pleasing sight. Even Ritva woke up and swayed there for a moment until she fell into the arms of a passing fire-fighter and was carried aside to await first aid. Siiri and Irma sat on the uncomfortable Jugendstil sofa to enjoy the efficiency of the rescue team. It was the only couch Tauno had been able to rest on in any way with his badly twisted and hunched back. They now missed Tauno, since they knew that of all their friends, Tauno would have appreciated the moment the most. The rats had gnawed apart every connection slithering between the basement and the outside world, and as their final deed before falling, the chips, sensors and electrodes had called for aid. Finally someone was worried about their machine-controlled existence.

Muhis gently woke up Tanglethatch and confidently extracted her from the arms of the robot, and two medics with a stretcher strode up to check on her condition. She was taken to the ambulance just to be sure. The fire-fighters ran up and down the stairs and cleverly forced the elevator doors open; no one was discovered languishing behind them. The police officers examined the machines and devices and couldn't understand why not a single one was working. A few officers chatted with the wheelchair brigade, while another two yanked Margit up and out of the massage chair, but no one disturbed Siiri and Irma. The residents unearthed from their apartments were brought down to the lobby one by one, as the emergency crews felt that each and every one of them required a health check and no one could be left at Sunset Grove now that the systems had crashed.

'Will we be staying in a hotel?' Irma asked in excitement, but the fire-fighters and police officers couldn't say where the residents would be evacuated.

'I see, evacuation. Well, it's not like we've never stayed in bomb shelters before,' Siiri said blithely.

Aatos was led into the lobby in his nightshirt and checked slippers, a dirty toothbrush in his hand. He was utterly disoriented; he tried to order a double whisky, neat, from a police officer and demanded one of the medics play roulette with him. The seasoned rescuers led Aatos to the ambulance, which drove off to conduct Ritva, Tanglethatch and Aatos to one of the nearby hospitals in siren-free non-emergency mode. They were in no danger. As a matter of fact, no one's life appeared to be at risk, which was an enormous relief to Siiri and Irma.

Muhis appeared at their side, looking concerned. He had removed his helmet and looked peculiar, as he no longer had his magnificent Rasta mane.

'Did you have to shave off your beautiful hair when you became a fireman?' Siiri asked, but Muhis didn't answer. He explained that he'd found hordes of rats in the basement, and some cables that had been gnawed in two.

'This wasn't an accident,' Muhis said. 'It was sabotage, vandalism. What do you think, who could have done something like this?' Muhis was very serious; apparently he found the act villainous indeed. Siiri and Irma glanced at each other and immediately announced in one voice, as proudly as naughty schoolboys: 'We did it!'

Muhis gaped at them in disbelief. 'You? Why? You understand you'll be caught, don't you?'

'If you'd been forced to live in a space station like this for months on end, you would have pulled the same stunt. This is no place for human beings,' Siiri explained.

Muhis' erect back slumped a little, and he said he would have to report Irma and Siiri to the police. He looked so sad that Siiri felt sorry for him.

'Don't you worry on our account! We've planned every detail of this adventure!'

Muhis disappeared and returned a moment later with four police officers. They were all exceedingly young men, barely old enough to shave, and they looked concerned. One of the fuzzy-cheeked fellows questioned Irma and Siiri, asked for their birthdates as if it were a memory test, but showed little interest in listening to Irma's catalogue of every Finnish president since the country gained independence. He wanted to know what they had done and why, and they told him freely.

'So you confess to the crime?' the officer asked. Siiri and Irma nodded in satisfaction.

'Did you get help from anyone? Do you have any accomplices?'

'No. We came up with the idea and did everything ourselves,' Irma said. 'We surveyed the cables and servers, hacked open the doors, orchestrated a suitable architecture for the rats, including the necessary vitamins of course, routed the clouds to the service and waited for the sky to come crashing down on us. It was that simple! Hey, c'mon guys, it's the latest, dig? Are you going to arrest the army of rats, too?'

The police muttered among themselves, and three of them started walking out the doors towards their vehicle while the last one pulled out his phone and made a call. Off to the side, Muhis shook his head, and when Siiri looked at him, they both started laughing.

'Siiri, my love! You're crazy.'

'I'm happy to hear it. That's a downright honour. Have you been baking *pulla*?'

A lovely white smile spread across Muhis' face. Gesticulating animatedly, he explained how his Nigerian friends had all fallen in love with the Finnish *pulla* Siiri had taught him to bake.

'We have *pulla* nights where we compete to see who can braid the best loaf. We drink milk and cry.'

Siiri felt incredibly happy. There she sat on the sofa next to her dear friend Irma, chatting with Muhis about baking, offal stews and Muhis' friend Metukka, who had also found a job, at a day-care centre. And Mika had returned to Siiri's life, too. He had helped them once again; they had successfully carried out the plan and Mika wouldn't be at risk on their account. All of her boys were doing well. Sunset Grove had been freed of chips, crumbs and contraptions, and not a single resident was in danger. She laughed, doubled over, at Muhis' stories, even though they weren't particularly funny, but because she was happy to see her friend again and because the laughter banished the sadness and suspense that had consumed her life over the past few months.

The fire-fighters had discovered many more residents than Siiri and Irma realized still occupied the building. The lobby slowly started to fill with people they'd never seen before. Temporary vagabonds of every description appeared with walkers, three-point canes and wheelchairs, some in tracksuits, others in nightshirts, a handful dressed appropriately. Most looked younger than Siiri but acted much older, with unfocused eyes and dragging feet. A decrepit crowd, all in all, and it was difficult to say how much they gathered of what had happened. A whiff of urine wafted across the lobby as the diapered diaspora filled the chairs, benches and corridors.

Suddenly Siiri saw Sirkka the Saver of Souls in the middle of the elderly flock. She was still wearing the same old turquoise tunic and speaking intently into her phone. A familiar-looking young man stood behind her, whose name Siiri couldn't recall. Might he have been one of Pertti's paladins, one of those who forced Anna-Liisa to sign the will Siiri later devoured? She smiled to herself as she thought how the document they had gone through so much trouble to draft had ended up in her mouth and eventually her bag. She hadn't remembered to clean out the masticated clump from her handbag until days later, when she finally flushed it down the toilet.

'Tell them it's complete chaos, that we need backup,' the young man urged Sirkka.

'What? They're coming. What's that? I wasn't talking to you, I was talking to Tuomas. He's standing right here. Yes.'

'It's a disaster! What did he say? We're never going to be able to handle this. Ask them if we can just drop them all off at the hospital,' Tuomas said to Sirkka.

'Yes, right. The police and fire-fighters, a few ambulances. Tuomas, not to the hospital. I wasn't talking to you; I was talking to Tuomas.'

'What do you mean we can't take them to the hospital? Where, then?'

Tuomas's agitation grew and he tugged insistently at Sirkka's sleeve. Siiri had often witnessed such multi-party calls on the tram, when the person next to the caller forcefully inserted themselves into the conversation, making a complete mess of it. Sirkka the Saver of Souls was about to go mad talking to two people at once. She shouted at both and the conversation didn't make the slightest bit of sense.

'They can't just dump us at a hospital,' Irma said. 'We're perfectly healthy. Old age isn't a disease or a cause for death, and that's that.'

'I must say, I thought we'd be able to stay here,' Siiri added. 'The building still has electricity. We have lights and heat and the stove works, too.'

They chatted about this and that and engaged in a running commentary on what they saw, as if they were watching a confusing television series. There were lots of them these days, programmes where the camera followed fires, emergency rooms and night-time police patrols with no sign of a reporter. If this had been a television broadcast, it would have been far better than the ones that were normally shown, but nevertheless, they would have changed channels long ago.

'What would we watch? Oh, if only Jeeves were still on! I love him almost more than I love Hercule Poirot,' Siiri sighed.

'Okey-dokey! Hey, guys, no cause for panic!'

Jerry Siilinpää's familiar voice echoed above the din in the lobby of Sunset Grove. No one paid him any attention, but Siiri gathered that Jerry found the situation a little challenging, but no worries, everyone would be back in their homes in a jiffy. Then Jerry and the police officers spoke for quite some time. Jerry kept on glancing at Siiri and Irma. They returned his glances with their most irresistible smiles.

'Do you see? He's not wearing his gorilla feet.'

'He's pulled on a pair of sneakers, since he was in such a rush to get here.'

'I think they caught him when he was out jogging. Look at the rubber suit he's squeezed himself into. That's what they all run in, even our ministers, hacking up phlegm along the seaside paths.'

The ambulances were the first vehicles to pull out. After the one that carried off Ritva, Aatos and Tanglethatch vanished, two more first aid cars appeared outside, and the most addled patients were packed into them, even though it was unlikely there was room for them at the hospital. There were more police officers now, and the fire-fighters continued to bustle around most speedily. Uniformed men kept running down to the basement. From what they could make of the rescue crew conversations, Siiri and Irma deduced the firemen were intent on exterminating the rats. Before that, the traces of the destruction had been doggedly photographed and documented and more than one police officer had inspected the scene of Siiri and Irma's crime. Fuzz-face had asked them to press their fingers into a square that looked like an ink pad, which was very exciting, and it turned out not to be an ink pad after all, but some sort of smart-alec screen that sketched their fingerprints directly into the criminal register. Then they were allowed to continue watching the entertainment unfolding before their eyes. The old Somali woman came over to thank them for their heroic act and said she was going to sleep. A few more maintenance men had appeared from somewhere; Siiri recognized the winking fellow with the dead fobs whom she had let into Sunset Grove. The maintenance men were hustled off to wrestle with the elevators and residents' apartments and get them running again.

Jerry gave orders as if he had just completed his reserve officers' training.

'Automatic systems are down; we need locks and elevators that function mechanically. The security system should have issued an emergency command; I don't get why this action point wasn't executed according to the roadmap.'

'Maybe it's night-time in India and his cloud engineers are sleeping?' Irma suggested in her tinkling coloratura laugh.

Gradually the lobby emptied. The residents were either directed to their apartments or carted off, but Siiri couldn't figure out where. The maintenance men fought to get one elevator into functioning condition. The locks to the doors were still jammed, and as an emergency measure Jerry proposed an open house. No one seemed to be bothered by the notion that they wouldn't be able to shut the door to their apartment. As things gradually calmed down, some of the fire-fighters and police officers left. Siiri and Irma were starting to think that they had been completely forgotten on their bench, but then Muhis came back over.

'Siiri, my love, the police are going to take you in for questioning. Do you know what that means?'

'Of course I know. They'll ask us questions and when we confess everything and explain why we did what we did, they'll understand and be grateful and everything will be over. Or then we'll be charged and end up in court. We're fine with any of the alternatives.'

Muhis laughed a little nervously at Siiri's nonchalance and shook his head. He promised to come and visit them no matter where they ended up and said he would be in touch the very next day.

'We can always appeal to our old age, claim we aren't responsible for our actions on account of dementia or allow ourselves to deteriorate so badly they free us out of sheer pity,' Irma said, and Muhis chuckled loudly, looking relieved.

Muhis hugged Siiri first, then Irma, then shook their hands just to be sure, because according to him that was the custom in Finland, one always shook hands. He said he had more pressing tasks to attend to, as there was a fire in Pitäjänmäki and one of the cars had to start up its sirens and rush off. But Muhis wanted to see Siiri and Irma to the police car. The young, almost-whiskered senior detective who had so conscientiously stored their fingerprints in the criminal register came over and respectfully asked them to follow him. From a distance, it looked as if he were asking them both to dance. It didn't occur to anyone to put Siiri and Irma in handcuffs.

The dignified duo lowered themselves into the back seat of the blue police vehicle while the officer held the door open like a butler. The car smelled of plastic and leather, the way new cars always did, and they started feeling like they were important figures on a state visit. Muhis helped Siiri with the seatbelt and looked his friend in the eye, a little concerned.

'What's going to happen to you now, Siiri, my love?'

'Irma and I will be just fine,' Siiri said, taking Irma by the hand. 'With Irma at my side, I've never had a care for the morrow. Watch out; you might die before I do.'

'Yes, we still have the most exciting thing in life to look forward to!' Irma said.

Muhis looked at the women in concern. 'Most exciting thing? Prison?'

Irma and Siiri shook their heads, exchanged glances and cried in a melodramatic vibrato:

'*Döden, döden, döden!*'

Read the complete *Lavender Ladies* series

DEATH IN SUNSET GROVE

Good detectives come in all manner of guises . . .

Siiri and Irma are best friends and queen bees at Sunset Grove, a retirement community for those still young at heart. With a combined age of nearly 180, Siiri and Irma are still just as inquisitive and witty as when they first met decades ago.

But when their comfortable world is upturned by a suspicious death at Sunset Grove, Siiri and Irma are shocked into doing something about it. Determined to find out exactly what happened and why, they begin their own private investigations and form The Lavender Ladies Detective Agency.

The trouble is, beneath Sunset Grove's calm facade there is more going on than meets the eye — will Siiri and Irma discover more than they bargained for?

Escape from Sunset Grove

It's not easy sharing a flat.
Especially when you're ninety-five years old.

Change is afoot at Sunset Grove retirement home, and its residents aren't impressed.

Under threat from falling masonry, best friends Irma and Siiri are forced out of their home to negotiate twenty-first-century living in the centre of Helsinki. Their new surroundings throw up an endless number of daily challenges, from caring for the ailing Anna-Liisa to the mystery of which of the many remotes controls the TV.

The pair are joined by growing numbers of friends in their flat-share, and their new close-quarters living raises some unexpected questions. As the Lavender Ladies begin to dig a little deeper, they find themselves following a trail of corruption, deceit and intimidation that might just lead them to their own front door . . .

The Lavender Ladies must steel themselves for what is set to be their most dangerous case yet.

www.panmacmillan.com

www.panmacmillan.com